W9-CMJ-573

THE
HERE
AND NOW

ALSO BY GREGG EASTERBROOK

THE
H
ERE
AND
NOW

GREGG EASTERBROOK

THOMAS DUNNE BOOKS
ST. MARTIN'S PRESS
NEW YORK

THOMAS DUNNE BOOKS.
An imprint of St. Martin's Press.

THE HERE AND NOW. Copyright © 2002 by Gregg Easterbrook.
All rights reserved. Printed in the United States of America. No part
of this book may be used or reproduced in any manner whatsoever
without written permission except in the case of brief quotations
embodied in critical articles or reviews. For information, address
St. Martin's Press, 175 Fifth Avenue, New York, N.Y. 10010.

www.stmartins.com

Book design by Jonathan Bennett.

ISBN 0-312-28647-3

First Edition: December 2002

10   9   8   7   6   5   4   3   2   1

To Molly Benton, 1977–2001

And to her mother, Sharon, and sister, Cheryl,
who carry her memory

To what then will I compare the people
of this generation, and what are they like?
They are like children sitting in the marketplace
and calling to one another,
"We played the flute for you,
and you did not dance."

Jesus, in Luke 7:31-2

THE
HERE
AND NOW

CHAPTER ONE

It wasn't the sellout so much, for many are led by life toward that moment. Rare is the person whose youthful dreams are not exchanged for the quotidian, and most are fortunate to receive ten cents on the dollar. Carter Morris, at least, had arranged to sell out on attractive terms. The ethically ambiguous arrangement into which he was about to enter would, in return for no product, labor, art, or invention, provide him a substantial purse of money. If nothing else that sort of transaction seemed very current: by the standards of the day, practically patriotic. What vexed Carter Morris was that the remnant spirit of his young awareness might witness what was about to unfold. He wanted his early self to approve of what his adult self had become, and the odds were not favorable.

Carter and the rest of the attorneys stood in the elongated shadow of the Whole Life Tower, a glass-clad skyscraper built by an insurance trust. Unnatural winds curling around the base of the spire made Carter feel lightened, as if he might lift off the ground. Limousines and car-service Town Cars idled along the drive up to the base of the tall polygon, exhaust rising as engines ran with no passengers inside. Drivers of limos like to keep the motor on when it's obviously unnecessary, wastefulness being part of the point of such vehicles.

"They must already be up there," one of the attorneys said, spying the limos and black cars. The other lawyers were anxious

1

to get positioned and get started, or at least get into climate control. On the way over from the hotel, one had complained into his cell phone, "We're running almost three minutes behind."

Fronting the skyscraper was a large public square of terraced concrete. Through this quadrate space moved office workers and aroma-therapy vendors and bag ladies and bicycle messengers clad in sheen fabric suits that seemed designed for colonization of distant planets. At the center of the square was a famously awful piece of federally financed plop art—an assemblage of crudely welded metal lamina shapes that supposedly represented man's inhumanity to man but that, by appearances, was a monument to the discovery of the bridge abutment. The work, *Prometheus on Toast*, drew no notice from the crowds that maneuvered around it. The fine-arts panel charged with selecting a piece for the location had originally chosen as recipient of taxpayer funds a sculpture that was to be a giant vagina people could walk through. The city council put a stop to that, citing technicalities of the building code which, after close textual reading, was found to contain a passage that appeared to prohibit giant walk-through sexual organs. The mayor then announced that he favored a sculpture of Daniel Boone in a canoe, "something for families." Eventually the abstract steel-girder monstrosity won as a compromise, acceptable because it represented nothing to anyone. Supposedly, *Prometheus on Toast* was incredibly daring. Passersby had long since learned to deal with the metallic lump by delivering to its sculptor the ultimate rejoinder, namely, not even bothering to be offended.

The reason a large sculpture placed where it now stood was to make Whole Life Square less attractive as a location for demonstrations. In youth the greatest event of Carter's life, a tumultuous uproarious delightful demonstration, occurred in this square, before the place was defaced by art. Carter had not returned to Whole Life Square since that day, avoiding the lo-

2

cation because nothing that ever happened there again could be as good as what happened there before. Now, owing to a coincidence of corporate ownership, the settlement conference that would make Carter wealthy was scheduled for the building that eclipsed this commons, leaving him no choice but to come back. Carter feared that his young spirit might still linger in this place, and through the effluvium of time glimpse his present self.

Looking out into the square, deliquescent emotions came over Carter, as one might feel when discovering a forgotten item of a lover's clothing after she had left for good, and holding the garment only served to remind that she had once been warm and present. Carter recalled his youthful conviction that what had happened in Whole Life Square was significant, that the world would really change because he and his friends demanded it must. What a crock. He turned away to admire the strong lines of the skyscraper.

Kendall Afreet, the firm's managing partner, stopped the group of lawyers before they finished crossing the commons, asking, "Hey, isn't this where it happened?" He gestured out toward the square.

"I guess so."

"People, a history lesson," Afreet announced. He was the alpha wolf; the other wolves settled in to listen according to pack rank. "This is Whole Life Square, where our own Carter Morris and five hundred thousand of his closest friends staged the last great event of the sixties. And what a relief it was the last one, too. Here our man Carter was interviewed on national television by Walter Cronkite who, fortunately, did not ask about his LSATs." The wolves howled on cue. "Now Carter stands again in the same place, only this time his values are in order—he's not here to make love nor war, he's here to make money!" The wolves clapped. Afreet continued, "What this tells us is that in this magnificent country of ours, even a faded flower child can grow up into a modern-day mercenary who is just hours away from a $6 million personal payoff in the most innovative tort litigation since *Grandits v. Forever-Freeze*."

The wolves pawed the ground respectfully. "Modern-day mercenary" was the highest compliment Afreet accorded to an attorney; the firm's associates strove for the moment they would hear themselves called this. And though word had been out that Carter managed to arrange for himself a special share of the settlement, no one would have guessed the sum that high. They were as much impressed with the figure as with the fact that their colleague had the balls to seize it for himself. Naked rapaciousness is much respected in the law.

They all looked at Carter, expecting him to say something about the square. Weakly he pronounced, "The past is behind us. Now the future lies ahead." Who knew he was quoting Dwight Eisenhower?

"There's the spirit!" Afreet seconded. "Who cares about bygone times? It's hard enough to remember last week. Let's hit the beach!" He plunged forward and the others followed. Kendall often employed military analogies, referring to Churchill or Rommel and not caring much about the distinction.

As they walked Ginny Intaglio, one of the young associates, fell in line next to Carter. She was the firm's tomato, the sole practicing attorney Carter had ever met who actually wore short skirts like the babe lawyers on TV. And she wore them well; no train of thought was safe around her. Usually Ginny paid scant attention to Carter but now was eager to chat him up, as if the words "six million dollars" had commanded her to do so. In the great contest of gender superficiality, men want women for their bodies, women want men for their wallets, and each side considers its true motives cleverly concealed. Males fantasize about lingerie models and females about heirs to petroleum trusts, forever finding the opposite sex wanting when held against these

4

impossible standards—mutually assured destruction applied to the relationship.

Carter braced for some joke from Ginny about how she knew who Walter Cronkite was because she'd taken the history distribution at Stanford. The post-boom generation hates hearing about anything even remotely related to the sixties, and those who lived through the period and dreamily exaggerate its significance hate hearing about what the current generation hates hearing. It was infuriating how, with their knowing looks and ingenious code words, the under-thirty crowd had become so proficient at dismissing the experiences of their Baby Boom predecessors. Infuriating, too, how often their judgment was right.

"This is so cool, you were a hippie once?" Ginny asked, coquettish.

"The whole period is vastly overrated," Carter replied, trying to sound world-weary. "I don't want to talk about it." He said this aware that if stated with the proper inflection, no words interest a woman more than "I don't want to talk about it."

But I do, his younger self declared.

"What the fuck?" Carter said audibly, just as Ginny was following up his previous claim not to want to talk with, "Really? Tell me more."

Carter heard *But I do* as an autonomous voice, as someone speaking aloud; heard through his ears, not within his mind.

Remember what you were the last time you were here, the voice pronounced.

"I don't want to talk about that," Carter said, answering what only he heard.

"Well, if it's real personal or something," Ginny purred. "But you could trust me, I'm discreet."

Some bit of Carter's younger self was striving for his attention. The voice intoned, *Remember the daffodils. Remember what you promised Jayne Anne.*

"Don't ever mention Jayne Anne again," Carter declared, loudly and sharply.

"Jayne Anne? Oh, so it was a girlfriend thing," Ginny said. That explained a lot.

Remember what was possible, his younger self said.

"Nothing was possible, and we know that now because nothing happened," Carter said, addressing the air. "We thought we were going to make a better world and we failed. The whole period was a big stunt. It was all prolonged adolescence, media hype, and pretexts for sex."

Ginny gave a puzzled look. "Media hype and pretexts for sex sound pretty good to me, tiger," she said, employing the kind of voice that normally makes a man advise a woman she'd better come in and lock the door behind her.

"I was just—recalling a conversation I once had with someone here," Carter said. He was unsettled and needed to change the topic. "Why don't you tell me a little bit about yourself."

Carter had chosen Ginny's favorite subject, but there was no time for her to begin a soliloquy for they had arrived at Whole Life Tower, a stunning, inhuman structure that eclipsed the sun for blocks. Within the building's lobby, affectational opulence ruled: gilded trim and polished mirrors made everything glisten in a disorienting manner. Along the inner corridors were works of second-rate contemporary art, indistinct globs of color selected for their vagueness. Some had plaques announcing the purchase price.

The thirty-fourth through forty-eighth floors were the home office of the holding company that owned Value Neutral, a fashion chain that was the subject of Carter's lawsuit. Electronically locked security doors blocked the way in. Armed guards laboriously checked each person's date of birth and Social Security number against a list of expected guests, as if the arrival of unauthorized attorneys was a major security concern at the company.

Waiting for the guard to finish verifying their names, Afreet instructed, "All wireless off now."

Some of the lawyers were disconcerted by this directive, reacting so as to suggest they'd been instructed to unzip their flies. "Cell phone interruptions are a power cue," one said. "I always arrange to have people call me during negotiations."

"That was last year's tactic," Afreet said. "Now high school girls have themselves called during algebra class. Janitors talk on hands-free headsets while they sweep. Been in a 7-Eleven lately? Minimum wage, no green card, but every clerk has a cell so advanced it's not yet available to the general public. So what's really strong is carrying no phone at all. That says, 'I'm so important no one dares call me.' " Thereby the attorneys of Malison & Afreet dutifully deactivated all portable communications devices. To accomplish this, one had to pull three different phones from pocket, briefcase, and belt clip. Three cell numbers: first for business calls, second for the wife, and third for the mistress.

The group was shown into a conference area, with a grand table for principals and a second row for aides. Microphones, earpieces, and speaker boxes waited at each seating point, as if Israeli and Palestinian diplomats would be joining them. Assistants scurried. Floor-to-ceiling windows framed panoramic vistas of the city skyline. Kendall Afreet stood admiring the view; among his goals was to move to a high floor of a skyscraper, the way it had been at the State Street firm in Boston where he'd gotten his start. "We are a third-floor operation today, but someday we will be thirtieth floor!" he would bellow at staff meetings, by way of motivational speaking.

Lawyers and executives of the other side began to enter. Afreet eyed them with a mix of contempt and admiration, as a thief might regard the detectives closing in on him. Then he bounded toward the Value Neutral team with a broad smile on his face, whispering to Carter, "Take no prisoners." The other side's principals were all white males, though a few sported female or minority assistants. They radiated inauthenticity, particularly from indoor tanning and obvious surgical touch-ups. The ostensible point of cosmetic surgery is to make a person look younger, but on most men a face-lift is so easily detected the true point must be to proclaim that you can afford it. Most of the Value Neutral male executives proclaimed this.

These are the kinds of men who pay themselves millions in bonuses, then cut health benefits for the hourly workers, Carter's young self said. *The kinds of men who are celebrated in the business pages for abolishing jobs. You are about to help them.*

"I am about to enter into an entirely legal business arrangement that complies with all relevant federal and state statutes," Carter replied, sotto voce.

When someone takes pains to insist what he's doing is legal, that's when you know it shouldn't be, the voice said.

The CEO of Value Neutral, a mechanically tanned and surgically rejuvenated man named Jennings Guerdon, took the floor and declared to Carter and his fellow attorneys, "You've put together an excellent case against us, exceeding our best hopes." It wasn't the sort of thing a defendant in litigation was supposed to say. "Before we go any further," Guerdon continued, "let's review the confidentiality clauses. The settlement only works for us if confidentiality provisions are bulletproof."

Ginny had taken the seat next to Carter. To keep his mind off the communiqués from his younger self, he was attempting to concentrate on the fact that whenever Ginny leaned forward to listen to something, her skirt hiked up a little farther—an effect Carter was supposed to think she was completely unaware of. But concentrating on Ginny's legs was not working.

You've put together an excellent case against us, exceeding our best hopes, Carter's younger spirit repeated, not bothering to add a sneer.

Years ago the decision to enroll in law school, resisted as a surrender to the workaday world, had been justified in Carter's mind on the grounds that he might someday participate in a landmark decision or textbook case. Civil rights, access to government secrets—that was the kind of landmark he had in mind. Now instead Carter was on the verge of going down in legal history as the inventor of the phantom class-action suit.

Value Neutral, officially defendant in Carter's lawsuit, was the hottest name in clothing retail. A creature of focus-group marketing, the firm had ascended to the status of the nation's leading full-price apparel retailer by relentlessly exploiting the coplanar overlap of celebrity worship, runaway materialism, and status fretting. Or "reference group anxiety," as sociologists call it. Everyone from affluent teenagers to Fort Lauderdale retirees flocked to the chain's outlets to snap up its droll mix of shapeless oversized garments, fitness apparel for the sedentary, vaguely eroticized leather miscellany, and the year's must-have status item, oil-rig roustabout boots with brass safety clamps. The chain led a charmed life, deflecting criticism about its daunting superficiality and developing-world sweatshops by strategically timed donations to environmental organizations, gay groups, and the Brooklyn Academy of Music.

At last Value Neutral had stumbled, selling thousands of running suits that a factory in Jamshedpur had treated with unsymmetrical dimethyl chlorofluorine monomer. This compound, marketed as Simu-Sweat™, made fitness apparel appear to be soaked with perspiration so that it would seem the wearer had been working out really hard, regardless of whether he or she ever left the SUV. (Simu-Sweat™ cologne and body wash sold separately.) But unsymmetrical dimethyl chlorofluorine monomer had not been certified for use in the United States; of equal importance, the chemical had an incomprehensible name that sounded ominous when slurred through by CNN announcers. On the morning the news broke that Value Neutral had been caught using an unapproved substance, there was joy in law offices across America.

Shortly afterward, Carter began a traditional class-action lawsuit against Value Neutral. Following the filing of some initial briefs, he received an unusual call from Value Neutral's house counsel: the company would not oppose Carter's suit, so long as the settlement entailed no cash payments to consumers and eliminated the defendant's entire exposure. Should Carter be able to arrange an outcome that met these conditions, Value Neutral told him, the company would agree to an abnormally high sum for the legal fees that a losing class-action litigant may pay to the victor. That payment would, of course, go to Carter's firm.

Through daunting application of legalism, Carter found a way to meet Value Neutral's terms. He signed up some buyers of the running wear, had his clients agree to waive future claims, then got a Delaware judge to certify them as representing the class of all buyers. This meant that once Value Neutral registered the settlement with the judge, its liability would disappear; even potential plaintiffs who'd never heard of the litigation and never signed a thing would lose standing to sue. The settlement would be announced as a huge victory for consumers, with the press release emphasizing Carter's background in social causes. Buyers would receive nothing more than coupons for discounts on future purchases at Value Neutral—"losing" the lawsuit becoming a promotional device for the company—while Malison & Afreet would land the largest fee in its history, $35 million, with a special portion designated for Carter personally.

All in all, the agreement was situated just slightly north of fraud. Kendall Afreet was tremendously excited that Carter had arranged it. He not only drooled over the fee but over the possibility they were creating a new kind of legal product in which

Malison & Afreet would be the pioneers. Companies would shed liability by appearing to lose lawsuits, paying opposing counsel handsomely for quiet collaboration. Afreet was already calling the approach "cooperative litigation" and mailing brochures about it to the Fortune 500.

Initially, Carter struggled with rationalizations. There was no evidence unsymmetrical dimethyl chlorofluorine monomer had actually harmed anyone. The settlement would cost an arrogant company millions of dollars. And if that sum went to the lawyers, well, they'd spend it and help stimulate the economy. Carter just wanted to get everything over with and hold the money. He hadn't counted on his earlier awareness emerging from the well of anamnesis to protest.

You've put together an excellent case against us, Carter's young spirit said again, now mocking. *Why don't you bring Beelzebub in on the deal and make everything official? You might as well be signing up as director of your local draft board.*

"There are no more draft boards," Carter whispered to his younger self. "The military has been all-volunteer for years."

Then I take everything back. This is the best of all possible worlds.

"What are you doing here?" Carter whispered to himself, trying not to attract notice. He had spent years working to erase cognizance of his younger self from his thought. Why did he hear that self now?

You always said Whole Life Square was a magical place. You told Jayne Anne that just before the police van took you away.

"Took you away maybe. I'm not you anymore."

Oh, dear thing, you must be heartbroken, his younger self said in a pixie tone.

Actually Carter was glad, and not just because any sensible person now denies the way he or she looked in the sixties. Carter denied the entire period, even its fond ideals of social progress and human happiness. He felt relieved to have shed his cosmic illusions and put on a Rolex Cosmograph.

The morning passed in technical discussions of clause wording. Among other things, Malison & Afreet was promising never to disclose the nature of its negotiations with Value Neutral—not the sort of stipulation often found in settlements that are announced as consumer victories. Since disclosure of such an agreement would be highly embarrassing, so far as Carter could tell the main purpose of the confidentiality clause was to prevent anyone from finding out about the existence of the confidentiality clause.

Each time the various lawyers made some reference to the formal signing of the deal, Carter's younger spirit chanted, *Hell no we won't go.* Occasionally this keening seemed so loud it made him fidget, drawing the attention of the others who heard nothing.

At 12:30, bargaining was adjourned so the parties could retire to the private dining room of L'Argent Folle, the city's most expensive restaurant, to eat, drink, and smoke cigars that would be offered on silver. Recently arrived Filipinos, Mexicans, and Pakistanis had begun assembling at L'Argent Folle at 4:00 A.M., eyes blinking into the still-dark, to commence the slicing, simmering, and spiffing that would allow the gold-card contingent to experience a perfect lunch hour. A typical day's proceeds for the restaurant exceeded the value of all property combined in the home villages of the immigrant workers, who were grateful for employment in this place and terrified about losing their positions.

As the conference participants began to put away their legal papers in anticipation of the meal, Jennings Guerdon approached Carter.

"When this deal closes you're going to be established as a big-league litigator," Guerdon told him. There was a slight torque to his expression that was not sincerity but neither was it sarcasm.

Carter thanked him for the compliment, having reached or perhaps it would be better to say having fallen to the point in life at which the opinions of people like Guerdon were beginning to matter to him. Guerdon seemed the sort of man who would confidently hold out a sheaf of junk bonds and say, "It's alright, Grandma, just sign everything."

"Have you seen our press packet yet?" Guerdon continued. "There's quite a bit about you, your background. Of course it's why we picked you to sue us. If the media challenges the settlement we can say, 'Look, plaintiffs' counsel was a former street protester, he really took it to us, this guy wiped the floor with us.' That's the strategy. Smooth, no?"

"I'd rather you left me out of this," Carter said, formalistically.

"Little late for that," Guerdon replied. "For what we're paying, you can't object to a little exploitation. Corporate research even found some old evening-news footage of you flashing a peace sign while being led away by a couple of cops as Walter Cronkite shouts a question about the First Amendment or something outdated like that. Were you really once known as the Daffodil Man? Priceless. We're going to distribute a still from the TV clip to the press with a now-and-then comparison, you know, the hippie you and the three-piece you. Primo PR."

That was a fabulous picture, the one with the cops and Cronkite! Remember the poster version? His younger spirit spoke with excitement. *Women who saw that poster just couldn't keep their legs together. That's certainly how I remember it, anyway. Though it stopped working on women in the 1980s and you then hid all the copies. Say, that's not what soured you on the counterculture was it?*

"Be quiet about the damned poster," Carter said aloud.

Guerdon gave a querulous look. He might have wondered mildly about Carter's sanity had he not been distracted, since he had positioned himself so as to seem to be looking at Carter while pretty much openly staring down Ginny's blouse.

"You should be promoting your former self, not trying to deny it," Guerdon suggested to Carter.

First intelligent thing you've said! the phantasm voice declared.

Guerdon's leering made Carter realize he had often daydreamed about his fellow attorney's legs and derriere but never quite zeroed in on Ginny's bosom. A generational thing: the fifties produced breast men, the sixties leg men, since it was for the Baby Boom that *Playboy* began shooting below the waist. Carter realized he must be losing his joy of life to have been around this woman so long, and daily, and failed to take note of her two bouncy, athletic talents.

Speak for yourself. I noticed her boobs immediately, his young spirit interjected.

Guerdon continued, "Sell yourself as a former street protester who now works through the free-market system. Get that old photo blown up into a retro poster, at the bottom have your Web address. Put the peace-sign icon on your business card. Not too large, you understand, just as a branding device. Have a graphics shop make a merged-image picture that shows you standing backstage with Bob Dylan at Woodstock. The press, your clients, they'd eat that with a spoon. Nobody's going to check authenticity. And Dylan certainly wouldn't mind, he's doing a sitcom pilot for Disney right now, you know. He plays some zany, wacky space alien who can only be seen by this zany, wacky bunch of kids in a zany, wacky household."

Woodstock: the notion of a rock concert, a thrilling experience in youth, now made Carter's flesh crawl. The current generation was right to be sick of hearing Woodstock lauded, and not just because it occurred during a phase when Joe Cocker was considered an artist. What exactly was momentous about standing in a muddy field listening to music? If anything Woodstock established the notion of the rock concert as an exercise in conformism, huge numbers of people coming together to act alike.

"I don't think about that part of my life anymore," Carter said.

"Prefer not to remind people of controversy, eh?" Guerdon said. "A good rule in business. The thing is, it was contentious once but now it's just retro. Take peace-sign accessories. They're big movers at Value Neutral stores. We wouldn't stock them if they were associated in the public mind with something controversial like peace. Now they merely connote fashion, and fashion sells. So market your background. Exploit yourself. Nobody else is going to do it for you, you know."

Carter had no wish to prolong the conversation, but tried to explain: "This is a sensitive subject to some people my age. We had a chance to change the world and we didn't. Now it's too late."

"You really think it's too late to change the world?" Guerdon asked.

"Yes."

"Then we did pick the perfect person to front this lawsuit," he said. Guerdon slapped Carter on the back in a practiced gesture of false camaraderie, turning to mingle with the others heading off to lunch.

Soon the group had left the skyscraper and was moving across Whole Life Square toward the restaurant. Some of the executives popped into limos and black cars to be driven, though the day was pleasant and the distance negligible; presumably, this was done to insure the others knew they had cars waiting. The rest strolled and, feeling the hard part of the negotiation was behind them, were in good humor, as evidenced by some jocular jockeying to obtain the ideal walking position behind and slightly to the side of Ginny Intaglio. The smell of outside air, mixed as it was with pretzel, perfume, diesel, and other scents, was refreshing after hours breathing through recirculation.

Ginny took Carter's arm. "You were marvelous in there," she said.

He barely remembered what he had done during the morning's maneuvering, other than try not to give away his running discourse with an inner voice.

"It was all just shameless grasping for money," Carter said.

"Right!"

At that moment Carter felt that the strivers of his day, with their forthright pursuit of status and dollars, were the ones who held the high ground. At least they knew what they believed in. For him, all convictions had faded to ambiguity, and passion was a word in the dictionary.

During the early postwar period, men wore gray suits to stifling jobs they hated, women accepted the confines of the home, families offered their sons to the government for war, and people were shocked if you questioned authority or so much as alluded to sex. Yet in this environment, Carter and his cohort had grown up perceiving the world as a place on the precipice of great, positive change. Today men complained unless their jobs were nurturing and fulfilling, women had so much choice that choice itself had become a source of anguish, sexual fixation was close to obligatory, even traditionalists regularly denounced the government, and people had become so skeptical about institutions that they wanted to know what the Girl Scouts did with the proceeds from sales of their cookies. Yet in this open, fluid society it seemed nothing could change. It was too late to try for a better world, and too late to hold out much hope for the self and the heart. That was Carter's view, in any case.

I can't stand that word "faded," his earlier spirit protested.

Carter pressed his hands against his temples, trying to silence the uninvited guest.

As the group walked toward the center of the commons, Carter struggled to push back memories of what this place had once been to him on the day a jury-rigged speaker's platform stood where the sculpture now did. There was a reason he'd never returned, to avoid those very recollections. The hullabaloo, the childlike exultation . . . the belief that people were making contact with each other on some plane other than the ordinary . . . the impression of removal from the normal flow of time . . . everything taken so *seriously*. Carter took nothing seriously now, other than perhaps his waistline.

He put his hands into his pockets and let his eyes lie on the facade of the restaurant. Still he could feel some small fraction of what he had once felt here, of being a man-child running joyously amid cheering men-children and women-children, throwing daffodils.

"Did you have anything planned for tonight?" he heard Ginny asking.

He also heard chanting, singing, sitar music, cat-calling, police bullhorns, people making the Zen sound *ooooommmmm*. These clamors, palpable, grew in decibel so rapidly that Carter spun his head around to see what was coming. For an instant everything was sufficiently deafening, and it seemed to him a circus train must be approaching. Yet all he saw were austere faces of people worried about their checking-account balances, hurrying to the office.

"—and I'm staying in this really nice small hotel, if you need a place," he heard Ginny saying. "There's a great view from my room. The bed is four-poster."

They crossed exactly the point where it had happened. *Thanks for bringing me back here at last. I'll repay you*, Carter heard. Then his younger spirit was gone, no longer a passenger.

Ginny was eyeing him with a mix of offense and bemusement. "Men don't usually ignore me when I proposition them," she said. Then added, "What's all that?"

From nearby they heard commotion, laughter, and clapping, caught a glimpse of a figure running. Someone was dashing through the center of the plaza and leaving a wake of bystanders. Skyscraper-accelerated wind carried away the specifics of the sounds.

Ginny stepped toward the disturbance, and came back a moment later, laughing prettily. "Hey, look what some guy just gave me," she said, holding out a fresh daffodil.

Carter felt slightly faint. "The guy was dressed like a hippie," Ginny went on, "period costume, running around handing out flowers. Must be some kind of promotion."

A long-forgotten phrase surfaced from the accretion disk of Carter's memory. He looked at the daffodil, looked at Ginny, and said, "Lady, you would flatter that flower if you wore it."

For a moment Ginny did not know how to respond. Women now rarely blush when hearing the indecent, vulgar talk between the sexes having made the historical transition from forbidden to mandatory. But civility throws today's woman completely for a loop.

"What a nice thing to say," she answered, flustered. Ginny mounted the stem into her lapel. Her face changed in some subtle way, making her seem slightly more a female human being and slightly less a well-put-together shark circling for prey.

Carter's mind spun. "Lady, you would flatter that flower if you wore it" is what he had said to Jayne Anne, leaning from the police van, as he handed her the last daffodil. "Until your return, my prince!" Jayne Anne had cried back as the door slammed shut. Carter cringed to recall that exchange, which at the time had seemed to mean everything.

"I need a moment," Carter said, and Ginny commented that

he did look pale. He told her he wanted to stroll a bit for air and would catch them up at lunch. She cooed, "Don't forget the four posters," then disappeared toward the restaurant.

Walking Whole Life Square, Carter passed several people holding daffodils. Just as you can find the ice-cream vendor by following backward a stream of people licking cones, Carter followed backward those holding the yellow flowers, and soon neared the man he and Ginny had previously glimpsed.

"Who will accept love," Carter could hear the figure calling to passersby. "Who will accept my flower?"

Hearing this, Carter's instinct was to run. But he could not, and drawing closer saw that the figure's period appearance was exquisite—embroidery vest, shaggy hair, patched blue jeans from the point in social history when jeans were a way of saving money rather than flashing it.

He called out, "Carter!" The figure turned to face him. It was the Daffodil Man, the young voice in his thoughts given form. The figure's eyes twinkled in the sly way Carter's once had, and the prior man regarded his present self with abstract sympathy, as one might when coming upon a car wreck from which the victims had already been removed.

"You are not real," Carter sputtered.

"Doubting your senses? I'm the one who does drugs, not you," the figure said. He attempted to hand a flower to a passing businessman, who pushed it aside with harried disgust.

The figure swept his arms around, histrionic, and indicated the passing crowd. "These proud realists one encounters in their determine guise, shoulders pitched against the wind, minds reeling with concessions they long to make. May I ask what is real about them? Don't you feel that if you stuck your hand into them it would go right through? No realist leaves an impression on the world, not even the supposedly powerful ones who run the big companies and governments. They're just sitting in chairs. Time and again the realists march off as prisoners upon the bayonets of completely disorganized dreamers." He gave a flower to a middle-aged woman. "Everything new and constructive—inventions, art, progress, even profit—comes at the instigation of someone who denies that reality is a barrier, pushes against it and finds that his hand goes right through." Then he addressed Carter only. "Because I am a dreamer, I am real. You can't dream. It is you that has ceased to be real."

Carter noted from the corner of his eyes that several people in the vicinity were holding entirely corporeal flowers.

"Once you were naive, mad at the world, misinformed, and had a hell of a good time. Now you're sophisticated and bursting with knowledge, accepting of everything you see, and miserable. And don't put this off to the normal process of aging," the figure said. A group of teenaged boys, in triple-sized pants with headset stereos, passed. When the young man attempted to offer them daffodils, they scattered. "Once you were limitlessly optimistic about the future, which is to say, American. Now you're so fashionably defeatist you might as well be the last Hapsburg."

"You had plenty of faults, as I recall," Carter stammered to the specter.

"Alas I am beyond critique, as nothing can change the past," the Daffodil Man replied cheerily. He handed a flower to a passing secretary. "The philosopher Charles Hartshorne once noted that the past continuously influences the present, whereas the present can never have any influence on the past. So which is more substantial, past or present? Answer quickly or you'll lose points."

The figure did a little dance. Good grief, now he's quoting, Carter thought.

Then the younger man's face acquired a stolid countenance. "But though being a shadow of the past I can never change, those in the here and now still hold their fates in their hands."

"It's too late for me," Carter said.

The Daffodil Man scoffed. "First it's too late to change the world, now you can't change yourself. Tell me, are you still capable of changing your shirt?"

Off in the distance, Carter heard Jayne Anne's recorder. The figure glanced at his Nixon watch and declared, "Time to go, have a flower!" In a period so brief it seemed to consume no time, the Daffodil Man evaporated. The plaza was restored to mundane bustle.

Carter dropped onto a concrete-block bench. No younger manifestation, no melody of the recorder. The passersby with daffodils—now he didn't see any. Some kind of memory-induced hallucination? How festive. He was about to surrender his principles, and as a throw-in, was also losing his mind.

The bewildered attorney hurried toward L'Argent Folle. Waiting for a stoplight to change, Carter paused across from the restaurant entrance. He saw Afreet and the others emerging from the front door, looking sated and mildly inebriated. Some puffed the final third of cigars. To Carter's perception, it had been only a moment since he took leave of them. He looked at his watch; two hours had passed.

"I'm confused about time, too," a child's voice said. Carter turned and saw a boy, crew cut, smelling of Brillcreem and Testors airplane glue. It was him, tumbled out of the past.

"Wow, you do look like Dad," the boy exclaimed. "People say that happens, but I never thought it would happen to me."

"Not funny anymore," Carter said to himself. "Wake up now. Not funny anymore."

"We have to go right away," the boy declared. He was craning his head around at the commons, trying to take everything in. "Except I really wish we could see a movie first. I bet they're way beyond 3-D by now." It would have been cruel to tell him movies had instead gone in the direction of one-dimensional.

"Stop seeing this," Carter instructed himself sternly. "Wake up. Stop seeing this."

"You need to touch me," the boy said.

Some impulse—parental?—told Carter to place a hand on the child's shoulder. Immediately his adult senses filled with forgotten impressions: excitement over toys; the longing to hold a baseball bat; the ambrosial taste of ice-cold grape Nehi on a humid summer evening; the reek of gymnasiums; a glimpse of a lunar eclipse seen when his father held him up, groggy, to the window in the middle of the night; his own bones loose in his body, aspiring to grow.

In addition to many sensations felt and lost, Carter became aware of a tactility he had never experienced. The hand that touched the boy's shoulder began to feel as though it were expanding outward from itself. The perturbation spread up Carter's arm and took command of his body, every point of which now seemed to be moving rapidly away from every other point.

"Creepy feeling, huh?" the boy asked. Then the city square became a vapor, and Carter Morris tumbled back to the past.

CHAPTER TWO

HEADS DOWN, EVERYONE! Keep those hands on the tops of your necks!"

Along the clammy halls of Millard Fillmore Elementary, girls and boys were taking up positions for the air-raid drill. Classes shuffled single file along linoleum corridors to the building's inner walls, painted institutional lime-green and papered with kids' drawings of stick-limbed people or houses whose chimneys skewed sideways. A few children giggled or exchanged whispers.

"There will be no talking during a nuclear attack!" the assistant principal exclaimed through a bullhorn. He'd taken the device from a kit marked with the yellow radiation-warning symbol, was handing out civil-defense armbands to teachers. His voice seemed enormous. The halls were cold, and cold somehow accentuates sound.

Each class came to a halt at an assigned place; hollow metallic tones echoed as children bumped into the banks of lockers that lined the corridors. They sat cross-legged facing inward, head bowed low with hands covering the neck, assuming a posture similar to an airline impact-brace position. The reasoning was that if a distant nuclear detonation blew in the windows of the school, it would be best to be crouched into as small a form as possible, turned away from the flying glass, with hands protecting the vital arteries of the neck. This had been explained to the children in clinical detail.

"My dad says these drills are a waste of time," Carter's boyhood friend Wardman Louvain hissed, furtive. "Unless you're in a fallout shelter when the big one hits, you get blown straight to hell."

"Don't say that," one of the girls injected. "Don't say bad words like h-e-double-hockey-sticks."

"Girls are sissies about dying," Ward announced.

"If you say bad words, Jesus will hear you," another girl murmured. "And *he'll tell!*"

"Ward, be quiet," Carter whispered in urgent susurration. "You're going to get us into trouble."

"I won't get in trouble," Ward answered with a slightly superior tone. "You can get away with a lot if you act confident. My dad says."

At that point the school's air-raid siren blew. Fortissimo and bellicose, the device made the air heave. The boys and girls fell silent, fearful. Ears hurt as the sound seemed to press the skull inward. Some of the younger children began to cry.

The siren had been installed a few months before by a National Guard unit. The men mounted the spar pole and horn not in a removed location but prominently on the school's front lawn, adjacent to the flagstaff—as if to suggest that attack and sudden carnage at this place were possibilities daily to be kept in mind. The guardsmen seemed to view the arrival of the siren with a mix of dread and pride in the growing power of martial science. Many had fought in Europe, the Pacific, or Korea, looked the horrors of modern fighting technology in the eye and survived. Now everyone would have to do the same, no matter how far from the gates of the enemy. The siren's multiple tocsin projectors pointed in every direction.

After the air-raid blaring ended, students listened for nearly another minute as the siren's chamber spooled down, pitch descending. The assistant principal, Mr. Eggert, then announced through his bullhorn, "We will now count down to the simulated explosion. Ten, nine, eight . . ."

At zero the building custodian flashed the hall lights, tripping circuit breakers at random. "Keep your eyes closed until your teachers tell you it is safe to open them," Eggert bellowed. "The light from a hydrogen bomb will arrive well before the explosion. Anyone who faces nuclear light will be blinded. The eyeballs will melt." Many of the girls made soft noises of disgust. Ward said, "Wow!"

During the course of regular air-raid drills, the children were repeatedly instructed on keeping the neck covered and the eyes closed, though nothing was ever said regarding what would happen in the next instant, after their school's walls fell inward, the shock wave hit, and their teachers died screaming. The reasoning seemed to be that since a properly coached child might avoid looking toward a nuclear flash, schools should teach this information. But since nothing could be done about what would follow an instant later, why mention it?

Every Wednesday at noon, air-raid sirens sounded throughout the town. The first time Carter heard this powered ululation, he shook with panic. Knowing the blasts were simply tests, he still trembled each week as the mechanized howling picked up, and could not regain repose until half an hour after the sound ended— when enough time had passed that he could be sure the sirens truly had been a test and not the proclamation of a doomsday attack that by coincidence was commencing exactly at midday Wednesday.

It was one thing to do the heads-down-in-the-school-hall drill, a marching exercise for schoolchildren who must learn many silly ceremonies. The siren represented something else altogether. Its wailing heft and presence adjacent to the national flag suggested this device was there because the cataclysm of which it gave notice might happen. Like every boy of his generation, Carter obsessively read books about the glories of World War II: D day, Midway, the air victories above the Marianas and London, triumphalist subjects from the safe distance of childhood. But the reason London and all those German cities had air-raid sirens was because they were *bombed* and people died. Now there was a siren on the lawn of Carter's elementary school, warning of an ultimate bomb.

Unseen, a sledgehammer was being banged against a large sheet of metal. "That is the explosion," the bullhorn voice said. "Now comes the pressure wave. Thermonuclear detonation is characterized by overpressure that may equate to several dozen atmospheres."

Mr. Eggert was reading from an AEC booklet he'd taken from the kit. To suggest the arrival of the shock, the janitor threw the master circuit breaker so that all building lights failed. Sudden darkness set most of the kindergartners to crying. "We will have complete silence as we wait out the prompt radiation," said Eggert. "Continue facing the wall. You must not move for four minutes."

Cross-legged and hunched low, the children's jocularity had expired. Walking the ranks checking for proper position, Eggert was saying, "Mrs. Sheridan, your sixth-graders are old enough to learn civil-defense fire fighting. I will give you the relevant pamphlets." His black tie, clipped to his white shirt, strained when he moved.

Ward, a moment before giving defiance to death, now spoke in murmur, hoping no classmate would overhear his anxiety. "When the bomb comes your dad is going to let me in, right?" he asked Carter. "He'll let me in, right?" A pause. "Right?"

"Be quiet, follow instructions," Carter hissed back. As a boy, he dreaded getting into even the slightest trouble.

At the same time Carter the grade-school kid was trying to hush his confidant, Carter the adult was trying to say, "Ward, you're going to grow up to make a very serious legal mistake. Let me warn you about it now." But Carter could not cause his child form to say that. After all he didn't say it then, and you can't change the past.

CARTER'S ADULT COGNITION had just extended through the body of his grade-school self. He felt lightened, limber, infused with energy as though he had stuck his finger in an electrical outlet without harm. The expensive watch with the never-used skin-diving features, his credit cards, identification were all gone, swapped for a pocket knife, quartz rocks, and real silver quarters and D- and S-series dimes. Carter's dull low-back pain had vanished, replaced by a coiled stored vigor insisting his legs really, really needed to run and jump. *This is not a memory, I am here*, Carter thought.

The skin of his face was smooth and delightful to touch; the acetous aftertaste of decades of alcohol and smog gone from his palette, which at that moment reliably could have detected the tiniest distinction of flavor among brands of peanut butter or ketchup. There was also the shocking sensation of his cock and balls being much smaller than they should be. But try as he might Carter could not make himself give his crotch a quick grab to be sure all was in order. The boy Carter did that regularly, of course, but had not at this particular moment, and you can't change history.

Looking through his boyhood eyes, Carter found it good to see Ward again—the comrade and consolation of his awakening to the world. Good, especially, to see Ward carefree and not yet accused, just a boy whose thoughts revolved around bicycles and Popsicles. As boys there'd been an uncomplicated happiness to their friendship, whose points of contention were never anything deeper than who should pitch and who catch. Prospects for the next day were always eagerly bright. Now Carter looked on his young friend again, saw the mischievous eyes, felt the nearness of a good heart, knew what bitterness lay ahead.

Stand up, Carter's adult awareness tried to order his young form. *Speak!* But he couldn't.

If you won't warn Ward, at least tell the pompous fuckup Eggert he hasn't got long till he wraps that overpowered Olds around a strut of the Elmwood Avenue bridge and the autopsy finds a blood level of pure martini. Carter could not recall the exact timing of something from so long ago, but it felt like he was observing a moment close to that day. The teachers had been tight-lipped when their assistant principal died. Carter's mother, who usually took him aside to tell him what the score really was in life, had avoided the boy's questions, saying only that God called people when their time had come. But Carter remembered how the facts gradually filtered out and how he'd puzzled why the Maker, if He wanted a particular soul in heaven, would summon that person via a painful, destructive action. Young Carter trembled in apprehension of Eggert's authority; adult Carter felt sympathy for the things the man was trying to compensate for. Nothing Carter's adult consciousness could do, however, could make boy Carter stand up and speak what his older awareness knew.

As his boy's head swiveled around, Carter peered up and down the rows of children. The school halls that had looked interminably long to him in youth now of course seemed short and narrow. Carter noticed one of the teachers comforting a sobbing girl. Mrs. Sheridan, who had once seemed a tower of friendly stability, now appeared a nervous totem figure with the tinctorial veins of obvious aging. Carter remembered how the boys mocked Mrs. Sheridan behind her back for the pancake and eye shadow she wore to mask her years. Adult Carter spent considerable time telling himself he wasn't "really" getting old, yet he was now older than the frail, failing Mrs. Sheridan. Though at the moment Carter wasn't exactly sure where he stood chronologically, or how to regard terms such as "now."

The school's bells rang. "That is the all-clear signal," Mr. Eggert called, bullhorn lowered. "You may return to your classrooms. Had this been an actual attack, we would have proceeded to the fallout shelter. Further drills will be held without warning."

The reference brought to Carter's mind those Cold War radio interludes during which a station would hand off to the Emergency Broadcast System and for sixty seconds transmit an ear-splitting screech. Just what was the point of that inscrutable squeal? The interruptions might as well have ended, "This has been a test of the Emergency Broadcast System. This has only been a test. Had it been an actual alert, the last sound you would ever have heard would have been this high-pitched screech." Or, "Had it been an actual alert, the system would not have worked." Each time the Top 40 was interrupted for this somber electronic exercise, boy Carter felt a wave of nervousness.

The place in the school that Mr. Eggert called the fallout shelter was a boiler room, where some tinned foods and jerry cans of water had been stored. The boiler room was also where the janitor lived, his cot and boxes of possessions set on the oily floor, the whiskey empties and bean pots often not cleaned up. Whether he made a home there by agreement or covertly because he had nowhere to go was the sort of question children did not ask. The boiler room was the custodian's strange zone, not even the daring boys would go near. Anyway, if the school's population really was sealed in that area for weeks while a radiation storm blew, competition for whatever food and water were available would quickly turn Darwinian.

Carter the boy thought about such details because his home was unusual in having an authentic fallout shelter—a concrete cube with air vents and lead-lined door, sitting mostly below

29

ground in what had previously been the backyard. It had started the day his father brought into the living room the family's first television, that magical device. As Carter and his brother Mack watched, their father fiddled with rabbit ears until grainy black-and-white semblances materialized in phosphor, and among the first images they saw was a public-service spot urging responsible homeowners to build fallout shelters. Allan Morris took this directive to heart, bringing the backhoe home one weekend from the small contracting firm he owned and ripping up the yard. Some neighbors laughed, others gawked; most kept their own counsel. The presence of this shelter did not lend Carter the slightest comfort. Its brooding, disruptive mass mainly served to give the boy more reason to think the bomb was really coming.

"Children, file back to class quietly!"

Carter turned toward Mrs. Sheridan as this command was spoken. She would die of stroke the year he left for college; he had been intending to visit to tell her about the scholarship and thank her for setting him on the right course, but didn't get around to it in time. To see her again in her glory was gratifying. "Can I go to the bathroom?" Carter whispered to his teacher. "Of course, dear." The child answered "Thank you," adult Carter trying to influence the words so they would carry sincerity.

The remainder of the school day passed. Young Carter returned to his desk, a hard single-piece unit with chair fixed to writing surface by a bend of iron, and fidgeted and doodled helicopter rocket-cars as his adult consciousness tried to roam the room. It was like being inside a robot of yourself: Carter's mind doing as it pleased but his body controlled by the scaffolding of time, his senses confined to seeing again or touching again whatever his self of that day had seen or touched.

When the dismissal bell rang, Carter ran out of the building and started home, Ward calling, "Wanna play Cooties after dinner?"

Adult Carter strove mightily to force the child's body to turn and walk toward the high school where so many of his important memories would reverberate, or toward the old bowling hall, where pin boys would still crouch behind screens at the end of each lane. But the young body would not answer the commands of the grown mind it hosted. Carter headed home as his mother had told him to, carrying schoolbooks folded into plastic protective covers.

Walking the streets of his boyhood did not cause Carter to experience sensations of lost idyll. Most people bear through life strong attachment for their memories of awakening to the world, and the connotations of rightness that their earliest impressions carry. Carter in contrast hardly ever thought of his young years. As a boy he viewed childhood as a period of unimportance: even at a green age it seemed to him nothing mattered until you were old and aware enough to make your own choices. Returning to his youth, Carter's attitudes about this were unchanged.

As Carter walked, noting lawn signs touting Hubert Humphrey or John Kennedy or Henry Cabot Lodge, it struck him that the town looked less different than he would have guessed. Basic arrangements of daily life have not been changing as much as generally assumed. Americans have been living in single-family suburban homes and arranging their lives around automobiles for half a century. Car culture, especially, has been present considerably longer than most realize; Willa Cather wrote about the ways car ownership affected life on the prairie. Still, there were distinctions between the time Carter had left and the one to which he had returned. His adult awareness noticed a stinging in the nostrils, something his boy self was inured to. He realized he had come back to the time before air-pollution control.

As his child's feet carried him closer to home, Carter tried to develop a theory of what had happened to him. Things seemed too tangible for a memory-illusion. Couldn't be actual time travel, there was the little detail of needing a time machine. Could it be psychosis? Carter began to entertain the notion that he had died on his way to the restaurant across from Whole Life Square and was now in an afterlife. Debating himself in his own head, then encountering a happier, youthful manifestation who criticized his adult choices: perhaps those had been review-of-life experiences he suffered while lying in a crosswalk, struck by a bus and breathing his last. With a start Carter wondered if some freak of pure physics had propelled his consciousness backward along a flaw in the empyrean, and that he would now relive his entire life. The notion was ghastly. To return to his brother's induction ceremony, to see Jayne Anne again that night—the prospect made him tremble. Finally Carter thought, *I'm assuming this is unique to me. What if it happens to everybody?*

The boy reached home, a stucco refuge guarded by an oak. Carter expected a rush of emotions on seeing the house again—it had passed out of the family years ago from his perspective, and toward the end Carter had rarely been welcome there, especially during the long phase of Mack's recuperation. Rather than powerful emotions, Carter was struck most by how compact his childhood dwelling place seemed. A weathered pickup truck sat in the drive, bearing the emblem AAAAAA-1 AL'S GENERAL CONTRACTING, this the name chosen to insure first listing in the Yellow Pages. The truck meant his father was home early.

Carter picked the evening newspaper off the porch, evening rather than morning papers then being the standard. The old evening paper was timed for delivery when the workingmen were coming home from the factory first shift, which began at dawn and ended at three in the afternoon. The modern morning paper is timed so white-collar men and women can read it before rushing off to a day that starts at a more civilized hour but lasts into the evening.

Atop the paper the headline read SUMMIT CANCELLED AS REDS

DISPLAY DOWNED PILOT. Adult Carter had hoped to look at the
newspaper's dateline in order to be sure of the moment, but the
child's eyes refused to rest on anything other than the sports
summary box. "They lost *again!*" the boy moaned. "How could
they lose *again!*"

Inside the house two enchanting aromas filled his nose—tuna-
pea casserole in the oven and beneath that a lesser fragrance of
lemon cake, already baked and cooling. While the sight of his
childhood home had not brought to Carter any powerful emotion
these scents did, triggering recollections of pure contentedness.
Carter felt his young self immensely hungry and knew that a
serving of casserole, cake, and milk would at this moment be
more fully gratifying than the most elaborate four-star dinner in
New York or Paris could ever be to his mature self. Adults view
meals as moments of indulgence but children *crave* food, which
for them conveys primal satisfaction. Nothing that will ever cross
an adult's tongue can taste as good as macaroni and cheese or
cherry pie at age twelve.

"Hey, I'm home," the boy called.

"Hay is for horses," his mother answered. She would not
brook children to employ certain words, among them "hey" and
"lousy," that bespoke lack of refinement. And Carter to this point
in his life had not even heard terms like "fuck" or "dyke," vo-
cabulary children of later years couldn't avoid even if their cul-
tural exposure was confined solely to church and PBS.

Carter ran toward the kitchen smells. His adult awareness was
startled to behold his mother again in her prime; his last sight of
her had been in the Sarasota nursing home, she pallid and insen-
sate, "fuzzy as a peach" in the words of the attendant. Here Marion Worth Morris stood in her domain, centered and assured:
member of the final generation of American womanhood where
there was consensus that the term homemaker was a commendation. "Any woman can be in the house, but not all women are

homemakers," Marion liked to say, *in the house* being period lexicon for wives holding no wage employment. And she was right, Carter now knew; with the addition of adult perspective he could recognize that his childhood home had been made, reflecting his mother's will.

"How soon is dinner?" the child inquired. His adult self longed to ask his mother if she was happy, if she loved her husband, if life brought her whatever she sought. But Carter hadn't asked when the chance was apparent, and the past cannot change.

"Early, because your father came home early," the slightest turn of the lips indicating his mother's disapprobation about any departure from the habitual. Having Dad home early was not a treat; it was a break from routine and a sign of disturbance. "He's working on the shelter." Regarding this she also inflected disapproval. "You should take his newspaper to him."

Carter drank the glass of milk his mother offered. The fluid was magnificently cool and substantial. What wine could rival this gratification? He headed for the backyard.

To Carter's adult awareness the family backyard was a provocative sight, though his young mind has long since stopped noticing its strangeness, the young able to update their frames of reference on a daily basis. A concrete carapace had taken over much of the yard, as if a large industrial turtle had settled just below the surface. An entryway descended to the shelter, its door currently open. Air vents with radiation filters jutted up, as did a periscope. The vent openings, Carter's father once explained to him, had been sized so as to be too small for hand grenades to be dropped down. Various tools and burlap bags of supplies were scattered around the yard, which had not yet been reseeded, leaving a salt-flats quality. Carter's father had promised his mother he would eventually install flower boxes along the shelter perimeter.

Allan Morris stood in the safe haven doorway, an acetylene

torch in his hand. "Got the paper? Let's see it," he said. Carter waited silently as his father read the latest about the CIA pilot shot down over Sverdlovsk. A much-anticipated Eisenhower-Khrushchev summit had been canceled as a result, and the newspapers were full of belligerent talk.

"He should have bitten the capsule," Allan pronounced, folding the paper in disgust.

"What does that mean, Dad?"

"He had a capsule of cyanide. He was supposed to use it if the mission failed, so that our government could deny everything. But he didn't, and now the president has been forced to admit the United States broke its word about spy flights. Wars have started over less."

"The pilot was supposed to swallow poison? But he would have died," Carter said, simply and plaintively.

"He knew there was risk when he took the job." Carter's father had been working on some aspect of the shelter door, and lit his torch to resume the task.

"Our side isn't like that," the boy protested. "It's their side that kills people, not our side."

"The man failed to do his duty because he was afraid to die."

"Dad, aren't we building this shelter because we're afraid to die?"

Allan Morris regarded his son. "Everyone is afraid to die, but people in the service may be required to. There was a time in France when an officer could have ordered me to die. When they put you in the service that time may come for you. This Francis Gary Powers with the three names, his time had come and he should have accepted it like a man. Because he didn't, millions may perish. These are facts of life, son."

"What do you mean, someday an officer might order me to die?" Both young and adult Carter couldn't believe how casually his father had said this, as though to offer a son's life to a government functionary was merely the order of things.

"We'll talk about that some other time."

"God can't want it like this," the boy said.

"The Bible tells us life is a trial and our reward comes after death. That corresponds with my experience. I've seen lots of trial and little reward. So I wouldn't worry about it much."

His father flipped down the welding visor and resumed work. Like many adolescents, Carter thought God should be the trump card in discussions with adults, but instead often found that mention of the Almighty only dropped the conversion downward to fatalism.

Growing up on a farm in Nebraska where life was hard, surrendering hope of college to support his family through the Depression, Carter's father viewed history as carried on the back of the common man. "Average people like us can find our places in the world," he would say over Sunday dinners, when he liked to discourse on current events, secure in the knowledge that his wife had been raised never to contradict a man on politics. "But we cannot hope to change the world, it takes us where it wants to," would be his benediction.

During World War II, Allan Morris had seen for himself how readily nations commit resources to destruction. Like many of his age group, he regarded the progression from Gatling gun to mustard gas to forty-ton tank to aerial bombardment to intercontinental thermonuclear missile as horrible but perfectly natural, considering that nations always acquired any weapon that became possible. To him, human nature made the use of nuclear munitions close to certain, and he was obliged to give his family a chance to live through the next round of escalation.

Carter and Mack had been taught how to read dosimeters, how to purify water, what radio stations to tune the transistor to for official information. Allan drilled the boys on the point that once the shelter door was sealed no one could be admitted, not even their mother, because anyone arriving after the blast would be hot and contaminate those within. One weekend, the father and two sons stayed in the shelter from Friday night to Sunday morning service time, and practiced rationing food. Allan had been distressed by how quickly it went.

Carter's father also warned his sons to steel themselves for the fact that he might have to shoot neighbors. Two rifles, German issue brought home as war trophies, were mounted inside the shelter door. When the awful day came, he cautioned, neighbors would try to force their way into whatever shelter they could find; but allowing in more people than their redoubt was designed to serve would only mean everyone would starve. Civil-defense manuals reluctantly endorsed force of arms at shelter doors, "to insure the preservation of the race." Once Carter asked his father if Ward Louvain would be let in. His father replied that Ward could be allowed into the shelter only to replace Mack or Mom, if they were not present or already dead. Then his father added that if Ward was caught outside the shelter and thus doomed, it would be merciful to shoot him so that he would not suffer death by radiation poisoning. Allan Morris, his son thought, talked just a little too often about the possibility of shooting neighbors.

"Dad, the arms race is crazy," the boy said loudly over the torch.

"Of course it's crazy, but it's happening," his father answered. Carter's father squinted at him as he dialed up the torch and it issued the swooping sound of rapidly moving gas. "There's a lot a person has to learn to accept."

"Why'd you come home early, Dad?" Carter shouted above the flame.

"When I heard about this U-2 thing I figured I'd better get back here and finish this seal in case the big one comes tonight. Figured I'd better let the guys off early so they could be with their families. Flight time of those missiles is less than an hour. Might not have had enough warning to get back from the shop."

"What do you mean, 'comes tonight'?" The boy shook.

"You can put your baseball glove and favorite toys inside here before bed, and I'll sleep with the radio on. The emergency tone will wake me. We'll get inside here in time."

Young Carter began to sob. The sob grew to a blubber, through which the boy spit out in almost infantile tones, "I'm afraid to die." His father shook his head and called toward the kitchen, "Marion!"

It's going to be alright, adult Carter tried to tell his wretched young self. *By my time the United States and Russia are running their nuclear factories in reverse, taking warheads apart instead of putting new ones together. Society does crazy things but is also capable of reason. It is up to us to determine which will prevail.*

"Marion, the boy is crying. Take him inside."

Young Carter was lost in dread and anxiety, watching his father labor over the concrete capsule in which he and his family would huddle for a few miserable weeks at the end of the world. In his mind the boy was hearing the air-raid siren blow in the night, running with his family toward the shelter in disoriented panic, watching his father warn pleading neighbors back with a rifle, seeing the house, the school, and the sports fields he so loved going up in blazing hellfire because adults thought they had no choice but to accept the drift of history. The bomb and later Vietnam would make Carter's generation think their own parents did not care if war and destruction came. To these children was given the chance to alter the current of history that carries nations toward awful fates. But the children misunderstood and viewed their parents, rather than the current, as the problem.

Carter saw his mother hurry out, rubbing her hands on an apron. She looked on the scene with unspoken disapproval and ushered a shaking boy back to the bosom of the kitchen.

Watching this unfold, Carter became aware that his consciousness was no longer accompanying the child, but viewing the scene as if from above. He did not reenter the house, did not receive his mother's consolation, did not sit to the plate of warm cake that was proffered to stanch the tears.

Instead Carter saw his father continuing to toil with the acetylene torch, swearing and mumbling. He saw his weeping boyhood form through the kitchen window, saw his mother's indecision. He began to perceive a change in consciousness, as if every part of his cognition were expanding in every direction. Then the smell of casserole was gone, his childhood home became a vapor, and Carter Morris tumbled back into the present.

CHAPTER THREE

Aꜰʀᴇᴇᴛ ᴡᴀꜱ ɪɴ ʟᴇꜱꜱ than ideal humor. "Where the flying fuck were you?" he howled. "Biggest payday our firm has ever seen, the table is set, and you disappear." Kendall's face had assumed a ruby tint and his neck veins were dilating to an unhealthful circumference. He looked as if he might soon need a helicopter ambulance. They'd have to carry him up to the roof, since the firm was on a low floor.

"An aberration took place," Carter said, using the passive structure of contemporary admission. Nobody lies to anyone; misstatements are given. Nobody causes injury; inadvertent harm results. Nobody defrauds; inaccurate information is released. Nobody violates the law; oversights occur. Above the portals into the White House, Congress, and big institutions of government and business ought to hang lovely Doric arches engraved ᴍɪꜱᴛᴀᴋᴇꜱ ᴡᴇʀᴇ ᴍᴀᴅᴇ.

"Middle of a settlement conference, the lead attorney disappears. A dozen senior counsels, a CEO, a CFO, mucho enchiladas grande. All with cars waiting. Two with *jets* waiting," Afreet thundered. "Suddenly no lead attorney. We recon the perimeter, search the city square outside the building. Top corporate suits and three-hundred-dollar-an-hour senior partners fanning out to foot-search. We call the cops, ask if there've been reports of foul play. 'No sir,' they say. 'Everything's shipshape.' But we have a missing person, we say. 'This is a free country,' the cops answer, 'sometimes people plain skip.' Everybody heads home, leaving millions of greenback dollars on the table. *Money is left on the table.* Total fucking fiasco. I go back to my hotel, drink all the vodkas in the minibar, use my laptop to find the most expensive nearby escort service, choose between guaranteed actual part-time supermodel and girl-next-door who's working her way through college, and tell them to get the honey over fast so I can fuck someone like I've just been fucked. Not as hard, mind you. I am not capable of fucking as hard as I've just been fucked. You would need the driveshaft from a battleship to fuck anyone like I've just been fucked. She comes up to the room, I do the needful, she even compliments me as she's hooking back her bra that I give a nice hard fuck. Instead of being flattered I have to say, 'I'm an amateur, you want to be fucked until you have been clinically speaking totally, utterly, completely fucked then you call my friend Carter, okay?' " Afreet had barely paused to breathe. "Am I getting through here? Has the word 'fucked' registered with you in any way?"

At last his pace slowed. "Finally at 3:00 A.M. I pick up this message you've just left with the hotel operator saying you'll see me back at the home office." Kendall looked Carter up and down. "Oh, okay, well then, as long as you checked in at 3:00 A.M. Where the fuck were you?"

"It's complicated," Carter said. "It won't happen again. I will patch this up and we will get the money."

"And the whole time you were somewhere where you couldn't have used a phone?" Afreet bellowed.

"I was near phones but I doubt the call would have gone through," Carter said. Kendall looked at him uncomprehending. "It's a long story."

Afreet paused. "Whatever it is, I have to know. You got some psychological issue? Obsessive-compulsive, post-traumatic, re-covered memory, multipolar? Or a physical challenge—blackouts, apnea, sleep deprivation? Anything that could count as a federally protected disability? Anything cutting-edge, like self-kidnapping complex?" Carter was shaking his head no on each point. "Illegal substance abuse? Substance proper use? Actionable dosage error in a prescription drug? Unconventional sex addiction? Latent transgender chromosome overlap?" More shakes of no. Kendall's eyes narrowed. "Look, this is like a security clearance situation, you can have something untoward in your dossier but you must level with me about what it is, so we can have our denials straight."

"I've done nothing to be ashamed of."

"So what was it?"

"Something that will remain my private affair," Carter said, attempting to sound decisive.

"If you think—" Afreet's intercom rang and the sugary voice of his secretary provided interruption. "Your broker on two. He used the word 'urgent.' "

"Danny, ciao," Afreet said, lunging for the receiver. "Sure I filed the disclosure. Definitely put it on my to-do list, anyway. Date? Sure I could get you the date. What do you mean the SEC disqualified my—wait a second, there's somebody in my office." He cupped his hand over the receiver and commanded, "Out!"

Carter slipped from the office, grateful. He smiled and nodded to Afreet's secretary, unanimously addressed as Miss Lockport. She carried herself in a British manner, and her uncertain ethnicity—mildly dusk skin, perhaps a London-educated Farsi—rendered her an exotic commodity. "Morning, luv," she said as he passed her desk. "Several FedEx on your chair. Six certified already this morning." Lawyers send a considerable amount of paperwork via registered or certified mail. Usually this is unnecessary, slows things down and generates process costs. None of those outcomes is perforce objectionable.

Carter walked the main hallway of Malison & Afreet. Everything in the interior of the firm was plastered with one kind of appliqué or another, from chrome facings to plastic veneers to a substance, fabricated from recycled loading pallets and Canadian tree bark, that was supposed to suggest cherry wood but pretty much suggested recycled loading pallets. Law-firm decorators strive for a soothing ambience so clients won't become too emotional when they hear about their invoices. Displayed on a narrow fake-cherry table in the front hall was a bronze cast of a Remington of horse and rider; Afreet liked to joke that they should get the statue motorized so the horse could buck whenever a deep-pocket client walked by. Actually he hadn't said client, a word Afreet used only in formal settings, he'd said customer. Just as people no longer live in cities, rather now live in markets, lawyers and doctors now have customers, and the goal is to sell, sell.

Entering his office, Carter found the accumulation of overnight and special-delivery communications. Several were procedural actions in death-row cases. Carter had topped out as an associate at the lofty Kirkland & Ellis, then been asked to "look around"— that is, leave—because he'd never make partner. He'd never make it because he spent too much time on pro bono cases.

At the time Carter had arrived at Kirkland & Ellis, he was told the management committee wanted someone with an unorthodox background to balance out the unreflective careerists who comprised the preponderance of the firm's hires. Initially his bosses seemed pleased Carter spent considerable hours on capital-punishment appeals or helping a legal-aid clinic with the sort of commonplace challenges—credit judgments, garnishments, custody disputes—that can take over the lives of those without resources. But then the Kirkland brass began dropping hints about how Carter wasn't young anymore, pro bono was for cutting your teeth, it was time he got down to real work like representing banks. Carter resisted and soon was looking around.

All legal firms say pro bono work is essential to their mission, but they say it with the same conviction that suburban churches say their doors are open to the homeless.

When Carter landed at Malison & Afreet, his new employer knew he was someone whom life had taken down a few notches. Kendall liked to hire lawyers who had washed out at the elite firms, because they came in humbled, ready to discard their compunctions. "If you're desperate to get partner because you know it's your last shot then you will do anything, and people who will do anything make good lawyers," he'd said. Carter was chosen for this reason. He'd tried to take a stand at Kirkland, staged a huge argument with the management committee about commitment to public-interest law, and the upshot was, he lost and got tossed. Dismayed, and by that point most of the way down the waterfall over which ideals plummet, Carter told Kendall he was ready to bring home some money for a change.

As Carter turned away from pro bono and toward class-action suits, Afreet thought he was maturing quite nicely. In the last year *Grandits*, a cash cow, and the Value Neutral quasi-swindle had taken over Carter's billable hours. Once Carter would have felt unease about that. He didn't now. At least the plummet from the rapids of ideals to the flat sea of acceptance had simplified his life. Carter's young self held a child's expectant belief in the world's ability to become perfect, yet was wracked by vast fears. As an adult Carter believed in almost nothing but worried about little beyond tragic matters such as the difficulty of finding parking spaces.

Staring at the piles of accumulated materials, Carter tossed the pro bono letters aside. Some of the death-row motions traced back a decade, following him from his old employer. Ten years was common for capital appeals, twenty not unknown; clients had a pretty strong incentive to drag out the process. In that sense condemned men might be the lawyer's dream client, if not for the complication that most were indigent psychopaths.

Carter weighed what was happening to him. Probably he had experienced an unusually poignant assertion of memory, traveling nowhere other than his own synaptic corridors. Yet the part about disappearing from the settlement conference—that was bona fide, there were witnesses. Maybe he had fallen into some kind of temporary blackout and wandered for those hours, not snapping out of it until 3:00 A.M., when he placed the call. Still it was strange that his suit was in perfect condition when his awareness rebounded normal. If he had blacked out, wouldn't he have been rolling in the gutter or some such?

Considering everything currently seemed ordinary, Carter felt he could eliminate the fearsome possibility that some freak of physics would cause him to relive his entire life. He seemed left with these alternatives:

1. Time travel. But scientists say it is a physical-law impossibility, and besides, where was the time machine?
2. Memory incarnation triggered by the return to Whole Life Square. This would suggest Carter had deeply suppressed emotions so potent as to be capable of taking command of his consciousness. The thought made him shudder: he much preferred to be attenuated by cynicism.
3. A higher power was causing him to revisit his past, for some purpose.
4. A higher power was causing him to revisit his past to mess with him.
5. He was indeed dead, and in the afterlife, people in your office will still be mad at you.

Of these possibilities only 2. gave any comfort, and even then it was comfort wrapped within a psychiatric diagnosis he was not anxious to see.

After riffling through business cards in a desk drawer, Carter found the number of an old college acquaintance, a research psychologist at the University of Michigan. He'd bumped into the man, Abraham Wolsam, a few years before at a social event. Wolsam was a networker and, knowing Carter had occasionally been in the news, pumped him for information about how to get one's name before the media. Now Carter wanted to pump Wolsam.

On the phone they exchanged pleasantries in a conversation with no clear purpose. Wolsam said, "You're having some kind of issue aren't you? That's why you're calling."

"Well—"

"I get calls like this, from people I haven't heard from in years, when they're having some psychological issue. But I'm in research. What you need is to see a clinician. Researchers should not give clinical advice." Then Wolsam leaped into clinical advice. "There's no need to worry. Everyone encounters psychological setbacks at certain points in life. This is normal. Usually it's something minor like an adjustment disorder."

Disorder. Sure didn't take long to advance to one of those ill-omened medical terms.

Carter explained his situation in the most general terms. "I can't diagnose over the phone," Wolsam said. Then he leaped into phone diagnosis. "Some patients report experiencing memories so intense they cannot be distinguished from actual events. Sometimes called anamneses. Usually it's a passing anomaly and resolves itself, people get tired of reliving their pasts because most people's pasts are not worth reliving. Once in a while this condition means the person is going crazy. You're not hearing voices, are you?"

"Ha ha. Of course not."

The conversation went sideways from there. Carter skipped the fact that he was not only hearing voices but seeing and touching the people from whom they emanated. Wolsam gave him the name of a local clinician who had a national reputation. Then he asked Carter if he thought Katie Couric would be interested in his latest study, on the psychological stress caused by receiving unwanted e-mail.

After the call Carter returned to contemplating his desk. The FedEx was chock-full with paperwork from Value Neutral, including a graciously worded request that he provide them, under privilege, any medical records that may exist pertaining to his psychological stability. Asking the other side's lawyer for his medical files is not exactly Standard Operating Procedure, but then, this was the dawn of cooperative litigation.

Value Neutral did not expect the request to be fulfilled; it was a way of telling Carter he'd better get back on the beam. This company just didn't miss many tricks. Carter thought for a moment about Value Neutral's current signature item—exact duplicates of the underwear worn by celebrities. The product's success showed how savvy the company was. Value Neutral's tie-in department worked with movie studios to develop distinctive underwear looks for big-budget films. Once designs were completed, they were digitally scrambled and rushed by courier to sweatshops in Chengdu or Xiamen. There, factory officials who had once run reeducation camps would monitor faxed statistics on film openings in the United States, and as soon as they knew which movie would get the weekend's highest gross, instruct laborers to sew underwear that corresponded to whatever the stars of that flick had been flouncing about in.

A few months ago it had been men's briefs with a red band that had to be turned inside-out to be seen, matching what a young swoon star had worn in a disaster movie based loosely on the *Exxon Valdez* spill, but adding a volcano eruption at the Coast Guard base and twenty leggy young high school coeds on an all-girl ecology field trip who were trapped on an island that was slowly being covered with crude oil. This week the featured celebrity undergarment was a black bra with a patented tongue-operated release, matching one an impossibly buff blond actress wore in a film called *Lethal Bimbo* during a love scene with an alien bounty hunter from another galaxy. As each batch of bras was completed, the finished products were airlifted out of China by A340 jumbo jets that employed satellite navigation pulses to touch down perfectly on runways adjoining rows of workers' shacks made from corrugated scrap metal and held against the wind by stones. What the laborers who spent fourteen-hour days in the factories thought of all this capital and technology devoted to celebrity underwear, Carter shuddered to imagine.

For that matter, what the customers who lined up for these products must be thinking was almost as distressing. But like the policeman said, it's a free country. If people chose of their own volition a life of frenetic work-and-spend, and that choice compells them to scan the horizon for possessions that make it all seem worthwhile, and what gives gratification or just a moment's surcease was a Lexus with gold nameplates or numbered titanium golf balls or a tongue-operated celebrity bra, who are we to argue? The satisfaction the ancient hunter-gatherer felt when prey was bagged now transferred to the mall, and for all Carter knew it was a positive development.

As for developing-world production, wasn't the choice in many poor countries either two dollars a day for backbreaking toil in a sweatshop making frills for the West or ten cents a day for worse toil at subsistence farming? Carter had seen somewhere the results of a study comparing the low life expectancy for sweatshop workers in the developing-world with equally dismal figures for late nineteenth-century immigrants in the mills of Massachusetts. Subsequent generations of Massachusetts workers turned out well off, and so it followed that generations of developing-world children would thank their parents for suffering for Value Neutral.

Lining up these rationalizations, Carter vowed again to accept the wealth the settlement would bring him. Marx may have bungled the details but was surely right on his core premise: everything is economics. Only a fool or an idealist, Carter told himself, would walk away from this. And I'm not a fool nor any longer an idealist. He picked up the phone and placed a call to Jennings Guerdon.

WAITING FOR GUERDON'S SECRETARY to put him through, Carter pondered the fact that once he took the money he would finally depart from youth. Carter had already surpassed the average American life expectancy at the beginning of the twentieth century, was already older than ninety-nine percent of the Homo sapiens who had ever lived. But he thought of himself as not yet grown up, his cohort nursing an extremely flexible definition of youth.

Some of it was stylistic: casual clothes, first-name basis, beer and pizza, obsession with sports—anything that harked back to the callow years was clung to. Some of it was marketing: advertisers devising the concept of "mid youth," which now meant the fifties, after which advertisers would like you to take early retirement, skipping normal adulthood entirely. Some of it was physical defiance of aging: StairMasters and the like. Though on this point Carter and his peers were taunted by medical science, which was increasingly producing indications that the biotechnology of a much-longer lifespan would be developed just in time for the Baby Boom to glimpse it from the nursing home, Moses on Mount Nebo dying in view of the Promised Land. In previous centuries, one of the chief accomplishments of a person's life was becoming an adult and able to address one's parents as an equal. For Carter's age group, the goal was never to become like mom and dad. His millions of peers wanted to acquire the material benefits of maturity—money, career—but conceptually to remain in adolescence, mentally still arguing with parents and teachers long after surpassing the age these people were when the arguments began.

Jennings Guerdon came on the phone only after an extended pause, during which, Carter knew, he had scrambled to get a company lawyer to pick up another line as a witness to the conversation. Then Guerdon spoke with affected formality, the way a mob lieutenant does when he assumes the FBI is taping him.

"Mr. Morris, we feel quite concerned about your absence from the settlement conference," Guerdon began. "Naturally our sole consideration is for your well-being, and we do not wish to jeopardize your mental or physical health in any way. Still, my company has a material interest in the rapid resolution of this matter—"

It went on like that for the better part of an hour. Carter fudged, mumbled, or changed the subject whenever his disappearance was mentioned. A couple of times he made vague references to a woman having something to do with it, and that seemed to allow other things to be left unsaid, in the way a person can wriggle out of an unpleasant conversation by making nebulous references to religious belief. By the end of the call, it was clear the status quo had been restored: Value Neutral still wanted to do the settlement and still wanted Carter as its simulated adversary.

He walked down the hall to assure Afreet the situation was under control, but Miss Lockport shook her head about entering the office; they could hear shouting inside. So Carter went back to his desk and sent the boss a computer message, phrased in the most upbeat terms. He checked his own e-mails and found more than one hundred, most of them infuriatingly ending with a question that required reply, though usually on something too minor to have any import other than engaging the obligation of an answer.

There were also half a dozen messages from Ginny Intaglio, including a few with mild come-hither references. In one, ostensibly asking for a First Amendment opinion about a pornography case, Ginny wrote, "I'm tired of sitting here thinking about sin when I could be doing something about it!"

Carter now recalled half hearing her suggestive suggestions about a four-poster bed. He harbored no misconceptions she was attracted to his soul. But a businesslike affair might be just what the doctor ordered for Carter's ennui, especially considering the ego rocket of a younger woman. Businesslike affairs get a bad rap, Carter thought, owing to various true-love illusions. What's wrong with a nice dinner and then straight to sex without complicating emotions, neither party's heart exposed to harm because neither has expectations? What precisely is wrong with pleasure for its own sake? If sex was available only for money, like justice, everyone might be happier. Then there was the matter of the Intaglio physique. Ginny brought her gym bag with her to the office most days, and clearly was getting her money's worth. That spectacularly curved boundary where her dress-white blouse tucked tightly into her business-gray skirt was a region any man could be persuaded to explore.

Carter spent the rest of the day polishing a brief. He tapped out answers to everything from Ginny, struggling to come up with lines that hinted ever-so-slightly at prurience. He opened a file drawer and tossed in all the pro bono materials, unopened. Then he completed a medical-leave form, leaving blank the box "state reason/illness," and slipped out through the lobby-evading door near the rest room. After a quick stop at his apartment he headed for the airport, going to the departure gate and only then calling Ward Louvain to announce his coming visit.

CARTER HADN'T SEEN WARD in a quarter century. What an expanse of time that would have seemed to them as eager boys; the duration of the entire Greek golden age, perhaps.

Discounting the blur years of infancy, the first decades of Carter's life seemed to have pulsed with significance: awakenings, contentions, strong-bonded friendships, passionately unstable romances, colossal errors of judgment, endless excitement perceived as the natural condition. Since then Carter's emotional self had contracted like a collapsing star, while the daily issues he struggled with diminished from what-is-truth to eat out or call in? It was natural for a person's early years to ripple with assorted kinds of tumult, then the middle years to be a quest for family and balance; Carter never married, and that deprived him of many experiences of the second phase of life. But as he rode the plane toward Ward, knees pressed into his chest and for hours watching attentively from the corner of his eye for his chance to place an elbow on an armrest, Carter found himself unnerved by the realization that Ward would ask him what he'd done since the heady days of youth and Carter would be able to catch him up on the whole story in a few minutes.

About what had happened to Ward in that interim, Carter did know. Unfortunately, he knew it from reading the newspapers.

Ward had stayed home, risen in his father's commercial insurance business, entered politics as a moderate Republican, won a state representative's post in the old-line Democratic labor district he and Carter were raised in, later won the job of county executive. Next Ward made a minor name for himself as a pioneer of contracting-out government services—refuse collection, fire trucks, the county jail. This attracted the attention of President Ronald Reagan, who praised Ward in a Rose Garden talk as "an example of what makes America shine like a jewel the whole world would like to steal."

When Vice President George Bush came to inspect Ward's privately run sewage system, Bush hosted a fund-raiser to introduce Ward to the kind of wealthy men whose favor he would need for a planned Senate candidacy. It was the biggest night of Ward's life. Not long after, an auditor piqued by the publicity surrounding the Louvain name noticed that several of the contracting-out enterprises were insured by Ward's father's firm at excessive rates. The waivers that let these contracts over the low bidders bore Ward's signature. Ward hung in the gust of the scandal for a year, talking endlessly, wife and daughters by his side, about how he had made mistakes—"mistakes were made" was the phrase he used—but that there was no shame in trying to help your family. The day Ward resigned his face was briefly on *CBS Evening News,* where Carter's face had once briefly been. When they were gangly boys rushing out to play cowboys and Indians, who would have guessed that conjunction? In the future, we will all be humiliated for fifteen minutes.

One of the other lawyers at Malison & Afreet had been an assistant U.S. attorney and recognized Ward's name. He asked, "Who took him down, local DA or the feds?"

"Ward resigned the night before the committee was to issue its report, so no charges were ever filed," Carter replied, protective. "His record is as clean as yours or mine."

"Oh, like that's reassuring."

Landing at the Fresno air terminal, Carter picked up his overnight bag from the carousel. Like many before him wanting to forget an old life, Ward had decamped to California. "Men rush to California as if true gold were to be found in that direction," Thoreau complained in 1855, thinking the fad would peak any moment.

Renting a car, Carter drove toward Armona, a dot in the San Joaquin Valley, the state's heartland. Here was working agriculture, not the modish vineyards farther north—dairy and vegetables from level land, the farmer's ideal. Carter passed field after field, most adorned not with farmhouses but standard-design contemporary suburban homes. Some of the large spreads had buildings that looked like military dormitories; there lived the seasonal labor, seven and eight to a room. Carter had once heard a lawyer for an agribusiness firm assert that for migrant workers it really wasn't a problem being bedded down side by side on the floors of cramped rooms, because after double shifts in the sun they were so exhausted they never had trouble sleeping.

Armona went by fast—a Burger King, gas stations, a strip mall of single-story buildings. Carter doubled back and on the second pass saw a purple-and-yellow sign hanging over a glass-front office, LOUVAIN INDEPENDENT INSURANCE BROKERAGE. Purple and yellow had been their high school colors. He parked and waited, watching the office for an hour, thinking he'd go in when it did not look busy; the California sun beat hard, making Carter sweat with the car AC off. It all seemed vaguely unnatural, the concrete and the unshaded structures placed into the sun to bake. During the hour, no customers entered Ward's place of business. So Carter walked up, feeling mislaid in his gentleman's downtown clothes. Every person he'd seen come and go in the strip mall was dressed for farming.

A bell jingled when Carter opened the door, ringing needlessly it seemed, for the inside was so tiny no one could fail to notice an arrival. Two metal desks fit closely together on either side of a partition, the entire area not much larger than the space taken up by a parked SUV. At the first desk sat an older woman with a small fan blowing on her and a radio playing, tuned to one of those play-at-work stations.

"Do you have an appointment?" she asked imperiously.

Carter identified himself.

"Señor is due back shortly," she answered. "You can sit there."

She indicated the second desk, covered with calendars, print-outs, mailing envelopes. There were pictures in stand-up frames of two young women, one in graduation mortarboard, the other holding an oboe; surely his daughters. No picture of a wife. It took a moment for Carter's vision to focus on the stack of mailing envelopes, each of which was imprinted, next to the return address and the large words YOU CAN TRUST YOUR INDEPENDENT BROKER, with a thumbnail photograph of a middle-aged man. A forced smile, heavyset, two-thirds bald, someone the years had not treated well. That's Ward, Carter realized, the skinny, bouncy, endlessly energetic boy with whom he had played a thousand games and made a thousand discoveries all totally unique in human history. The Ward for whom the whole world seemed possible.

A door slammed just outside, and Carter saw Ward clamber down from a pickup truck. His stomach jutted past his belt and swung around, like an object he was carrying. He was sweating.

"Juanita, the Thurnherr application is a complete mess. That's the second time this month, Juanita, and I'm not paying you to—" he began as soon as he had the door half open. Juanita said nothing, merely nodding toward their visitor. Ward's demeanor quickly changed. "Ward Louvain, independent broker you can trust because I represent all brands. Sir, how can I help you?" he asked, extending his hand to Carter.

"Ward, it's me. Carter."

Ward's face fell. He had been distant on the phone, trying to discourage the visit. Carter moved awkwardly to hug him, and he stepped backward toward Juanita.

"Well—nice of you to drop in." A long pause. "What kind of business brings you to this hellhole anyway?"

"I don't have any business. I came here just to see you."

"Well—great. But I've got appointments all day, I'm sorry

that—" Carter could see Juanita making a gesture of "you have no appointments" and Ward waving her off. "Listen, if you're ever going to be out this way again—"

"Ward, I haven't seen you in twenty-five years. Let's talk."

"I don't think I—" He was edgy and uncomfortable. Was it Carter seeing his bald spot and waistline? How far he'd fallen?

"Why don't you ask your receptionist if she would like to go get a cup of coffee?"

It took Juanita mere seconds to gather herself and depart. Ward seemed to relax slightly after the door closed behind her.

"She overhears every word I say on the phone, looks at me all the damn day long," Ward said. And then, "I was sorry to hear about your father. I meant to send my condolences but things have just been crazy lately, they've been—"

"I understand. Things have been crazy for me too," Carter said. Practically everyone would agree with the statement "things have been crazy lately," although objectively this was rarely true, except in the consumption-of-time sense.

"Your dad was a fine man. People made comments, but they didn't understand him. He was always very kind to me."

"Thanks. You were his favorite, of the kids." Carter didn't add, He always said he would have felt really bad if he'd had to shoot you.

"When I was elected county executive, he sent me a picture he found when he was disposing of your mom's things. You and me as boys, arms around each other, both flashing the thumbs-up sign. One of those old black-and-white prints with the serrated border. It choked me up."

"Can I see it?"

"A lot went into storage when Marcy and I—you know she left me?"

"I didn't know. I'm sorry, Ward."

"My pet peeve: fair-weather friends," Ward said. Carter shook his head, uncomprehending. "In our high school yearbook from senior year that's what she said under her picture: 'My pet peeve: fair-weather friends.' Moment something goes wrong she's out the door. Only time I ever hear from her is when she needs extra money for a stone garden for the house, she needs extra money for new window treatments, she needs extra money for therapy because she's still working out her anger that I got into trouble. I'm supposed to pay for her to talk about how she's angry at me. And who just signed the note for Laura's six-thousand-dollar competition oboe? Not her for damn sure."

"Ward, how are your folks? Are they still with us?"

"Both fine, thank you. Mom still sharp as a tack. Dad still starting before noon."

"He can keep drinking like that at his age?"

"The man is already embalmed, so he can't die."

Ward's dad was a drunk but a jolly drunk; as a teenager Carter had treasured the Louvain house because there he received the open affection that was impossible in his own home. Carter's father built a bomb shelter and racked rifles by the door; Ward's father built a beach house and every friendly face was welcome. Carter always wanted to be around Ward's father, who would praise him, compliment him, offer him a Seven-and-Seven like he was a sophisticate. Ward in turn always wanted to be around Allan Morris, who possessed the seriousness, work habits, and knowledge of current events that Ward's father lacked. Some sort of grass-is-greener for both boys. But while Allan Morris's dourness masked nothing, for dour he was, Ward's father's joviality was a front. According to what Carter had heard, Ward put the fix in on the county contracts because the family firm was about to fail, owing to his father's alcoholic brume, and his mother begged him not to let her husband be disgraced. Disgrace came instead to the son.

"So—how's business?" Carter was desperate for conversation.

"Look, what's the reason you're here? Why now?"

"I had—let's say an unusually intense dream about childhood the other day, and it made me think of you," Carter said. Ward's eyes rolled as if to say, yeah right, a dream about childhood. "It made me think I made a fundamental mistake in life by letting our friendship lapse. We were once happy boys together, and maybe"—now he was deteriorating into relationship talk, and Ward was wincing—"maybe remembering that could bring some happiness to our adult lives."

Ward looked on perplexed, as if Carter had just proposed they paint their bodies blue and beat drums in the forest.

"Then was then, now is now," Ward said. "We had a happy childhood. Adulthood sucks. It's just the facts of life. And don't blame me for the drift apart. You were the one at the fancy college. I wrote you letters, I had to tell the guys in the dorm I was writing my mom so they wouldn't call me a fag for writing to a guy. How often did you write back?" Carter blanched to remember that in those wild first years of university independence, his new college friends had seemed so sophisticated and cosmopolitan, Ward in his mind had become something he had moved past.

"That was stupid of me, and unfair. Today I wish I'd—"

"So you're here for some nostalgia thing," Ward said. "I thought, you being a lawyer, maybe they set you up to tape me or something." Carter made an "impossible!" face. "Every few years somebody talks about reopening the investigation, since technically they never nailed me."

"Ward, there isn't enough money in the world to get me to sell out a friend," Carter said. Now my principles, that's a different matter, he thought.

Juanita was returning, clutching a coffee large enough to set on a soda fountain and drop two straws into. "I'm sorry, but my business is in bad shape and I've just got to get back to work. Thanks for coming," Ward said.

Carter got into his rental car and drove around. The local map had ominous markings like "dry lake" and "asbestos hazardous area," a ringed zone bigger than Fresno itself, but up in the Diablo Mountains. Carter pictured Ward driving his pickup from farm to farm, laboring to sell term life or auto or crop insurance.

About five o'clock Carter drove back to the strip mall and waited for Juanita to leave. He walked in again and offered to buy Ward dinner. Ward agreed and didn't stop to phone anyone; Carter felt pretty sure there was no one waiting for him to come home. They went to a steak joint in Visalia—"anything but Tex-Mex," Ward said—and ate well. Ward barely sipped at the one beer he ordered, though he called for soup, starters, the twenty-four-ounce porterhouse, and dessert.

Carter's friend talked in considerable detail about many forms of bitterness. Most of what he said was what you'd expect. Ward was particularly resentful that he had been unable to find new work as a city manager or county official. All the way to the West Coast the scandal had followed him, and the point that he resigned before any formal charge was leveled—something that meant quite a bit to Ward, since officially his honor was preserved—didn't resonate. The cities and counties Ward talked to about jobs were blunt in saying all that mattered was that he had been accused. Reporters and civic groups were looking for something to denounce, and anyone hiring Ward would give them what they wanted. A very modern viewpoint.

Ward explained that his father had begged him to find money that would prevent disclosure of the fact that the family finances were based on embezzlement. That's where the funds for the beach house originated; the father's expansive, self-congratulating style was underwritten by phony receipts and shell transactions.

The only way out for Ward's dad was to pay it all back quietly, plus fines. During Ward's youth, his father had endlessly advised that one could get whatever one wanted by acting with confidence. "And in a screwed-up way he was right because the stuff about him never did come out, I shoveled him enough business that he was able to settle with the creditors off the record since they didn't want it known they had been embezzled," Ward said. "He acted confident and took whatever he wanted, and everything worked out fine for him."

"But if he feared scandal, he got ten times the scandal with you," Carter said.

"Bastard never cared about my name, only his own," Ward said. "I went home the night I resigned. Needed to hear him admit I did everything to show loyalty to him. Mom locked her room and wouldn't come out. And you know what he said? 'Don't blame me for your mistakes, son. You took bad advice.' I said, 'Christ, Dad, I took your advice!' Again he insists, 'You should not have taken bad advice.' Was the only thing he would say. If I'd had a gun I would have dropped him where he stood, swear to God."

Carter tried to draw Ward into sentimental talk of boyhood, but attempts to breech this topic were deflected; Carter began to fear he sounded lachrymose, and so dropped the subject. He learned that Ward hated the San Joaquin Valley, hated the insurance business, really hated Juanita, was barely breaking even, was getting up in the morning and struggling to earn money solely because he wanted, when he received phone calls from his daughters, to be able to say he would mail whatever check they required. And how long until the ex managed to turn his daughters against him? Pretty much the classic profile of a suicide candidate.

Carter reflected on the inverse relationship between friends and time. In youth, most people can make a friend in an hour, quickly develop emotional attachment, and hold on to that feeling for years. By late adolescence it's still relatively easy to make a friend but losing them becomes a danger, since actions are more easily taken the wrong way. By adulthood it's almost impossible to form a new friendship, while an existing friend may be squandered by a single poorly chosen word. Thus the supply of friends declines over time, and the emotional risk-reward ratio keeps changing for the worse. As relationships wither, the number of people who care about your life's journey steadily drops. Owing to this, it is priceless to recover even one friend who knew and loved you when all was still in the distance. But contemporary life made this unlikely by scattering everyone to the four winds, adding physical to emotional distance. Those who lived their whole lives in one place at least had the consolation of nearness to ones who knew them when.

As it grew late Ward insisted on taking a taxi back to his place, but taxis are hard to come by in farm country. Carter guessed the reason was that Ward didn't want his old friend seeing where he lived. When Ward relented about the ride, Carter drove him to a block of cheap flats, one step up from a trailer park, pathways half lit by untended lamps. "This is the kind of place the seasonals move to when they've saved enough to get off the labor camp," Ward explained. "I'm the only one in the complex who has his own bedroom." There were tough-looking Mexicans hanging around, but Ward assured Carter they were harmless, because the last thing a migrant worker wants is trouble with the law. "Just stay away from them on Saturday nights, drunk as skunks, knives come out over nothing and they play the boom boxes till dawn," he said.

Then Ward, companion of Carter's boyhood, disappeared into a puddle of shadows near the building entrance. When they'd been children, anything that went wrong for Ward—bad grade, lost a game, fight on the playground—Carter instantly knew about and worked to solve. He didn't have the slightest idea what to do about the problems Ward had now.

Carter drove to a Best Western motel he had seen during the afternoon of aimless circling. He checked in, went to get his car to park it near the room. Standing by the rental sedan was a rangy teenager who seemed too young to be out at a late hour, and whose appearance—white socks, short cuffs, flattop cut—was out of sync, even by contemporary standards of the-worse-the-better fashion.

The boy was inspecting Carter's car and seemed bewildered. As he drew closer Carter recognized the figure—himself, in his teens.

"Where are the wings?" the boy asked. "I figured every car would have wings by now. That's what *Popular Mechanics* predicted. And the personal helicopters—I haven't seen a single personal helicopter go by."

"You're a handsome sprout," Carter said to his younger form.

"Touch my hand," the boy instructed.

"Shouldn't I put my stuff in the motel room first?"

"That doesn't matter."

Carter placed a hand on the teenager's shoulder. Immediately he felt himself course with disconcerted, imperative sexual longings. Lesser urges implored him to dribble a basketball and eat several cheeseburgers. Then he experienced the sensation of every part of his body expanding away from every other part, and tumbled back to the past.

CHAPTER FOUR

A WAFT OF AUTUMN AIR, chromatic and substantial, spun around Carter, who blinked into the declining afternoon sun and checked his footing. He was aware of the crowd murmur, various chords of it floating by on the wind. He thought of the group watching him as unfathomably huge, though the spectators numbered perhaps a thousand, and one day he would run to the cheers of far more. The teenager looked up at the scoreboard, just as he had done that day, and saw his school trailing reviled crosstown rival Roger Taney High by five points with the clock two ticks from zero. The punt was about to sail to Carter, he would be tackled, and the big game of the annual high school football season would be over.

Carter's adult awareness expanded into the boy and, like him, squinted toward the late-afternoon sun. Football equipment that made the teenaged Carter feel robust and powerful felt entertainingly silly to the adult, something a jester would don. Pads that didn't really fit, loose against spiny bones, pungent from being hung unwashed in a football locker. A helmet worn by many boys before him, much of its purple and yellow paint rubbed off by the pseudo-combat. Knee and elbow and hand and neck padding, all perspiration-stained and not quite put on right.

The teenaged Carter was thinking at this moment of the effort that had carried him to this point. He'd forced himself to do push-ups in the summer evening heat, forced himself to be friendly to the strutting popular boys who formed the core of the team, forced himself to endure the coach's rambling orations on who gets going when the going gets tough. His adult awareness considered those efforts quite trivial, and focused on the splendor of an autumn afternoon when life is new and everything lies ahead. The breeze slipped under the awkward football padding and brought cool sensations to the skin, brought back the awareness of biology that adults talk themselves out of feeling. Smells associated with youthful contentment—hot-dog aromas and cheap aftershave and even the sulfur bite from the nearby steel mill—made the draft of air seem a chemical medium. A train rumbled by toward the mill, across the trestle at the far end of the sportsfield plateau; its low oscillation seemed to make the very atoms of the teenager's body vibrate pleasingly, telling him all was in motion, all was purposeful. And every person who mattered to Carter's teen years was nearby, watching, making the moment exactly as the child imagines the whole of life will be, watched eagerly.

There was a whistle, a decline in the crowd murmur, muffled grunts, the pops of collisions between boys in plastic armor, and then the ball was spiraling end over end toward the teenager. Adult Carter stiffened, for he knew what came next—his brother Mack's voice, projected through the instant of crowd hush, encouraging and threatening as only an older brother can. Mack to whom it had come so easily to be the school's football star, back home for his first Marine leave and wearing full dress, Mack hollered to his brother, "Make me proud!" Teen Carter flinched when he heard Mack's challenge, took his eye off the ball, felt it hit his chest and roll away.

Many things then happened in a blur. Two players in gold and black sprung for the ball, but it followed an eccentric ricochet back to Carter's hands. Carter writhed from their grasp and ran toward the sideline. Many gold forms were there, so he doubled back toward the opposite sideline. A gold player slipped and caused a teammate to trip. Someone grabbed Carter's jersey but failed to get purchase. For a moment he was running in the broken field behind Carl Wabash, the street bully who menaced Carter and all kids who were skinny or had good grades, but who now lowered his big shoulders to clear Carter's path. An unseen player hit Carter in the back. Hands grabbed his left ankle, so Carter kicked his right leg forward with all his might, just as he'd seen Giants and Browns runners do on television, and the extra momentum broke the tackler's hold. Carter saw a gold form perfectly poised to bring him down and end the game. Then a purple streak came across his vision; Richard Delaware the earnest student council president, ever-praised by adults for his gift at impressing the grown, had thrown himself at the gold player and both toppled. Carter stumbled and spun, high-stepping to avoid the chalky streak of the sideline. He regained his balance and looked up. There was no one ahead of him.

For the next moment the teenage Carter's thoughts would be focused with consummate intensity on running in a straight line and not forever humiliating himself by falling down and blowing the game. Carter's adult awareness saw the action from a different perspective, examining those around him as he ran, seeing their young forms and knowing their fates.

Ward Louvain had dropped his sousaphone, bolted from the band, and was sprinting stride for stride with Carter down the sideline, urging him on. Carl Wabash was back on his feet, cheering and shouting obscenities at the other team. Richard Delaware and George Deerhurst were a few yards behind running in the convoy-block position, hoping the crowd was watching them, too. Richard: who would grow up to be a doctor owning one of the town's nicest homes, cheating on his wife and his taxes, for whom the whole of adulthood would be a search for the glow of laudation he was bathed in when young. George: whose looks and loping ease at sports masked the failing grades that were never mentioned, who would mature to a life of bad debts, impulse marriages, and hourly labor as a heating-and-ventilation repairman, endlessly apologizing for entering people's homes.

In the stands, Carter's adult awareness could see Peter Millersport: the uncommunicative math whiz who cowered so pitifully before the gang boys that they stopped pushing him around because his whimpers became embarrassing. Carter could see Shelly Hartford: the Yale-bound upperclassman whose friendship made Carter feel urbane and who was not jumping up and down as all others in the stands were now doing. Shelly would publish ardent collegiate manifestos denouncing his country, then make millions with a dashed-off screenplay about a defrocked priest turned invisible vigilante. He'd end up at Miramax as head of the Division of Formula Thrillers, settled in Bel Air with a succession of actress-slash-models whose breast measurements exceeded their IQs. Carter could see Ken Highland: the quiet, obedient only child of a divorced mother, who never told a soul about the diagnosis of lupus, both afraid of it and somehow ashamed, his mother sending around a printed death notice after a private funeral that was just her and a minister, at which she sobbed so long and violently for her lost son that the reverend called an ambulance.

As his young form ran, Carter's adult awareness also saw every high school girl who ever turned his head. The unattainable April Hazeltine: who lived with her grandparents for reasons unspoken, whose life was a paragon of pubescent female perfection—cheerleader's captain, homecoming queen, and National Honor Society. Marcy Wendover: whom Ward would marry at a ceremony on a golf course. Karen Deumont: who during homeroom showed her favor by sitting with legs crossed in such a way that whatever boy she liked had a clear view up her skirt, with whom Carter once made out so passionately it was a wonder the car's shock absorbers did not break, and who did not remember Carter when they ran into each other in an airport as harried adults. Bonnie Worth: who sang in school plays and acted at a professional regional theater and who would be typecast as an ingenue and discarded by Broadway by age twenty-three, yet well into her forties would still live alone in a studio on the Lower East Side, waitressing and teaching aerobics, hoping to get her break. Nora Cortland: who one day would have a full professorship in English lit at Cornell, but who in this year could think of no subject other than Joni Mitchell. Susan Englewood: the school's gorgeous girl, unanimously pined for, who would let herself go after children, never able to adjust to the loss of the automatic comeliness of a woman's nubile years, and one day be given up on as a hopeless case by the Jenny Craig clinic. Sharon Brighton: remembered only by the flowers and small crosses left by the side of the road where it happened.

He could see the adults, too. His father, mother, and Mack, who at that moment was standing rock-still and not breathing, sure that his little brother would fall down and blow it. Mrs. Sheridan at the side of the bleachers, by that time in her wheelchair and unable to peer over the crowd to know what was happening. Mr. Knowlton, the Goldwater-backing social-studies teacher who already thought Carter's views had too much influence with the student body, grimacing as he realized this event would increase the teenager's standing. Carter could remember Mr. Knowlton arguing, "If we have sex education, ultimately it must lead to the distribution of condoms in the schools!" Mrs. Sheridan replied that this was a ridiculous impossibility.

As his teen form ran, Carter's adult awareness found he could feel the complete sensory details of every aspect of the moment—the way the wind moved, the colors of the banners, the patchy mud, the sun glancing off the soot-shaken train, the sense of pleasing the town that had fathered him.

Even the highest satisfactions of adulthood can never approach the small satisfactions of youth. An adult man receiving a billion dollars or a Nobel Prize or a night to do as he pleased with the most beautiful woman in the world—such things could never be as profound as the joy of being a five-year-old at a birthday party, drinking orange soda and regarding the cake and pile of glittering presents, parents cooing and little friends clapping. Conventionally it is assumed that the child's gladness is greatest because the child is unknowing of the days to come when wants will not be satisfied. In many ways the child's joy is simply better, deeper, superior, more accomplished. If offered the chance to live forever in one moment, wouldn't an early birthday be a fine choice? A time when cake, presents, orange soda, and clapping friends were all the treasure that could be imagined; when there was still the illusion that the world existed specifically to welcome and applaud *you*. Carter might have chosen to live in the happy blur of this touchdown run eternally, the crowd cheering, friends and family in awe, the cheerleaders calling his name, the son bringing honor to his hometown, the kiss under the stands with April but a short time away—everything promise and possibility.

Gold gleams diving at his legs, teenage Carter crossed into the end zone. Uproar followed as most of the assembled ran onto the field, encircling the boy, who at one point rode the shoulders of Carl Wabash. The teenager was delighted to be lifted up by his worst day-to-day enemy. His adult awareness could think only of the day at college when he received the envelope from his mother containing the newspaper clipping with Carl's misspelled last name in that peculiar flag-bordered Vietnam column in the *Express*, headlined TO HONOR OUR FALLEN.

"Mack! Did you see it!" the boy called, and adult Carter felt his young self being transferred from Carl's shoulders to those of his brother, who would also fall in Vietnam, though parts of him would rise. Mack used his Marine's strength to lift Carter high for the crowd to adore. Held up for his friends, parents, teachers, and love interests to acclaim, the teenager entered a condition that might, technically, have been bliss.

Carter's adult awareness felt disdain for this jubilation. *It was just luck*, he thought. *Half the world's possessions, honor, and fortune are distributed through luck, and it means nothing except to those who aren't lucky.* The adult thought of Carl, with whom he had daily, disagreeable contact through boyhood. Carl had been beaten by an oafish father; lost his mother to emphysema when he was six, and was told that was God's will; died himself at age nineteen crying and moaning in a rice paddy where he went to serve his country and become a man in his father's eyes. In his few years on earth, Carl became an oaf too, that was true, but if anyone deserved through chance to be given a moment in the sun it was him, since fortune favored him in nothing. Carl should have been the one to pick up the fumble and score the lucky touchdown. Then, when he died, perhaps he could have gone on to an eternity of cheers.

Carter's adult perception remained in thrall to the sensations coursing through his teen self, emotions of elation, vainglory, and abandon, enough hormones flowing at that instant to start a small pharmaceutical firm.

As boy Carter listened to the words the others were exclaiming—congratulations, boasts of prowess—the adult realized that a cherished adolescent fantasy was coming true. The minds of his teen friends were turning transparent to him. How Carter had wished, at this age, that he could know his friends' thoughts; often he daydreamed about the advantage, titillation, and direction such power would confer. As his teen form began to realize this much-sought ability, Carter the adult resisted. *I don't want to know whatever immature, petty things they are thinking,* he told himself. *It'll be excruciating. Even Einstein's high school thoughts must have been obsessive nonsense about puberty.*

Despite inner protest, the thoughts of his young friends began to flow into his awareness. Carter heard:

Richard Delaware: I never aspired to score the winning touchdown myself, but I always dreamed of throwing the block that would allow my teammate to make the winning touchdown. That's what I'll say. That's perfect. Everybody will think it's the perfect thing to say.

George Deerhurst: Mr. Wilton won't flunk me out of chemistry now. He's a big football fan, he'll be in a good mood and he'll let me slide. Next year, though, I'm hitting the books.

Sharon Brighton: Richtie swears he got rid of the flask, but he could be using breath mints. Last night when he went across the median I was real scared. But if I say anything, he gets mad. I don't want him mad when he just put the ring on layaway. I wish I knew how to tell for sure if someone's been drinking. Maybe I should write to Dear Abby.

Nora Cortland: Above the clamor and raucous burly, I alone hear a faraway sound.

Carl Wabash: Screw those faggots from Taney, we showed those shitheads. Now they'll have to kiss my ass whenever I drive around there. We are number one! Number one!

Bonnie Worth: This just can't be happening. Anybody can be a month late, can't they? I've got to find someone who will help me without Mom knowing. I'm not going to give up my chance for New York. I will never, ever, ever get married.

Shelly Hartford: Owing to their limited intellects, they don't realize the farcical nature of this pale reenactment of warrior-cult rites. At the conclusion of ancient Aztec sporting events, the defeated were executed and the victors allowed to run into the crowd and rape women. Perhaps ticket sales could be maximized if these features were added to modern-day football rituals.

Ken Highland: Greatest moment in the history of McKinley

High and I am here. This is the greatest thing I will ever see.

Susan Englewood: Over summer is when I'll dye. If I go blond now people will make jokes, but when I come back from the lake they won't be able to remember for sure. Just wait till I walk in first day of senior year, blond. Half the girls will scream. Now Shelly Hartford, this is the third time you've looked down my cleavage.

Wardman Louvain: I told Dad band is for losers. That could have been me, I should have gone out for football. Don't think that! Carter is your pal, never envy another man's success. He's my best friend and I was at his side for the moment of glory. My best friend. Friends forever!

Marcy Wendover: Quit it, I was standing here first. Quit it! Some people. Oh, great, now I'm getting squeezed toward Ward Louvain, president of the united jerks society. He's looking my way. In your dreams, pal.

Peter Millersport: I wish my parrot were here. Cyrus understands what I'm thinking. I don't care if he's a bird. I wish he could be with me all the time.

Karen Deumont: Every time I think I've figured things out they hit me with something else. I can't even understand my own mother and I'm supposed to understand algebra. I wish I had an older sister, then I could copy off her. Maybe I should copy off Becky Moulton. Her life is perfect. Becky met Brian carhopping and Brian's got an Impala with an eight-track. Mrs. Hertel says I need to spend more time studying but if I took a carhop job I'd have twenty-five dollars a week. Things are too confusing! And just how exactly am I supposed to know which colleges to write to? I'm certainly not going to apply to any college that won't let me in! I can always go to the community college, Katy's sister met a guy there and you can park close to class. Gram says all things happen for a reason so everything must be part of a plan. Go Purple Weasels!

Carter was even able to hear the thoughts of the splendid April, in the hour before she would consent to his kiss. He hoped for some inkling of awakening desire, perhaps even of first love. Instead he heard:

April Hazeltine: He's sort of cute, I guess.

The kiss would not lead to much. Sporadic dates, rounds of petting followed by days when they would not acknowledge each other's existence, followed by petting of distraught intensity, followed by resolute mutual promises to write when he departed for a distant college and she stayed close to home. Once Carter was off at a prestige school, it wasn't long before he acquired the expensive-education worldview of believing his eyes fully open while the people he had left behind to have been hayseeds. Carter's adult awareness tried to turn away from the memory of that haughty thought. During his 1970s lonely years, when the counterculture was over but Carter had not yet found a place in the careerist order that supplanted it, in idle hours he sometimes marveled that he had actually had his chance at a life with a traditional hometown sweetheart, and wondered how different things might have been if he had worked to win her hand.

The glass between his thoughts and the thoughts of his friends clouded back into opacity. He heard their voices normally again, and became aware time had passed. The crowd was drifting away from the midfield celebration; in the distance, car doors were slamming and engines starting. Mack and his father had left in search of beer. The other grown-ups and the crowd were gone. Only Carter's friends remained, reveling in their moment.

Ward was enthusiastically telling the teenage Carter about parties they'd be invited to. George Deerhurst was trying to arrange that they'd all meet up again after changing out of their muddy uniforms; George was always happiest in a group. Nora Cortland was importuning Carter to drop football and get involved in the debate society. Sharon Brighton was tight by the side of Richtie, her slicked-hair apprentice electrician beau, the sort of guy who hung around his old high school for years after graduation, trying to show up the younger boys and impress the younger girls with his car and walking-around money until finally, finally becoming able to achieve the goal of having respect and a girlfriend within the aura of high school. April was gathering her things by the cheerleaders' area, in no apparent hurry to depart. All the people who made Carter's teen years were in this one spot, all at their moment of highest regard for him. The breeze that blew across Carter's body felt fresh as air must have felt when the world was new.

Adult Carter fought to tell himself, *These are but shadows of people who are now overweight and in debt and in bad marriages and have nothing to say and earn modest livings being told what to do and drink to dull themselves out and then sit in recliner chairs watching cable.* That's what he fought to tell himself. Acquisition of worldly cynicism had made his adult self believe it was a mistake to attach too much significance to the special excitement of anything, much less of the young years, which seem special mainly as an artifact of the coincidence that they come first.

Then Ward said something Carter's adult awareness thought for an instant must have been an epenthesis, only to remember it really had been said on this day at this time.

"We'll always be friends, won't we?" Ward asked him. "I mean forever. We won't drift apart and get all funny and closed off like our parents, will we? Friends forever, right?"

George Deerhurst overheard. He cupped his hands and hollered across the play field the age-old high school students' vow, "Friends forever!"

Several of the others picked up the call. Richard and Sharon and Karen began shouting the pledge, "Friends forever!" Soon everyone joined but Shelly, whose face betrayed a thin sneer.

"Friends forever!" they caroled at maximum decibel like a pep-rally cheer, trying to outshout the rumble of another passing train. Standing in the gathering twilight, a small group of joyful children plighted themselves to that which would not happen, chanting and hollering, "Friends forever! Friends forever!"

Carter began to feel his consciousness detach from his young body and expand away, seeing the group as if from a slight distance above. Children pitched against the world, fidgety and pimply and mostly on course to lives of surrendered dreams, and beautiful in a way the constellations themselves could not rival.

Carter again experienced the feeling that every part of his awareness was about to accelerate away from every other part, and realized he was being drawn back to the present without reliving the kiss. His spirits fell, and he felt the sort of true emotional pain that had not been pricked within him for any reason for far too long.

At that point his awareness began to wamble, the acceleration reversed, and Carter experienced himself being compressed back into the restrictions of his teenaged form. He was staying for the kiss after all. Someone or some office had decided to show him a kindness.

The teen Carter was now showered, changed into street clothes, and lingering in the concrete tunnel that bisected the grandstand. April was there, dappled sunset gracing her face. They were waiting for a passerby to round the far end of the tunnel and pass out of sight, leaving them alone.

"Could I—what I mean is—" Carter was saying, his emotional speedometer reading ten thousand miles per hour. *Call me in 1975*, his adult self struggled to make the boy declare.

April had her eyes slightly down. "You can," she said, and slipped her hands into his. Their forms met and the kiss, though unskilled, could not have been better if their lips had touched the chambers of each other's hearts. Young Carter felt, flowing through him, the current of another life.

His adult awareness was given an instant in which to reflect that this day of youthful happiness, adulation, and romance, awarded to him and not to others, might have instilled an expectation that he would live a special life, or alternatively might have made him know he carried a special obligation that should be repaid. Then his awareness began again to accelerate away, and he tumbled back to the present.

CHAPTER FIVE

CARTER STOOD IN THE PARKING LOT of a Best Western motel in rural California at midmorning, flaring sun already making the pavement radiate. He felt the aching thirst that parches the body after a strenuous sports event. His ankles were sore, as they always had been following a high school football game.

Without having to consult his watch, Carter knew he had missed the morning plane from Fresno. He walked back to the motel to check out. Central American cleaning women pushing carts the size of shipping crates were moving among the rooms, hoping to see a single dollar bill as they opened each door.

Encountering his teen-years companions again made Carter realize that he'd lost both them and the ideal they represented. Gone was the actual Ward and also the ideal of Ward, of the one Best friend who shares your discovery of the world and knew you when your eyes were on what sparkles in the distance. Nine out of ten men and women do not appreciate how magnificent is the first Best friend until the solitude and isolation of later life gives perspective, but by then the parties in the friendship have been cast to the winds by job changes and moving vans, which is why the youthful Best friendship is structurally doomed in modern society.

Gone was the actual April and also the ideal of April, of the one True love whose affection can never be corrupted because it was attained before the knowledge of duplicity that hangs over adult emotions. Nine out of ten men and women do not appreciate how magnificent is the first True love until the disappointments and bitterness of subsequent romances give perspective, which is why True love is structurally doomed in modern society. First True love exists, a physicist might say, in a negative feedback loop, rendered comprehensible only by the very forces that negate it.

Most in Carter's age group had chosen in youth to pursue the goal of having multiple romances, for excitement and to differentiate themselves from their square, repressed parents. Multiple lovers may help avoid the ill-considered marriage: though fooling around is not necessarily more fun, as surveys show that people in long-term relationships get more sex than swinging singles. Sometimes Carter found himself entranced to read the newspaper feature story about aging high school sweethearts who'd married young and never looked back. Such people must bicker and have bad days and wonder what they might have done differently, but live out their entire lives in the True condition, with someone who knew them when.

Flying back home that evening, the airplane rocking, Carter tried to keep his mind off what was continuing to happen to him. Two experiences now. He wondered anew if he was not at this instant in the process of being struck by a car in the drive-up of the Whole Life Tower, the other lawyers looking on aghast and already calculating how to grab his share of the case; whether everything from the beginning of the inner dialogue with the phantom of himself up to this airplane seat was occurring within his own mind in the seconds between the impact and his ascension to glory or disappearance into oblivion. One way or the other Carter Morris was experiencing the ultimate sixties flashback, and it was an honor he did not seek.

––––––––

RETURNING TO THE OFFICE THE FOLLOWING DAY, Carter expected to plash into hot water. Instead everyone was happy to see him—suspiciously so. When he entered Miss Lockport called out a greeting with such sincerity she had to be faking. "Man, you look great," Kendall Afreet said, passing him in the hall, effusing phony warmth.

Obviously it could not be actual human concern for his well-being. Turned out the Fifth Circuit had just attributed an important ruling to the reasoning in a law review article Carter had written; certiorari would head to the Supremes, where if the reasoning was upheld, Afreet & Malison would win considerable prestige. Further it turned out that a research journal called *Annals of Meiosis* had just published a study implicating unsymmetrical dimethyl chlorofluorine monomer as a haploid anaphase disrupter. Not many people knew what that meant, but everyone knew how it sounded. Suddenly Value Neutral was extremely anxious to settle its case. During the very period he was absent without leave, Carter's corridor status had taken two big upticks.

As Carter strolled toward his office, he was quickly taken over by the familiar work-arrival sensation of severed enervation. It was comforting. Carter actively liked the fact that so much of modern work culture is disaffecting and superficial. The new institutional ethos of round-the-clock careerist pursuit might be miserable and soulless, but in a way offered relief, since under miserable and soulless conditions, no one could be expected to accomplish anything beyond looking out for number one. Such lowered expectations were reassuring. Once Carter had dreamed of a life in which he would experience all, reveal all, and be engaged with great emotions. Now his goal was to be predictable and feel as little as possible, but eat in really nice restaurants.

The age group to which Carter belonged grew up detesting the fifties-style institutional culture of conformism, yet the new institutional culture it created was just as inimical. Careerism, workaholism, the cell phone that takes priority over love or family, the tyranny of the stock price; his enlightened peers bowed to them all. Especially careerism, that what you do is what you are rather than what you are is what you are. The postwar generation was going to start a kinder new human order, and instead the main social transformation it accomplished was casual Friday.

At one point Carter had been sitting with Jennings Guerdon and listening to him recount the downsizing of Value Neutral. Guerdon took delight in describing how putting eight thousand people out of work immediately bumped the company's trading price up twenty percent. Though, Guerdon confided, "Already with our Guatemala outsourcing we have labor issues, local organizers who are stirring things up, saying $2.50 a day isn't enough. We may have to leave Guatemala for a better wage climate." Carter wanted to feel superior, but weren't he and his peers the ones buying Value Neutral shirts and demanding that the firm's stock rise to inflate their mutual funds?

In Carter's office registered letters, FedEx envelopes, pink message slips, and other missives were stacked high. Before he could inspect them Afreet buzzed, asking that he "Come say hello to our good friends from Taegu Heavy Industries."

Afreet was squiring around a delegation of Korean industrialists who were offering stock in exchange for regulatory approval to acquire Pentagon encryption devices. "It is for our school systems, for the student privacy," one of them kept saying, barely even trying to be believable. Taegu had multiple image problems—a political bribery scandal and less than optimal publicity about an experimental fragmentation torpedo the company had tested by firing one at blue whales. But so long as campaign contributions went to the right congressional committee chairmen, approval of the export license seemed likely.

"This is the Woodstock lawyer?" one of the Korean businessmen asked.

"One of the outstanding legal minds of our generation," Kendall replied, shooting Carter an expression of nudge-nudge wink-wink.

"I was not at Woodstock," Carter said, wincing, sick of that word. "If someone says they were at Woodstock, you can be sure they weren't."

"We see this movie," the businessman intoned. "Jerry Hendrix, LDS, Thomas Dylan. Women with no shirts, sex in sleeping bags. Very American. This would not be tolerated in Korea."

"It was another time," Carter said.

Owing to the standoffish response the executive feared he had given offense, so switched to humor: "Sex in sleeping bag, no hotel cost!" The Koreans laughed heartily, Afreet conspicuously joining and motioning Carter to laugh too. Then the businessman noted, assuming a sudden air of gravity, "Sex not important, not like the blue whale."

"The critical issue of blue whale preservation is not in your talking points for this trip," Kendall interjected. When clients had public-image problems, it was essential to keep them on message.

"Taegu Heavy Industries respects the blue whale," the executive insisted, now grave. At this all the visitors made a slight, duteous gesture with their heads.

Carter excused himself and returned to his office. He began to clear his desk by dismissing the pro bono detritus. He knew what would be inside: pleading *habeas* claims filed by prisoners writing in laborious block lettering on yellow legal tablets, earnestly invoking *Marbury* or *Gideon* without realizing this would only make some judge's clerk chortle at such giveaways of the novice jailhouse lawyer. The letters would demand justice when what the poor fish needed was to find a technical error in the search warrant or the jury charge, and obviously the public defender hadn't been able to do that or petitioner would not be in the prison library looking up the meaning of *habeas* in the first place.

Early in his pro bono work, Carter could become deeply distressed by a prisoner's powerfully heartfelt claim of mistaken identity. Investigating, he would almost always find the convicted was in fact guilty but accomplished in the art of the fervent lie. What the U.S. legal system rewards is the persuasively asserted falsehood; those who spend their lives around courts become adept at lying, lawyer and defendant alike. Sometimes there were genuine miscarriages of justice, and once Carter uncovered one. How close Mayhew Collins had come to the chair, and what a rush it had been to walk with him through the state penitentiary gate to address the international media mob waiting outside. And the sight of Collins's wife, who had never lost faith, and driving up to find five hundred people lining that block of skinny row houses when he went home, every house decked with ribbons— that day of Collins's release, years ago, was the last time Carter had looked into the mirror and really liked what he saw.

Perhaps in the present stack of prisoners' petitions was the next Mayhew Collins, but Carter had no intention of finding out. What he intended to do was transfer riches from Value Neutral to himself. He left the pro bono envelopes unopened, wishing only that he could open his window. All glass in his building was fixed pane, the better to force the air conditioners to run overtime and expend fossil fuels. When the sun slanted in and greenhoused the room, it became stifling no matter how high the AC was set; when the sun eclipsed behind the adjoining office tower, the room quickly turned frigid. It was like having seasons inside a building, except the only seasons available were dead of winter and midsummer noon. Carter passed many hours in febrile contemplation of litigation that could end the outrage of the window that can't be opened. Questions like whether his window opened, or how long his computer took to download, now engaged him in a way that the guilt or innocence of a death-row inmate did not. That was the point in life he had come to.

But hadn't everyone? In contemporary society everybody has criticisms and few have causes. Once the burning issues of the day had been civil rights, free speech, free love; now the kind of thing people turned out to protest were auto insurance rates. What were once intense grievances against society had methodically been supplanted by issues more closely resembling consumer complaints. That was good, it was progress; better to have gripes than fundamental injustices. But all seemed so much less interesting. Evil, scheming presidents had given way to smiling poll-watchers; heartless Pentagon generals to officer-executives with masters degrees who fretted about not offending gays; malicious, public-be-damned corporate barons to cute-chick flacks who wore AIDS awareness pins and threw you completely off your anger by flashing a little leg. There was still poverty, thirteen percent poor in the most affluent nation in history. That could be a cause. But who had time to worry about the poor? It was their own fault they didn't cram for their SATs.

Carter turned in his hand the sheet of paper on which he'd written the number of the therapist recommended by Abraham Wolsam. He called and scheduled an appointment, being asked for his health insurance carrier and policy code before he was asked his name.

LISTLESSLY, CARTER REVIEWED THE LATEST in the Biogent case. A gene-therapy start-up backed by venture capitalists, the company had inadvertently invented a communicable vaccine—people could spread inoculation by contact, making each other well rather than sick. Biogent was furiously petitioning the FDA to recall lab samples of the product before an epidemic of immunity broke out, ruining its market share. All manner of citizen groups, pharmaceutical manufacturers, and tort specialists were now involved in a cascade of Biogent litigation, variously claiming the company sinned by releasing the communicable vaccine and also sinned by attempting to withdraw it. A lawyer's ability to generate business by filing lawsuits is as if stores could generate business by mailing out invoices, and the recipients had to prove they never ordered anything.

Carter flipped through the latest file on *Grandits*, the cash cow. Man sets a microwave oven to three hours rather than three minutes and is injured when the device explodes; blames the manufacturer for selling a unit that accepts a setting of three hours. Carter was glad to have won the lead client a hefty settlement, and never mind that Grandits didn't notice when it was two hours fifty-nine minutes later, he still hadn't had his snack and the micro was still pulsating. But in the aftermath of news stories on Grandits's millions, others with the same make and model of microwave had gone copycat, deliberately setting for three hours. One woman from Alabama instructed her fourteen-year-old son to go stand by the unit as the three-hour mark approached, and he lost an eye. The boy wasn't doing well in school, the mother told Carter in the deposition, so I figured this was the only way he'd ever bring the family some money.

Next Carter looked at a file on a promising class-action suit against Living Large, Inc., corporate owner of a clothing chain catering to the plus-sized—Milady Beaucoup outlets for the Rubenesque and Milord Grande for the Falstaffian. The company had begun to offer a range of products for the targeted lifestyle, including oversized china settings for serving double portions and a recliner armchair with a hidden hydraulic booster that helped the occupant regain his or her feet by discreetly pressing the seat bolster upward. One of the products, a seat-belt extender for those whose girth made standard belts uncomfortable, had strangled a man in Grapevine, Texas, when an extender flap snagged on a moon-roof latch and pulled the seat belt taut around the driver's neck as the moon roof opened. Company engineers swore this was physically impossible, but photographs taken by the county coroner suggested otherwise.

The lawsuit Carter was working turned on whether the seller should have known of this danger. It certainly knew of rising American mass. From a company marketing document he'd obtained in discovery: "The obese deplete more resources per capita, thereby fueling economic expansion. Yet they are too sluggish to commit crimes, do not demand costly environmental preservation because they never walk, and on average die eleven years sooner than the mean, which moderates federal pension spending. In short the heavyset represent the ideal consumers for the modern world." Another document described how the installation instruction sheet for the seat-belt extender would be done entirely in pictures "owing to current trends in literacy." A third document concerned an advertising campaign to make people feel dissatisfied with their existing seat belts. YOU MAY BE UNCOMFORTABLE AND NOT EVEN KNOW IT, the ad's headline ran. Living Large had made money on the belt extenders but cost one man his life, essentially by creating a dangerous safety device. Justice was out of the question; Carter did not plan to waste anyone's time bringing that up. His best hope was to win about half a hundredth of the company's profit for the year and split it with the estate of the deceased.

There was a knock and a voice asking if he had a minute. It was Ginny, her man-tailored suit jacket removed to uncover a shrink-wrap skirt and thin white-silk voile blouse through which her bra was distinctly visible. The combination of formal business attire and complete obviousness of the way the ensemble called attention to her bosom made Ginny's appearance more arousing than would the actual revealing of skin.

"You saw the *Annals of Meiosis* thing?" she asked.

"Yes."

"And did you see the district court decision in *Conoco v. Bowl-a-Rama?*" Ginny tossed a file about the case onto his desk. In the clipped manner of a young resident presenting the case to her attending physician, Ginny explained, "Oil company subsidiary manufactured a polishing agent for bowling balls. Workers in a California bowling alley say exposure gave them fear of developing covert carpal tunnel syndrome. Huge award. Company paid through the nose by going to trial instead of settling. Juries assume the worst about anything with a chemical name." She paced a bit, showing off. Her buffed, athletic figure made her seem slightly menacing; Carter was sure he'd lose a kick-boxing match with her.

"Covert carpal tunnel syndrome?"

"That's when you have the syndrome but don't exhibit any symptoms. Sure your hands work fine today, but someday they might not. It's a very pernicious syndrome because without symptoms, there's no way you can be treated."

"Isn't someone without symptoms normally considered healthy?"

Ginny pulled her chair closer to Carter's desk. "Plaintiffs put up an expert witness, guy with a Ph.D. in comparative allopathy, who specializes in demolishing the argument that being in good health means you are not sick. Anyway plaintiffs never claimed their absence of symptoms was scientifically confirmed. They only asserted that they were caused to fear they would someday develop a condition that could not be detected."

Ginny felt pleased to be telling Carter something he didn't know. "You see a factory," she said. "You worry that its emissions will give you cancer, or that the halogen bulbs in its outdoor lighting will cause retroactive amnesia or something like that. You sue and recover on the anxiety, even if you're completely fine. Fear torts are just this huge litigation growth arena, and every day the media get better at finding new things to be afraid of. I'm writing Kendall a memo on this."

"Doesn't the fact that the media keep fixating on smaller dangers mean many big dangers are being corrected?" Carter asked. "Crime down, less pollution, a lot of big trends are favorable."

This Ginny found offensive. Educated in the late-century instant-doomsday milieu, she was made uneasy by the idea of progress, whereas reports of crisis created in her an agreeable sense of encountering the expected. "Just scan the decision in *Bowl-a-Rama*," she said, testy. "Jury awarded $1.2 billion. Sure the judgment will come down on appeal, but it can come down a long way and still be a hell of a lot more than Value Neutral is offering us."

Carter skimmed the file Ginny proffered. A Fortune 500 company's litigation department had been slam-dunked in a case where there not only wasn't harm, there wasn't even any *claim* of harm. Value Neutral was a lot more exposed than that.

Ginny was excited and eager. "I say we fax Value Neutral the printout of this award, just fax it without comment. Bet you one night of your dreams they call back within the hour to up the settlement. You know, it could turn out that your weirdo vanishing act—" She stopped herself, having mentioned a topic everyone was avoiding. Resuming, "The brilliant way you delayed the first settlement conference, that could turn out to be a master stroke, resulting in the offer going up by millions. I'll send the fax right now."

"Let me run the case," Carter said. Not only was he selling out to Value Neutral, now an associate newly out of law school was advising him on how to do it.

"I've got to get in on the real action at this firm, Kendall is only giving me slag," Ginny replied, switching from all-business to emotional appeal. "He has me getting the waivers for that made-for-TV movie about the school murders, calling up the parents of the victims and sweet-talking them about signing permissions for a network to depict their children being shot to death. He has me on the Korean account, but it's just regulatory boilerplate and baby stuff like writing letters to the editor for them. You should see the one on my desk right now, to *60 Minutes*.

"Dear Sir,
Your recent report about Taegu Heavy Industries was completely erroneous. The workers at our Surinam waste reprocessing facility are all very happy and none have complained regarding the radiation leaks."

Carter smiled at that. "Taegu is smart to know they need a chick to sign that letter," he said. "Today's best corporate bullshit is delivered by minorities or women. The senior executive tier may be white male but the visible apologists must be diverse. The theory is that people will think, 'If a black or a woman is willing to say this, maybe it's true.' The result is that minorities and women are becoming just as proficient at lying for money as WASP males. It's one of the big achievements of affirmative action."

"It's not the lying I mind, it's that I'm only getting low-level lying," Ginny said.

Then she changed her tone to one that drew Carter into her confidence. "Kendall wants me to take the Koreans out to dinner tonight. Their boss looked at me and said, 'Get me sleeping bag quick.' What kind of innuendo is that supposed to be?"

"No idea."

Ginny continued, "Kendall suggested I wear an evening gown and made a comment about how we all do what we must to keep clients happy. I didn't go to law school in order to get to the top by screwing our clients. I want to make it to the top based on merit, by screwing people in court."

Carter had to admire that. By the standards of the profession, screwing people in court was the honorable path to success.

"So you figure if you get a lead position in this case, Kendall has to start taking you seriously. Are you asking for your own share of the bonus?"

"Oh, no, of course not," Ginny said with such a calculated, rehearsed air that Carter would later wonder how he could possibly have neglected to write out a memorandum of understanding on that point and have her sign it before another minute passed. "All I want is a chance to work on a major case with a pro like you, to really learn from someone I look up to," she cooed, subtly hiking her skirt to provide diversion from the fact that she was barely pretending to be sincere. "I've been reading up on the overlap between Value Neutral and *Bowl-a-Rama*. I can hit the ground running."

"Okay," Carter said. "I'll tell Kendall to hand somebody else the Taegu file, that as of now I need all your time." Ginny smiled broadly. "Just one thing," he added. "The reasoning in *Bowl-a-Rama*, is it legitimate or a crock?"

"Total crock. Scarcely rising to the level of science fiction."

"That was my impression."

"Does that bother you?"

"It would have once," Carter said.

Ginny got up to leave, doing so as sinuously as possible. This caused Carter to replay his mental tape of her earlier comment. "What did you mean, 'you'd bet me a night of my wildest dreams'?"

She winked and mimicked a spank of herself on the ass. "It's a bet I can only win," Ginny said, and left.

This woman is playing me like a kazoo, Carter thought, but was not sure he minded as long as no-obligation hot sex resulted. He closed his office door, not for concentration but to lend the impression he was engaged in such work as required concentration. Generally in offices people close their doors when they're not doing anything, rather than the other way around. Carter typed an E-mail to the boss, requesting Ginny be reassigned as his subordinate. Approval came back in five minutes. "Love the plan to fax them *Bowl-a-Rama*," Afreet added. Carter hadn't mentioned that. Ginny must have set a world's record in making sure she got credit for the idea.

Carter's mental state was confused and the sexual stimulation was not helping. He was certain only that he wanted to get his six million, then return his life to its humdrum cycle of work, exercise, meals, sleep, unfocused desperation, and no entanglement with any person or cause.

His interoffice e-mail indicator flashed with several messages. One from Kendall: Ginny was now busy so would he take the Koreans out to a fancy dinner that night on the firm, then to a strip club, high class of course. Of course! Kendall suggested the Pudendum Palace, which he seemed to know and assured Carter was "strictly platinum." Ask for Chrissy, was Kendall's suggestion. Client entertaining was unavoidable, so Carter messaged back yes. Another from Miss Lockport: Catholic Relief Services needed an answer to its request that he become a legal adviser to its refugee placement project. Carter messaged back that she should tell them he was in a meeting. One from accounting: Kendall had just approved three thousand dollars cash for the evening for "miscellaneous entertaining" and for such a large amount he would have to come down and sign. Officer of the court spends a night introducing visiting plutocrats to lap dancers—how postmodern. Maybe buying sex was the better way, at least both parties were sure to get something from the deal.

Next a message from Ginny: Value Neutral had already answered and was prepared to "substantially increase" its settlement offer. They'd called her instead of him.

THROUGH THE AFTERNOON, office door closed, Carter conducted a series of computer searches and phone calls trying to locate April Hazeltine. Several calls were awkward, to old neighbors or retired teachers, people who were surprised to hear his voice but who recalled Carter's juvenile persona and the events of his high school years as if they had happened the day before. A Chinese proverb gives this advice to those who would be leaders or sages: Never return to your home village, because an old woman by the stream will remember what you looked like as a baby and address you by your childhood nickname. Most of those Carter telephoned asked after Mack and didn't know much else to say beyond that. Nobody could say what had happened to April, though everyone remembered her youthful aura of most-likely-to-succeed.

By dusk the Nexus research system had found the following in the archives of the *Cincinnati Inquirer.* Printed the year before, Carter felt sure the obituary was hers, owing to the distinctive middle name:

> April May Hazeltine passed away peacefully yesterday at the Balm of Gilead Hospice, where she had resided for several months. Cause of death was not announced. The deceased, a former National Merit Scholar, had been a part-time clerk at Magnificent Muffins downtown. Kevin Euclid, assistant shift manager at the bakery, said that "While we did not know her well, she will be missed during the morning rush." Rev. Duncan Woodcrest, who counseled the deceased in her final days, told the *Inquirer* Miss Hazeltine wished others to know she had endured a series of hardships in life, including loss of her parents, substance abuse, loneliness, and mental health challenges. "But

whatever her trials, April Hazeltine was infinitely loved by her God and will now sit at the Lord's hand through eternal rest," Rev. Woodcrest said. Miss Hazeltine never wed and leaves no known relatives. Magnificent Muffins will donate $100 to the hospice in her name.

If the article said that the pope had just announced mandatory homosexuality, the surprise would not have been so great. Carter felt sure he would find that April was now a state senator or a small college president, or at the least married to a CEO or diplomat, reading to her three perfect children and running the local volunteer center. *April never married.* She was a catch, and loved kids. *April worked the counter in a muffin store.* She'd been offered full scholarships to Chicago, Swarthmore, and Yale. After a while Carter realized he was focusing on the wrong things, the lowly circumstances and the unfulfilled promise. *April is gone.* There could be no nostalgic reunion, no pleasant evening drinking wine and reminiscing, no chance to say what had not been said. He'd never see her again.

Feeling panicky, short of breath, Carter called Ward. During his phase in politics Ward had known everything about everyone. Carter could have started with him, but wanted to avoid admitting how far out of touch he'd fallen with a key person from their mutual past.

Ward sounded distracted—something about a review by his district manager. He knew she had died, hadn't heard the exact cause of death, and was surprised Carter was unaware of her decline, to say nothing of never hearing the real version about her parents. "Her father was a suicide, in her early childhood. The mother was a falling-down alcoholic," Ward said. "It's amazing she did so well, considering."

Then he told April's tale in short version. The "grandparents" she'd grown up with were foster guardians to whom she was awarded by a juvenile court. By the time of their high school graduation, April's mother had become clinically despondent and went through hour-long screaming jags even on medication. April passed on the scholarships to excellent but distant schools in order to stay near her surviving parent. Kept away from her mother during youth, April held herself together and displayed her promise. Once reaching age eighteen her foster relationship with the guardians became voluntary, and what she wanted was to spend time with her mother. Soon the signs began to appear in April, too. She lost her focus, began to drift, took her mother's medications, turned down suitors, didn't finish college. Eventually, there were no more suitors or prospects.

"Something genetic, the best I can figure," Ward concluded. "Born with the proclivity. We shouldn't judge."

Genetic. Today DNA is blamed for everything, but the idea that genes simultaneously create people and sabotage them didn't sit well with Carter. Too much like the theory of original sin, that God made us but then placed an obstacle right where we'd be sure to trip over it.

"I should have been paying closer attention to this," was Carter's useless comment.

"She could have used help," Ward agreed. "Maybe ten, maybe twelve years ago I tried to get her to head up my fund-raising. She still had it then—the glisten, the way she could make you think she was doing a huge favor by speaking to you. I thought if I could get her into something where she'd employ her talents, she'd snap out of it. She said yes, we picked a start date, she signed the W2s and never showed up at campaign headquarters. So I called her to say why aren't you here and she acted as if she had no idea what I was referring to. All she wanted to talk about was how much she wished she was back in high school, when everything had been perfect. It was spooky. Later I heard she moved someplace in Pennsylvania. I think she moved a lot."

Ward said he needed to get off the line. Carter wondered, Was April now in paradise, to exist forever in the moment she was named homecoming queen?

His eyes were red from crying when he heard someone rap hard on his office door. It was the Koreans, ready to head off for steak, scotch, and strippers. Carter pulled himself together and made it through the dinner portion of the program, five courses with cocktails and wine. There were rounds of numbing chitchat, Carter struggling to say things like, "Well, at least you didn't deliberately electrocute those dolphins." He thought, *I'm devoting an evening to three total strangers whom I hope never to see again, but did not have ten minutes to send a letter to April when it might have mattered.* An obvious sort of regret. It is the obvious regrets that hurt.

Soon they were driving up to the Pudendum Palace, its tuxedoed bouncers in view. A tasteful, dignified marquee advertised that the establishment's platinum-class entertainers specialized in private-room lap dances and "table showers," whatever that meant. By the entrance a white stretch was disgorging Arabian playboys, ne'er-do-well cousins of some emir. High-rollers were handing over their just-detailed Porsches and Jaguars to nineteen-year-old parking valets about whose driving records they knew nothing. A few men were arriving with dates, women who must be either unusually fun-loving or, alternatively, were stockpiling valuable relationship bonus points.

Carter might have given anything to have the next two hours already over. It had come to the point that he was so burned out he didn't want to eyeball naked babes. He handed the wad of cash to the Koreans, so they could decide whom to tip and for what, on the theory that in the presence of the breasts of tall blondes, they'd burn through the money fast. He dropped his guests by the door and drove down the block to find a parking place, spurning the valets just to get a moment alone. Carter parked and started walking back, drowsy and debilitated. His nose caught the syrupy pungence of marijuana, which he hadn't smelled in many a year. A young man in early-hippie guise— not the current vogue high-priced interpretations of period wear, but real faded jeans with flag patches and embroidery belt—was walking ahead of him, puffing. The man's locks swelled outward in the disheveled "gimme a head with hair" fashion that made one's noggin seem twice normal size.

"Be prudent with that joint, friend. I saw a police cruiser up by the strip club," Carter said, overtaking him. The figure turned. It was Carter, when he was an aspiring draft dodger.

"Where are the People?" his younger self demanded. "Why aren't they marching in the streets?"

"The People are home watching HBO," Carter said.

"Is that a new faction?"

His younger self was pleasantly intoxicated, unlike the disagreeable though much more expensive intoxication the grown man felt. The young figure raised both hands skyward in histrionic display. "Students and workers unite!" he shouted for all to hear. "March on the Pentagon, march for your rights! March in the day and march in the night! Students and workers must do what is right! Time to unite! March for your rights!"

Carter looked around. His younger self was making a considerable commotion but no one paid the slightest heed. Whether others couldn't see him, or were accustomed to deinstitutionalized orators on the street, Carter could not tell.

"You expect me to touch you," the grown man said.

The younger man took Carter's hand in the outdated, excessively hip soul-shake gesture. Instantly Carter felt his body course with illimitable energy, disdain for sleep, eagerness to talk, and a nearly round-the-clock erection. Bursting in his mind were poignant, pressing questions about politics, history, art, and sex on which he had to have, simply *had to have*, immediate answers. Then Carter began to perceive every aspect of his being accelerating away from every other aspect, and he tumbled backward in time.

CHAPTER SIX

Marxist-Leninist theory demands action against the means of oppression," a student in metal-rimmed glasses was saying with teeming agitation. "That's why we have a moral obligation to take over the gymnasium!"

Perhaps a dozen students had made it inside the glassed vestibule of the sports fieldhouse. Hundreds of others milled about outside, chanting death threats or playing Frisbee. There were demonstrators, counterdemonstrators, counter-counterdemonstrators, townies, faculty, reporters, and the curious of every stripe. University security and a few local police, irritable about having to deal with unruliness by the privileged, cut off the line of approach to the gym just after Carter's group rushed the entrance. Now everyone was waiting to see what those who got inside were going to do.

Nobody was really sure how the fieldhouse had been chosen as a target. One theory was that someone in the chaotic throng that formed that evening in the quad fronting the student union had started a rumor the ROTC would be recruiting there. Now, from beyond the glass foyer doors of the fieldhouse they could hear scattered exclamations of "Hey hey, LBJ, how many kids did you kill today?" and "Get a haircut!" and "Ho Ho Ho Chi Minh, the NLF is gonna win!" and "America, love it or leave it!" along with a stray labor sympathizer using the opportunity to bellow apropos of nothing, "Let the bosses take the losses!"

One of the broad door panes of the fieldhouse entrance was shattered. Glinting glassy fractals, transparent yet easily visible, spread across the foyer floor.

"We should sit passively and practice disobedience," one of the group inside the fieldhouse was saying. "When the cops come in we will join hands and sing 'We Shall Overcome.' Or something by Gandhi. Does anyone know if Gandhi wrote any songs?"

"Smash the rest of the windows!" another declared.

"Shouldn't we use the pay phones to call the black power group to see if they'll join us?"

"The Negro cause is greater and purer than ours. We are not worthy to contact the black power group."

A woman asked, "Isn't somebody going to help me unfurl this banner?" She was struggling to string an elongated pennant, painted in Day-Glo with Tao symbols and flowers, that read MAKE LOVE NOT WAR—today a fleered cliché, but at the time fresh and a promising thought.

"We should be inciting insurrection, not hanging banners!"

"That kind of New Left dogma is revanchist and neo-determinist."

"The Old Left is atavistic! It must be criticized!"

"The New Left has caused backsliding. The New Left is solipsistic!"

"Let's join hands and sing 'Age of Aquarius.' "

"Let's make a stand against the oppressive university system that controls our fates by issuing meal cards. All meals should be free to the masses, man."

"Let's smoke a joint!"

"People are chaining themselves to military bases and you're thinking about dope?"

"Castenada says the ancient Indians purified their minds by doing peyote before council meetings."

"I can't believe you brought stash to a sit-in. Didn't you read the Official SDS Pre-Takeover Checklist? Point number four says, 'Prepare your person for police search.' "

"Damn, I left my Angela Davis poster in the dorm."

"Do you think the cops will charge?"

"They can't actually arrest us while we're on campus, can they? My dad would cut me off if I got arrested."

"How dare you call the New Left revanchist! That's reductionist solecism!"

"Hey, earthlings," Carter shouted above it all. "We're in a gym. Anybody want to shoot some hoops?"

Buoyant energy coursed through Carter's collegiate self. The other student rebels wore on their faces expressions of fury or severity, but Carter was carefree. He was playing at saving the world and there were even girls present!

Carter broke off from the excruciating earnestness of the main group to help the woman who was struggling to raise the make-love banner. Like him she seemed jovial and confident, grinning. Carter had met her at the initial demonstration and tried his best to flirt, but failed to learn her name. Though the cause was solemn, no one could fault him for noticing her inclined smile and braless glory. Life is miraculous, the young man thought.

"I'll help you raise that," he said. Then, gesturing back to the main group, "I'm trying to get them to loosen up, since we could be here all night. They're too uptight to do anything but argue. I suggested a game of basketball."

"Spot me five for your height advantage and I'll play you twenty-one, one on one," the woman replied with an impish grin. "Winner's out."

"You want to play me one on one?"

"If you had any balls you'd accept my challenge," the woman said. And then, suggestive, "Unless you're afraid to guard me close."

"You're on."

She and Carter chased each other across the foyer, laughing, stopping for one instant to encourage the main group to join them, catching snippets of ardent disputation about Maoist line of analysis and lackey tendencies and Lowenstein's rules for community engagement. Carter felt totally alive and vital, a great cause on his shoulders and a beautiful, brassy woman running before him, leading him on.

At that moment Carter's adult awareness settled into his college self and was nonplussed by the very things that excited the younger man. The fecklessness of it all—petty vandalism, smashing university property while secure in the knowledge there would be no repercussions. The self-importance of demanding that an institution come to a halt to listen to the ill-formed babble of intellectual amateurs, who knew enough Herbert Marcuse to sound portentous but who had never paid a month's rent and couldn't tell you who the Secretary of the Treasury was if their lives depended on it. The silliness of the student strike itself, of society's favored striking against the very thing—education— that made possible their freedom of thought and the affluence in which they exercised it. The dissonance of kids chanting about victory for the NLF, when Carter knew that as adults they wouldn't even remember what these initials meant but would obsessively follow the NFL. Carter's older mind saw his fellow radicals in their early hours and beheld not courageous dissenters but kids on their particular generation's particular lark. The whole thing made him wince.

Carter's adult consciousness was discomfited all the more to realize he was once again at that place where he first heard the name Jayne Anne LaMonica. *A gift from God to the temporal world*, he thought. *Please don't make me see her again.*

The woman had turned on the court lights while Carter found a basketball. "Shoot you for first out," she exclaimed merrily. "My name is Jayne Anne."

As she confidently arced up jump shots, his younger self was already lost in wonder and love. He stared at the shape of the back of her jeans and marveled at her poise and tried to disguise how intently he was watching her breasts bounce when she dribbled the ball.

Exultant as his young self was, Carter's adult awareness was as claustrophobic. He knew that in a few minutes Jayne Anne would do something spontaneously brilliant—turn an ugly, dangerous scene at the fieldhouse into a storied event. Hearing the police charge the foyer and begin to assault the other students, she'd run out to plead for peace and failing to get their attention, strip off her flannel shirt and, festively topless, challenge the cops to a shirts-and-skins basketball game. Jayne Anne would instantly become to the constabulary what a magnet is to iron filings; the police would end up inside the gym playing the protesters, officers as the shirts team and Jayne Anne leading the motley skins. The about-to-happen scene of Jayne Anne, shirtless, pausing the game to explain the pick-and-roll to another bare-chested woman while the cops looked on was strictly for the you-had-to-be-there file. Young Carter would first be dumbfounded by her nerve and quick thinking, then impressed as the tensions vanished and Jayne Anne and the sergeant in charge negotiated a friendly outcome of takeover. The underground press would devote considerable ink to the shirts-skins game between demonstrators and cops, and begin to follow Carter's and Jayne Anne's careers. The game itself, by the time the sixties ran out of gas, would be remembered as a legendary moment.

Beyond that Carter's adult consciousness knew what also lay ahead for the two of them: years of emotional intensity and enchanting lovemaking, the triumph at Whole Life Square—then the milieu in which their love bloomed came to its close and it all turned sour for them for reasons neither ever quite grasped, leading up to that awful night at the farm in Vermont and the break Carter's mind refused to contemplate. Young Carter was at this moment gazing on Jayne Anne with exhilaration, wondering if he had found the love of his life. Adult Carter was regarding her bitterly, as the wellspring of his life's deepest disappointment. Desperately he wished he could will himself back to the time whence he had come. He wanted the ennui, irony, and reassuring emotional vacuity of the Internet age in the worst way.

"Stop letting me score," the flower-child Valkyrie was protesting. "Play me hard."

"I'm trying to be nice to a girl," Carter said. At the time even feminists still called each other girls. Later "girl" would be so thoroughly banished from correct speech that female children, who *are* girls, would be referred to as women. By the end of the twentieth century, "girl" would come back into usage among women as slang, and in culture acquire the meaning of sexualized woman, the way a swimsuit model or Hollywood bombshell can only be addressed as a girl—the term then stood on its head, like saying "bad" when you mean "good," since actual (chronological) girls are not sexual.

"Play me hard!" Jayne Anne insisted.

"Do you hear that?"

They stopped and listened to sounds of hostile commotion from the fieldhouse foyer—doors being flung open, pounding of heavy footsteps, shouting, plangent reverberations. Then the sounds of hitting. Carter and Jayne Anne heard their friends exclaiming, "Stop that! Stop that!" When one of the women from the group gave a scream of pain, Jayne Anne bolted in that direction like Teddy Roosevelt riding toward the sound of the guns. Carter trailed, aware he was a male following a female's fearlessness.

In rapid succession a horrible scene of swinging nightsticks and crunching sounds against flesh, unslowed by Jayne Anne's appeals to reason, turned to instant quiet and priceless expressions when her shirt hit the floor. Next Jayne Anne the stripped and proud Greek warrior—she would later point out that Hellenic women went into battle with their chests bare, or at least did in the imagination of Renaissance painters—led the bluecoats, seemingly hypnotized, into the main gym for one of history's least probable sporting events. The highlight of it all, Carter thought, was when the policemen removed their revolvers and stacked them in a corner, where no one from either side paid any attention to the weapons during the game.

As midnight neared, the cops announced it was time for them to clock off shift and for the students peaceably to vacate. Jayne Anne and the sergeant in charge agreed on a mutually self-serving fairy tale of tense, respectful negotiations, skipping the game and the bare-breasts part, though of course all parties would be boasting of these things on the morrow.

Emerging from the fieldhouse into the ebon midnight, Carter's group found many students and others still milling around. University officials asked that reporters be briefed from a makeshift podium. The sergeant stepped to the microphone and stuck to the agreed cover story, speaking in the clipped, institutional tongue of peace officers: "At 10:18 P.M. an apparent incident situation was observed. Subsequent to receiving authorization, uniformed officers entered . . ." Carter then took the mike and gave a much too long, too wordy oration on the antiwar movement. Finally Jayne Anne ascended the low riser behind the podium.

"We don't blame our soldiers who are fighting far from home," she said. "They are brave and noble, and what we want more than anything else is to have them back." This brought hoots and hisses from many students, cheers from the cops. "We don't blame those who oppose communism, for none of us would wish to live under its tyranny." More hisses, mixed with "hear hear!"

from a few. "We simply want a country where no citizen is ever asked to kill or to die in an unjust war. We can have that country. But we don't have that country yet." She sat down.

There was stillness followed by hearty, extended cheering. The subsequent evening, national newscasts played Jayne Anne's time at the podium in its entirety. She seemed instinctively to know that concise comments are the ones picked up and relayed, though this was easier to achieve at a time when the typical network news clip was about forty-five seconds, not about eight seconds as it is today. Had she rehearsed these words or dreamed them up on the spot? Either way, it was obvious to young Carter that he had met a woman with many gifts.

Gradually the crowd drifted off. A reporter from United Press International asked Carter whether he favored the violent overthrow of the United States government. The police sergeant stopped off to arrange the next basketball game. "I tried marijuana once but I didn't inhale," he declared with a wink, and everyone joined in laughing at the absurdity of such a statement. To young Carter the sergeant seemed a chiseled, aging, fatherlike presence; to Carter's adult consciousness the same officer appeared shockingly boyish for such a position of responsibility. The assistant dean of students told Jayne Anne he appreciated her comments, then observed that he'd just bought the new "Protocol Harlem" album and "really dug into it." One of the New Left kids, intense and humorless, told Jayne Anne she was a dangerous accomplice of the military-industrial complex. One of the Young Republicans favored them with a dissertation on how the CIA was fomenting the draft resistance movement in hopes of diverting attention from the Warren Commission cover-up and were they aware that Martin Luther King, Jr., took secret trips to meet with his masters in the Kremlin? Then the Young Republican asked Jayne Anne whether lesbians like her wore their strap-ons all the time or only at drug orgies. Everyone realized it had come to the point that it was time to say good night.

Carter and Jayne Anne found themselves the last ones standing atop the embankment before the fieldhouse. As young Carter looked toward her fondly, his older awareness dreaded to remember the clumsy come-on line he was about to use to try to get her to sleep with him. The line was so excruciating, it will be skipped here for humanitarian reasons.

Clumsily propositioned, Jayne Anne replied, "It was nineteen to sixteen when we had to stop."

"What?"

"Me nineteen, you sixteen, game twenty-one," Jayne Anne said. She shook her hair back in a way Carter would come to adore. "Let's finish the game. Whoever wins gets to decide what we do with the rest of the night."

"Okay. If I win, I can predict the next two hours of your future," Carter said. "What if you win?"

"I dunno. Maybe I make you listen to my life's story."

They went back into the fieldhouse, stepping through the broken door. When their pickup game was ready to resume in the light of security lamps, Jayne Anne grinned and again peeled off her shirt, tossing him the ball. Carter was not so much aroused as warmed by the gesture, since now she was doing this generous and intimate thing for him alone. Highly motivated to score baskets, Carter won, and anyone can guess what the next two hours held. As the lovestruck children dribbled a ball and laughed together in the half-light, adult Carter wondered how the years that followed might have differed if she had won and he had listened to her life story.

Carter began to be aware that he was viewing the basketball match as if he were at a distance overhead, in the position of a sports-event camera. He would not remain to experience again their first night of lovemaking—and just as well, for emotionally he was no longer able to handle such transport. Then every part of Carter's awareness moved away from every other part, and he tumbled back to the present.

CHAPTER SEVEN

DESUETUDE OF LATE AFTERNOON prevailed on the street in front of the Pudendum Palace, where Carter found himself. The early happy-hour crowd was straggling in, masked behind mirror sunglasses. Platinum-class dancers, or at least molybdenum-class, were arriving to prepare for their labors, causing little whitecaps of commotion as their idealized forms swiveled by. The dancers reflected one of the iron laws of present-day American society: the better a woman's figure, the more ridiculous her line of work.

Carter walked to his car, took the parking ticket from under the wiper, and saw that it was time-stamped to the day after he had encountered himself smoking pot on the street. He got in the car and dialed his cell phone. Once again he hadn't been fired. Instead there was a glowing message from Afreet telling him he handled the topless club situation brilliantly. The Koreans had the time of their lives. They assumed Carter abandoned them deliberately so they would not feel inhibited, and from the sound of things, inhibited they had not been. In addition to numerous lap dances in the VIP room, apparently they had gone onstage and done the Watutsi with tall naked blondes, to the cheers of assorted rounders. Plus, each had a table shower. Carter still didn't know what that meant, though presumably it made no difference so long as breasts were involved. They ran up a sixteen-hundred-dollar bill for regular charges and went through the entire three thousand dollars in dancer tips. "Chrissy says she owes us a favor and just let her know when we want to collect," Afreet noted ambiguously.

There were other miscellaneous messages. Several e-mails from Ginny concerned tactics in the Value Neutral case. One clipped in the URL of an erotic Web site with a note from her attached reading, "I was safeguarding my First Amendment rights by looking at some of these pictures, there's so many things here I would like to try." Another e-mail, tabbed URGENT, was from Catholic Relief Services. Carter didn't open it.

Instead he guided the sedan along rutted downtown streets and up onto an expressway ramp, experiencing the sense of relief that suburbanites feel when their cars break the magnetic field of the city. Twenty years ago the suburbs had scared Carter; now the city was beginning to have that effect. Up on a suburban freeway a person could blend in with others whose faces he'd never see, all rushing purposefully, none interacting. Carter wondered if he should give up the downtown place and get something detached.

It was the day of his appointment with the psychotherapist. Carter drove toward the address of a Dr. Sonora Andorra, whose name seemed vaguely familiar—was she a brand of gourmet mustard? There was no one in the waiting area of her place of business. Presumably therapists didn't overbook, otherwise patients would have to sit looking at each other and thinking, Okay, so what's wrong with *him?* Carter filled out many insurance forms, and the receptionist took impressions of all three credit cards he carried. "Can't be too careful," she explained cheerfully.

A door opened and a woman slipped out of Andorra's office. She left as quickly as possible, avoiding eye contact. This departing patient's face bore the expression of some nameless, tapering sorrow.

A second woman appeared. "Carter Morris?" Dr. Andorra asked, and shaking hands said, "Abraham called about you." She looked him over. "Yes, I think I do recognize you. People must recognize you everywhere! I mean, since you and your fascinating career were recently featured on *Good Morning America.*"

"No, just a head shot on CBS News, and it was a long time ago."

"Well. He said featured." Andorra was plainly let down. "Have a seat."

Sonora Andorra's cheeks were sallow despite what appeared to be hours in the tanning booth and cost-no-object facials. Her office was decorated in bright contrast colors, like a page of layout in a woman's magazine. On one wall hung a framed copy of a newspaper advertisement for a psychology seminar at a Hilton hotel, headlined: DR. SONORA ANDORRA (MEDICALLY LICENSED) ASKS, "WHAT ARE YOU HIDING?" In large type was an 800 number to call. A paperback book by Andorra was displayed on a stand on the desk, her photograph prominent on the cover, and titled *Day Care for the Inner Child.* A second displayed paperback was titled *What to Do When Mom and Dad Countersue.*

They went through introductory discussion, medical history, Carter's general circumstances. This consumed the first forty-five minutes of the scheduled fifty-minute session. Andorra slowed down and pressed for what seemed like excessive detail whenever Carter made glancing references to publicity or the media. He was anxious to get to the heart of the matter, if only to determine whether he was wasting his time consulting a professional.

"Can we talk about what I came to talk about?"

"Many sessions are normally required to establish a baseline, before we begin to regress."

"It's not regression. It's something happening to me right now."

"Something you *think* is happening."

"Right. That I think."

Carter gave a bowdlerized, carefully redacted version, emphasizing the power of memory images that seemed real, leaving out the sense that he was actually in the past rather than reliving it, not mentioning the prior versions of himself with whom he conversed.

"So you are in complete blackout during these memory episodes, wandering for hours."

"No. The event ends and I am standing exactly where I started as though no time had passed, except that it's much later or the next day. And my clothes are always in perfect condition, as if I hadn't moved. That's kind of what bothers me."

"You have stress factors in your life but no secondary indicators of psychosis. You're not hearing voices, are you?"

"Ha ha. Of course not."

Andorra seemed pleased. "*Very* innovative," she said. "Extended palpable memory-induced illusions with witnesses but no physical evidence of blackout location. This isn't a named syndrome. Would you be interested in participating in a journal paper?"

The receptionist announced the end of the session. Dr. Andorra reported that she was eager to see Carter again and accompanied him to supervise the scheduling of the next appointment. A middle-aged man in the waiting lounge, by appearances the headwaiter of an exclusive restaurant, gave Carter a look that said, What's wrong with *him?* Carter made the second appointment having no intention of honoring it; agreeing to the date was a means of getting out swiftly.

IN THE LOBBY CARTER CALLED someone he hadn't seen in years, then pointed the car toward the outlying suburbs. Twenty minutes later he stood inside the thing to which his generation's culture war had been lost: not a military installation or an evangelical church or a libertarian think tank but a mall.

Carter stood in the central esplanade of the nationally praised

Mall to End All Malls, a faux-aureate, ersatz-inlaid, appliqué-spritzed shrine to that which is unnecessary. As far as the eye could see in every direction, glittering stores opened to causeways congested with shoppers in various states of abundance-induced anxiety. No matter how far a person walked through the mall the number of stores in the distance appeared to remain unchanged, as though the place were an infinitely expanding universe.

Locations and dimensions of footpaths, escalators, and aisles in the mall were designed by a firm that specializes in the psychology of the impulse purchase; a Cold War surplus supercomputer had been used to calculate the permutations of stairwell placement. Thirty truck ports and two rail spurs served as merchandise debarking areas, busier than the ore docks of Cleveland. The mall's twenty-thousand-slot parking facility, larger than a medieval town, was so much in demand that perilously affluent teenagers rose early on Saturday mornings to be assured of getting a space for the day. When preparing to leave a good space near the doors the mall-mad of all ages called friends or relatives so someone could drive over to take their parking slot as it opened, keeping the precious vacancy within the kin structure. Shuttle buses brought in clerks, stockboys, and other service workers from satellite lots miles away, overworked Peruvian and Moroccan and Senegalese immigrants whose minimum wages were a tiny cut of the mall's renowned thousand-dollar-per-square-foot take. Airlines offered Mall to End All Malls excursion deals in which shoppers flew in from other cities in the morning, shopped the day long while periodically dropping their packages with express-shipping services, then flew home that night. Hilton and Hyatt built premium hotels within the mall itself, like the lodging within the grounds of Disneyland. The well-to-do booked afternoon-only rooms not for passionate assignations but to have someplace to rest a few hours between shopping rounds; sometimes they stayed overnight, just to sleep in the proximity of complete material superfluity. The mega-mall represented consumer technology and market economics at their highest coupled to culture at its lowest. The combination proved irresistible.

Entering the Mall to End All Malls gave Carter the sense of being an operative who had penetrated enemy headquarters, and who must appear decisive or be given away. So he walked confidently down the glittered arcades, passing every emporium and trading house imaginable to the mind. Department stores, shoes, electronics, upscale apparel, discount apparel, CDs, DVDs, stores for climbing gear, synthetic emeralds, natural herbs, a store that sold only dust ruffles (separate counters for imported and domestic). Engagement rings with no cosigner. Exercise equipment that converts into furniture: *You've Got to Try Our Combination Sleep-Sofa Stair-Climber to Believe It!* Instant marriage counseling. Custom laser eye surgery in about an hour. California pizza, Memphis ribs, cholesterol-reducing French fries, pressurized cryogenic ice cream, Iranian takeout. Sleep disorder management. Cartier, Coach, Tiffany, Vuitton. Steak Knife World, Pager World, Gurlz World, Dollar World, Instant Self. Hair removal, hair replacement, weight loss, weight gain. Spiritual weight loss. Home genetic screening. Day trading for beginners. Books 'n' asiago panini, all sexual violence bestsellers forty percent off every day. Counterculture stores established by Fortune 500 companies. Super-sized Rapafrapazapachino; will that be shade-grown or sun-grown or hydroponic? Personalized key chains with digital find feature. Try our new mood-adjustable bras with remote control. Cloned Barbie, now with programmable attitudes. Invisible disinfectant infused gloves for discreet germ protection. Theme stores based on Judy Garland and Lou Gehrig. Theme restaurants based on James Bond and Herman Melville. A theme restaurant based on rock stars who died of overdoses, and another whose theme was cleavage shots of starlets. Child Zone, The Fun Place to Ditch 'Em While U Shop. (LIMIT EIGHT HOURS PER CHILD, ALL PARENTAL NO-SHOWS WILL BE PROSECUTED!) Refinancing, debt consolidation, and credit reconstruction. Eighteen-screen multiplex with entry-point body scanners able to detect unauthorized candy.

Carter paused to purchase a Rapafrapazapachino. "Melp yew?" the woman behind the counter asked. "Nezzinline. Melp yew?" Her job was to dispense the product and his job was to consume it. The drink was excessively sweetened, igneous in consistency but frigid, tasteless, served in a thirty-two-ounce cup. Many shoppers were waiting impatiently for one.

Pausing at the glassed entrance of the credit-problems boutique, he saw young couples not long out of high school, single mothers trying to hush fussing toddlers, truck drivers with packs of Winstons stuffed into shirt pockets, smooth-looking yups in nice clothes, all hunched staring in muted stupefaction at the wording on legal forms. Carter knew this look from court experience. It was the look of someone confronting the formal documentation of a personal stupidity and finding out just how high the charge would be merely to get back to zero.

Carter paused, too, at the Dollar World, where recently arrived Pakistanis and Ecuadorians worked grueling hours hoping to earn a permanent place in this order. Who could blame them? Any rational person would choose shallow material excess over the social realities of most nations of the globe. One might sensibly choose the designer-label lifestyle over most systems of philosophy, too. After all, if the postmodernists are right—nothing matters and there's no truth—might as well go to the mall.

Farther along the loggia Carter encountered the Value Neutral outlet, or to be precise, encountered one of them. There were three Value Neutral stores in the Mall to End All Malls, each identical to the next, duplicated throughout the structure to take advantage of patterns of foot traffic in the way that a suburban turnpike might have a McDonald's on the right-hand side and then another on the left-hand side a block later, each serving a completely different set of customers.

Carter wandered into the Value Neutral. An auditorium of lights, mirrors, and polished surfaces intended to daze, the store was chock-full with patrons—none disoriented by the mirrors, this for them a conditioned environment. Incomprehensibly money-eyed teenagers jockeyed with SUV moms and middle-aged executives to purchase $185 prescuffed hiking boots, $85 teenagers' jeans and $45 adults' jeans, disposal clip-on eyelid rings and $25 plain T-shirts identical to those sold at Wal-Mart for $8 but prized for a sleeve stripe where appeared in tiny stitching the chain's slogan, *More of Same.* The motto was to be ironic, to prove the wearer's cutting-edge independence and ironic detachment. How ironic that everybody wanted one.

The celebrity underwear feature this month, Carter found, was an exposed-nipple bustier worn by a swimsuit-model-slash-actress in a recent action-movie scene set in a tent atop Mount Everest, where the buffed-to-the-point-of-genetically-engineered heroine and her love interest had climbed to escape a germ warfare attack by aliens from another dimension. And quite a tent it must have been, as in her love scene the actress seemed comfortable wearing the bustier and nothing else, though the outside air would be minus seventy Fahrenheit.

In the days of Truffaut and Fellini, when provocative film-making began in earnest, there were wild stories about how, in order to entice actresses to shed their clothes, directors got them drunk or offered LSD and soon a Dionysian atmosphere prevailed on the set. Today no urging is required to persuade a movie babe to disrobe; often the agent specifies that his client wouldn't do the film unless the contract guarantees that her shirt hits the floor, as marketing and career promotion dictated this. But the resulting movie scenes are the reverse of erotic, about as risqué as watching software code being written.

The porn video business arose in part to compensate for the end of screen romance: no seduction, but authentic if excessively choreographed lovemaking. As porn grew closer to mainstream, its lingo became corporate. Porn began to refer to itself as "the industry" and its starlets to refer to what they did as "working." Thus, in certain parts of Los Angeles "I work in the industry" came to mean I have sex on film, and the fact that it was work not fun somehow made everything respectable. In this way, even as porn grew more adventuresome physically, and the performers more luscious, the product became less erogenous, more labor-focused—kind of like watching really good-looking naked people replace roofing tile. The impulse here is fundamentally Puritan, suggesting sex is dirty if done for pleasure but acceptable if a business proposition. The viewpoint has spread to all areas of commercial entertainment. Removal of the erotic from nudity and even from lovemaking, a trend begun by the entertainment industry, now proliferated throughout society. Pretty ironic, huh?

Carter wandered toward the customer service counter of the Value Neutral. There the manager, an exceptionally stylish young man of unclear ethnicity whose name tag read Hazur, was politely explaining the phrase "card declined." The shopper to whom he spoke wore lace-up high heels, jewels, a plunging halter top and full facial makeup, and could not have been older than fourteen. Carter spied a small plasticene rack, placed where it was unlikely to be noticed, holding a brochure titled ISSUES CONCERNING SUPPLIER RELATIONSHIPS. For a company that specialized in targeted communication, that seemed pretty cryptic. Carter read,

Well-meaning interest groups such as the Catholic Church have questioned Value Neutral's practice of outsourcing certain

114

aspects of production (up to one hundred percent of production) to developing-world nations. This is done solely to create economic opportunity in developing nations.

While it is true that, in certain contract production facilities that comply with all local labor laws (note: if there are local labor laws) and over which Value Neutral has no control, conditions sometimes called "sweatshops" apply, it is important to remember that in many professions, people sweat. Autoworkers who make $25 an hour sweat. Lifeguards sweat in the sun, and labor activists have shown no particular interest in them. Professional athletes sweat profusely! So do stockbrokers, take our word for it. Thus, the fact that someone sweats on the job hardly means a labor abuse is taking place.

Nevertheless, in order to certify that Value Neutral contract production operations around the world continue to comply with minimal requirements, the company has retained as a public-image consultant Tiger Woods, who will lead a rigorous Fact-Finding Delegation* to examine certain contract production facilities over which Value Neutral has no control. The findings of this commission will be posted on a Web site at no later than an undisclosed date.

*Due to scheduling conflicts, Tiger Woods will not personally participate in the Tiger Woods Fact-Finding Delegation.

The drivel continued southward from there. Good stuff, Carter thought—no lawyer could have written better. Tiger would be paid a bundle to put his name on the whitewash, and his fee might represent enough to end much of the labor mistreatment in the first place. But while corporate executives don't mind showering excess on themselves or celebrities, most would sooner die than give an extra dime to seamstresses in Vietnam. The thinking flowed from market logic. In market terms, a celebrity definitely is worth millions, while a developing-world day laborer is worth considerably less than the equipment she sits at.

Holding the brochure, Carter toyed with the idea of taking Value Neutral to the cleaners in the legal settlement, then using the company's own money to start a public-awareness campaign about the hypocrisy of a suburban fashion food chain anchored in developing-world misery. But what if the economists were right and closing sweatshops just meant the people who once toiled there would be even worse off? The sorts of international fair-wage agreements that could resolve this dilemma to everyone's mutual benefit seemed hopelessly utopian. Carter let the idea go. It was a fight for somebody else to take on.

Leaving the Value Neutral, Carter continued toward the far end of the edifice, where the mall's management offices were located. He kept walking and seemed to draw no closer to the end, the edge of the shopping universe receding away. He passed teenagers with aggressively glazed-over eyes, spiked green hair, tattoos on their shoulder blades, pierced lips. For all he knew, these were honor students. Carter's peers had adopted the unkempt long-haired look specifically in hope of upsetting their older generation, so he could hardly object to the latest manifestation of the same impulse. But if things had already deteriorated from beards to body modification, by the time these kids were grown, what would be left for their teenagers to do to make them cringe?

Carter stopped for a frozen decaf mocha-apricot tea, but it didn't taste right. He kept walking. He stopped to check office messages and saw one e-mail from Value Neutral and another from a death-row appeals lawyer, both tabbed URGENT. Ignoring the latter he clicked the Value Neutral message. The company had added fifty percent to its settlement offer; that would raise

Carter's take to about nine million dollars. While mulling this he arrived at the mall's management domain. Two doors were beside a gold plaque that read SPRAWL PARTNERS TRUST. Carter entered and asked for the president, Marshall Lelchuck.

Shown in, he saw a trim, well-arrayed man of about his age behind an abnormally large blond-wood Scandinavian Modern desk. The man's manner was confident, time-pressed; he wore dock shoes, a short-sleeved golf shirt, and sunglasses. The walls behind his desk were panorama glass, and the broad window-panes looked out on the mall parking facility, ranks of vehicles extending to the horizon. Brilliant, glancing late-day effulgence refracted through, explaining the man's sunglasses. Carter had to shield his eyes against the angle of the sun.

"I never tire of that view, but with the sun this time of day, gotta have shades," the figure said. "Sure it's a parking lot. But it's the largest bond-financed private multidecked earthquake-resistant retail parking facility in the world, and I can't get enough of looking at it and knowing I did this, I started with nothing and I made this happen," he continued. "The endless shuttling of cars in and out, it's cosmic. Like amoebas at the dawn of time or something." The figure pushed an unseen button and the glare dimmed to an agreeable rich bronze luminescence. "Piezoelectric lensing glass," he explained.

Carter could take down his hand from his eyes. "Marshall, it's been a while," he said.

"Too long, man," Lelchuck said. "Saw your picture in the newspaper on that death-row vindication thing. What was that, last month?"

"Eight years ago."

"I was going to write you a congratulations note but it's just been crazy around here. Want a Cuban?"

Lelchuck held out a humidor. The glare damped, Carter could now see details of the office, prominently displayed walls of framed photographs of Marshall pumping hands with the connected or famous. One wall was political—Marshall meeting the mayor, the governor, Hillary Clinton, Clarence Thomas, Ed Muskie, Elizabeth Dole, Ted Kennedy, at least two George Bushes. The second wall was celebrities—Marshall beaming next to Cindy Crawford, Clint Eastwood, Heather Locklear, Dustin Hoffman, and several whom Carter did not recognize but concluded from their glistening teeth must be entertainment notables. In a few of the pictures, Marshall had his arm wrapped tightly around some strapless-gowned starlet's waist as if they were the dearest friends.

On an exhibition table near Marshall's desk was a well-made architect's model of what appeared to be an amusement complex; on the desk itself was enough advanced electronic equipment to control a space probe bound for the outer moons of Meepzor. Two ultra-thin laptops on the desk showed market results, two others the video feeds from CNBC and MSNBC. There was a gadget that resembled a miniature nuclear power plant, complete with tiny cooling towers. He'd gotten the device in Hong Kong, Marshall explained, and it was supposed to control the room's feng shui. A companion feng huang generator was on back order.

They began to puff the Cubans. Carter had noticed Marshall's name breaking the bottom ranks of the *Forbes 400*; it said something about the times that three-quarters of those on the list were billionaires.

"I tell you, man, life has been berserker since my REIT went j-v with Microsoft," Marshall said. "We're making plays in a dozen states right now, retail space, housing starts, mixed-use. Between the real-estate investment trust and my blue chips, I literally can't figure out my net worth some days." Lelchuck hesitated, as if he'd let something slip. "Don't mention the Microsoft thing, they haven't announced it yet and they're not sure the public is ready to know Bill Gates is buying up land. It's such a huge country, the most Gates can possibly acquire is maybe ten percent. But people are going to blow this all out of proportion. He's got to enunciate that it's for stewardship. Anyway it's not about money or real estate, it's about being change agents." Lelchuck savored the cigar, regarding its curl of smoldering luxury. "Not what we used to smoke. Those were the days. So what can I do for you?"

Marshall had been the student who, on the night of the fieldhouse demonstration, had wanted to set the gymnasium on fire. In the basketball game that followed he'd complained angrily about cooperating with pigs and committed more fouls than everyone else combined. He ran a hard-edge protest chapter that called itself the Emancipation Cell; it smashed up lab equipment in the science department, threw paint balloons at corporate recruiters, shouted down speakers during public events, and praised the Weathermen, the thug faction that planted bombs. Lelchuck had been a little dictator among his cell members, calling midnight meetings at which he held the floor interminably, expounding half-baked theories of human history and screaming at anyone who rose to go to the bathroom.

Marshall might have gone on to become the focal point of a UFO cult, living in some remote location and haranguing lonely, weak-willed followers about purity in their bodily fluids. But his father was rich and the call of capital proved inexorable, as if hereditary. Lelchuck went into business with his dad, smoothed out his social skills, and climbed toward wealth. He hit the big leagues by forming the syndicate that bought the land behind the Mall to End All Malls, using mainly Saudi money but outsmarting the Arabian bankers and ending up with proxy for a majority of the shares. Fleecing the oil princes made Marshall a hero to the Beverly Hills financial elite, his name becoming A-List in Santa Monica, Manhattan, Sag Harbor. That business about his arrest for beating a girlfriend with a pool cue and breaking her clavicle? Youthful indiscretion. Marshall's father arranged recon-structive surgery and a confidential settlement in exchange for which she dropped charges. After Marshall began mingling with the likes of Bill Gates and Cindy Crawford, he expended a pretty penny in legal fees to get records of the case expunged.

"Nice picture with you and Kissinger," Carter noted. "Didn't you burn him in effigy once?"

"I've learned to think outside the box," Marshall replied. "He's got juice with the mandarins. We're looking at China so we hired him as a consultant. Talking to some government robot types there, telling them if they let us put a people's cineplex into Tiananmen Square, all will be forgotten about that tanks-crushing-protesters thing. Consumer demand trumps political un-rest every time. Did you know that next to Marx's birthplace, in Trier, there is now the Karl Marx Fashion Mall? No lie, seen it with my own eyes. Good deals on Dockers, too. No alienated labor agitators at the Karl Marx Fashion Mall, they're all too busy shopping. Anyway it was a kick to call up Kissinger and give him instructions."

"You gave instructions to Henry Kissinger? Isn't he an insuf-ferable egotist?"

"I sign his check. He was extremely deferential to me."

Carter had never liked Lelchuck. Hard to believe they'd not only worked together on many occasions but once lived together at the farm, in the group house days, when Arcadia was supposed to happen.

One of the laptops on Lelchuck's desk beeped and displayed vacillating sine waves. Marshall smiled. "I've got a preferred position on an IPO today, biotech company that claims to have synthesized an Indonesian rain-forest enzyme that makes sleep unnecessary. Company hasn't got a prayer, won't last out the year, but investors don't have to know that, now do they?" Once everyone Carter knew had been devoted to civil rights, saving the environment, social equity. Now everyone he knew was devoted to making money. Who was Carter to question a social consensus?

Lelchuck began to seem antsy. "It's really great to see you but like I said, what can I do for you?"

"We've both become establishment. I've been thinking about that."

"What's to think?" asked Marshall. "Times changed. When our parents' generation was in college they stuffed themselves into phone booths. We protested a war. We've got nothing to be ashamed of. Times changed."

"I'm not outraged anymore, just grouchy," Carter said. "I don't wake up either mad or eager for the day. I don't dream of a better tomorrow."

"You have the symptoms of civilization, my friend," Marshall said knowingly. "Get out of your rut. Do Club Med, Canyon Ranch, the Hunza Valley. Take over a company, dump your wife. Take cabala instruction, I did that with Madonna and Tom Brokaw. Fly in a pair of *filles de joie* from the best L.A. escort agency, they're pricey but you won't be disappointed and you can book the whole thing over the Web. Mix Halcyon and Prozac. Do Vedanta kick boxing. Just shake yourself up."

Then in a lower voice, as if confiding that which others were not qualified to know, Lelchuck continued, "People like you and me, the high achievers, our genes come down from the elites of the ancient hunter-gatherer societies. Back then the top people like us, what did they do all day long? Kill and rape, rape and kill. This has been scientifically confirmed. So killing and raping were what made ancient life gratifying for the people at the top. Today that's what your genes tell you to crave, but it's really not practical for a democracy. So you've constantly got to find some alternative buzz to pacify your DNA. Maybe blindfolded skydiving. Anything that's a challenge. Pick out a challenge, then rape it and kill it. I promise you'll feel better." Marshall seemed proud of himself for this disquisition, as if he'd proven he could be a sympathetic ear.

"I once felt our challenge as a generation was to change the world," Carter said. "Now it's too late to change the world."

"That is where you are so wrong!" Lelchuck replied emphatically. He rose up and came around the desk, quick with energy. "Change is everywhere, change has never been greater. We're all empowered to be change agents." He slapped Carter on the back, hard. "Fifteen years ago this mall was a cornfield and now thirty-five thousand people come here per day, we have our own hydroelectric plant and our own mortuary, all new, all brought about by change. Anything can be changed! Zoning limits, securities rules, EPA regulations, the capital-gains tax—everything I've wanted to change in my life I have been able to change."

Lelchuck gestured to the architect's model near his desk. "If you don't believe in change, check this out. This is a new theme park based on horror movies, the park will be called Gates of Hell." He pressed a button. Red lights on the model began to flash, and a recorded sound of screams was heard. "We break ground next week in Florida. Awesome inferno rides where everybody gets splashed with simulated blood. Hall of slaughter, depicting all the most unusual ways people have been massacred through history. But it's no wax museum, we'll have college kids at six dollars an hour in costume acting out slaughter—medieval peasants and religious martyrs and coeds abducted from dorms by serial murderers. The gore is very convincing and very graphic. Though we won't show much skin, it's family-oriented. Working exhibits of torture with animatronic captives, you turn the dials and make the captives scream. You can pose in one, too; we anticipate long lines for having your picture taken while strapped into a torture device."

He went on. "And the huge, huge hit in our test marketing,

Slasher Zone, wait till you see it. Slasher Zone is a virtual-reality chamber with holographic illusions that enable you to watch your own friends and loved ones stalked, terrorized, and ritually murdered. You can choose to role-play the doomed victim or psycho killer from any of a dozen famous slasher movies. The teenagers in the focus group went nuts for this technology, we had to pry them off it. What seventeen-year-old boy isn't going to want a safe, healthy outlet for seeing his date scream in agony while she gets it with the butcher knife?"

Lelchuck was pumped. "Now you talk about change. When we first filed for the permits for the Gates of Hell park, there were people saying we'd never build it. They said it wouldn't sell, that it was questionable taste—all the predictable naysayer responses to innovation. Today I've got Time-Warner backing, they bought in for thirty-three percent. Disney is extremely excited about the marketing possibilities of personalized holographic violence. I've got MTV signed for a 'Who Wants to Go to Hell?' game show where you see the loser on each round dragged away and seemingly ripped to shreds by famished rats, while the winner gets to pick any one of the evening-gown models who turn the cards and appear to butcher her as she begs for her life! Audience roots for which model they want to see offed, people vote from home via Internet. Tell me that's not a fifteen share in the first week. Plus your better gift stores everywhere will be flooded with Slasher Zone fashion accessories. That's new, that's different, and that, my friend, that is change."

A buzzer sounded and Lelchuck said something briefly into an intercom. Carter got the distinct feeling that before he stepped in, Marshall's secretary had been instructed to buzz after a set interval with an "urgent call," to conclude the session.

"Let me get to what I came to ask," Carter said. "I've got a deal working that has a seven-figure payday. Getting wealthy, is it worth it?"

Lelchuck lowered his eyes, as if engaging the secret greeting of a covert society, rubbed his fingers together, and replied: "There is just nothing like money. With money you I can kill and rape all day long." His eyes sparkled. "When your deal is done call me and I'll sponsor you for the right clubs. Now I gotta go, conference call."

Carter left the office and wandered toward the teeming congress of the mall. Marshall Lelchuck might be wanton or merely unhinged, but he was rich and evidently having a fine time. Carter wasn't having a fine time. And the only thing about his life that seemed to stand within his power to alter was to acquire wealth.

Walking, or perhaps the verb would be hiking, back toward the doors from which he had entered the mall, Carter came up behind the figure of a young man in the scrubs of a hospital attendant. The gown was mangy and out-of-date, with short pant legs and a coarser fabric than could now be found even in the used-clothing bins of consignment stores. Carter had once worn such scrubs and by this point could guess what a glimpse of them meant. "Carter," he called out. The figure turned and was Carter Morris as a young nurse's aide, when he worked in a Veterans Administration hospital.

"I don't even understand what these stores are selling," the younger Carter said in a diffident tone, the Veterans hospital year having been his meek Buddhist period.

"It's the same stuff as before, just more expensive and now made in China."

"You know why I've come," the younger man said.

"Whoever or whatever is investing all this effort is going to be disappointed. It's too late for me to change. I'm faded. I am what the world has made me."

Carter the hospital attendant regarded his elder self. "I had hoped that by this point in life I would have freed myself of the delusion of control," the younger man said, managing not to slip on tense conditionality.

The hospital attendant held out his hand. Carter took it and experienced sensations of dejection and physical weariness, mixed with overpowering sexual urges ready to transfer to any suitable woman who might come within a hundred yards. Then he felt himself expanding away from himself, and tumbled back to the past.

CHAPTER EIGHT

AIR HUNG PERPETUALLY STAGNANT in the George McClellan Veterans Administration Convalescent Facility, on the military reservation of Plattsburgh AFB in the upper ledge of New York State. A commission of retired officers had chosen the site, a hill above Lake Champlain, in hopes that nearness to the lambent waters would soothe the spirits of those in recovery. But the low bidder built the facility, and corners had been cut. The parking lot ended up with the view; the wards looked out on a field of Quonset structures where spare parts for bombers and their tankers were inventoried. Reedy plaster walls within the hospital meant little privacy from the sounds of other patients' torment. And though the north winds howled through the building in winter, there was never enough ventilation to carry away the hanging sting of disinfectants and the scents of burned flesh.

The cut-rate setting reflected how little Congress cared to invest in soldiers who would have served better had they died in sentimental glory than come home crying from pain and wired up like amateur science projects. The continuing existence of the severely wounded was a visual reminder of the cost of conflict. Severely wounded vets were seen by Congress as somehow having screwed up by failing to expire on the battlefield in an abstract affirmation of manhood. But then Congress during the Vietnam years wanted courage and sacrifice from America's soldiers but was itself so timorous and obsessed with the preservation of its privileges that it never declared war on North Vietnam; not even the hawks had the guts for that.

Aromas of medicaments and singed flesh were sufficiently pervasive in the convalescent facility that when Carter smuggled in marijuana the patients could smoke without attracting notice, scent blending into the general redolence. Carter brought as much as he could afford, considering his light wallet and the fives and tens the wounded soldiers could offer. Some of the doctors knew the patients were smoking weed and seemed not to object, given that the hospital could offer them little succor and no pleasures. Plus the medical staff welcomed anything that discouraged patients from begging or stealing codeine and morphine. The supervisory brass who blew through the hospital now and then on "surprise" inspections whose schedule was always posted a week in advance found the patients' fixation on painkiller drugs to be disgraceful, pathetic—soldiers who'd only a short time ago stood tall beneath their nation's flag now reduced to pleading for an extra dose, crying or grabbing, not accepting their conditions like men. The medical staff would rather tolerate grass than listen to a blind or legless twenty-year-old entreat for another injection that would afford him an hour of groggy dreams that he wasn't where he was and wasn't going to stay there.

Once a week a civilian psychiatrist from Burlington made rounds and counseled patients on adjustment, which in the case of the really bad casualties meant the time it takes to accept that your life is over but you're not dead. For some it proved impossible to face the reality that they'd never hold a job, never use a toilet without help, and no woman would ever want them. Carter was cautioned when he arrived not to get attached to anyone, not to form friendships, because within a year of admission a third of the patients would lose their minds and a tenth would be suicides. One of his responsibilities was to monitor patients for signs of hoarding pharmaceuticals that could be used to make the dose that ends it all. To a portion of the patients, finding a way to commit suicide when physically disabled and under watch would be the only remaining possible test of manhood—the final ordeal to overcome and the last chance to leave while the memory of their bursting-with-promise young selves still existed.

Carter stood in one of the hallways of the hospital. He noticed an officer coming his way, a colonel who had some indeterminate supervisory role. Involuntarily he brushed his hair back upward into the hairnet he wore when on duty. It hardly mattered, as the colonel, on passing, shot him the customary look of contempt.

For a moment the building rumbled as a B52 lifted off from Plattsburgh and took the climb-out lane above the hospital. The facility shook at all hours from aircraft departures, not an ideal therapeutic environment. Carter looked through a window and saw the wide, flat airplane as it rose in the unusual buoyant style of a B52 takeoff, nose not pointing up but rather the whole assembly seeming to lift as if floated on a wave. Carter could now tell the different types of B52s. This one was the strategic nuclear variant, headed out over the subarctic on a training mission, its crew preparing for something even worse than Vietnam.

The colonel walked on, radiating dislike. Officers hated conscientious objectors such as Carter, whose presence ruined the grandeur of the military enterprise; officers tended to think COs belonged in jail, changing bedpans was too good for them. But few of the patients gave the COs a hard time, and the fact that the noncommissioned and the objectors got along made the officers even madder. Most soldiers understood that going CO was hardly the easy way out, considering you'd have to endure the opprobrium of parents and community and then serve two years in the army anyway as an orderly or corpsman. It was not the objectors but the Canada kids that made the soldiers mad, because the Canada kids simply walked out on their obligations. In a rehab facility, often the bravest and most daring of the soldiers—there was a link between courage and return on a gurney—were friendliest with the objectors. Disabled heroes and objector orderlies found themselves on the same side of the fence, both an inconvenience in the military's eyes. And every wounded soldier brought to a place like the one in which Carter now worked took little time to notice that there were no mangled officers present. Disabled officers were sent to Walter Reed in Washington, and had their pictures taken with the president.

As Carter's adult consciousness expanded into his younger form, he began to feel anew the mild neurosis he had experienced during his time in this place—the complex qualms that arose from being forced here against his will, yet feeling some level of self-reproach that he allowed himself to be angry when he knew he would be spared the ultimate price some soldiers paid.

Carter's adult awareness was taken aback by his younger self's skinny waist and bony arms. Living in a base dormitory and dining on peanut butter and apples purchased with his objector's nominal pay, Carter was the leanest he would ever be. His adult awareness also felt his head the calmest it would ever be, for this was the period he'd steeped himself in Buddhist and Mennonite thinking as protection against army mentality. Throughout his head were tranquil sayings, philosophical reflections, and antibody thoughts that chased after negative thoughts. Buddhism and pacifist Christianity also turned out to be useful for talking to wounded soldiers who sought repose.

As Carter the orderly walked down the hospital halls, his adult awareness struggled to remember the people behind the doors.

Behind number 283 was Sammy Weston, a slender black man from Cleveland, an only child in whom his parents had invested their whole world. His mother and father lived hand to mouth for four years to keep Sammy in college, so the boy could make something of himself and also so the deferment would protect their child from the war. Sammy had been called up three days after his college graduation, in Vietnam was hit in the stomach by an RPG fragment. He was now fed using TPN tubes grafted to the remains of his large intestine, and excreting through colostomy bags. From his hospital bed Weston passed his civil engineer's licensing exam via mail; he sat diligently reading engineering textbooks, sure he would soon be recovered and working in a big Cleveland A&E firm. Weston was almost eerily upbeat about his prognosis; the medical staff knew he had no chance. *I met your parents when they came to claim the body, Sammy*, Carter thought. *They wouldn't just have it shipped, like most did. They wanted to see where their child spent his last days. They were very dignified. Hardly said anything.*

Behind number 165 was Will Rutledge, who when he departed for basic at age eighteen was leaving his Appalachian coal-mining hometown for the first time, who flew for the first time on the 707 that bore him to Vietnam, who had been in-country less than a week when a mortar round blinded him. Will sat with the television perpetually on, volume cranked up loud so others wouldn't hear him when he burst out crying. Sitting with Rutledge for many hours, Carter realized that what caused the eruptions of tears was when a favorite show came on and he could hear the familiar actors but not see them. *I'm sorry, Will, I just can't remember what happens to you*, Carter thought.

Behind number 144 was Jack Sheller, a muscular twenty-year-old whose mother had come from Indianapolis to decorate the hospital room with his sports trophies and academic awards and framed pictures of his fiancée, a high school sweetheart to whom he'd given a ring the night of his induction. Sheller had been taken to the field surgeons with blood pressure scarcely detectable, they'd cut and stitched with abandon to keep him breathing. Now his face was permanently contorted, his legs mangled though usable, and his penis and balls gone, replaced by a bladder shunt that infected easily. He sat looking out the window all day, watching the arc of bombers moving skyward, mired in clinical depression.

She's coming, Jack, Carter thought. The hospital staff had been stunned on the day his fiancée appeared holding papers for his discharge. When they heard the news about their ruined boy-friends, girls back home always swore nothing was changed. But eventually every patient got the letter, if anything again at all. Jack's fiancée arrived in a rental car, then an exotic appurtenance, and had a garment bag with a new suit for him to wear. A delicate woman in a flounced, furbelowed dress appropriate for a high school dance—the way he'd want to see her, Carter realized— she walked straight into Jack's room showing only the slightest queasiness. Several of the soldiers thought the fiancée's actions were as brave as anything they'd seen in war.

You'll marry her, Jack, you'll honor her, you'll find your way, you'll end up as the principal of the same high school where you had your halcyon days, Carter's adult awareness thought. *Someday the whole country will read about you.* Carter gaped in amazement when he picked up the edition of *Newsweek* with the article about Jack and his remarkable family—he and his wife adopted three refugee children from the Vietnam airlift, and the stories ran when the third of three was admitted to Harvard. In the photo accompanying the article, Jack's face showed a man satisfied with a life well lived. Walking past the room where despondency now reigned, Carter wished he could offer a pre-view.

And then there was number 386. Carter couldn't possibly for-get who was behind that door. As his young form moved in that direction and his adult self struggled against the motion—any-where but there—he was glad to be interrupted.

"Morris!" a martial voice snapped. "Him again!" Carter could hear the howling and turned toward it. Several of the objector orderlies were scrawny guys, frightened of physical threats; Carter tried to help them by always allowing himself to be the one sent in to Mad Dog. So he stepped toward number 289.

Webster Philion, Jr., was among the few who at all times had his own room. Usually a private room happened only for a while as patients shuffled in and out; most of the men shared rooms, listening to each other's moans and farting. Nobody was expected to share a room with Mad Dog Philion. Entering, Carter felt amazed, as he did each time he came into the man's presence, to perceive not only how loud but how genuinely canine was the soldier's sound.

Mad Dog had gotten himself out of the wheelchair and into the corner by the window, as he did when in full bellow. He claimed he needed to face the moon to howl properly, and that he knew where the moon was in the sky even during daylight hours. Once someone had looked up a lunar chart and announced that Mad Dog did in fact know where the moon was, for he never howled when the satellite was on the opposite side of the world, but would howl when it was above unseen. Now Mad Dog was clattering around the corner of the room, his half-a-body rolling back and forth slightly on the fused area where his legs had been. He was howling and slamming his fists against the suicide-prevention bars. There was already blood on his hands.

"Mad Dog, I checked you an hour ago and you were fine. What brought this on?" Carter tried to remain blasé when the patients were in worst distress, having observed this trait in the doctors. "You're really messing up that new gown, you know."

There was a long, subhuman howl. Carter looked down on the soldier, towering over this man with much of his body removed, but felt no sense of the bathetic—only the wish to stop the fit short of once again having to have Philion tranquilized, which was carrying the animal analogy a bit far in Carter's mind.

More howls followed, and then a moment of clarity. "Apple

Jacks," Mad Dog screamed. "Want more Apple Jacks."

"I told you we're out. The next time they come in I'll give you the first box."

"Apple Jacks," the soldier said again, intently. "Apple Jacks. Need 'em. Fifty-five percent sugar. Goddamn it give me Apple Jacks or I'll keep at this till you have to sedate me and write it."

The docs did not like having to write up requests for narcotics, and so they gave the orderlies a hard time about not keeping patients under better control. Patients knew this quirk and the leverage it allowed them; the patients knew all the rules.

Carter was slightly disgusted by the thought of the new cereal, infamous as being the first to contain more sugar than all other ingredients combined. So he played his trump card. "You really think you can commit suicide with Apple Jacks," Carter said.

Somehow Mad Dog knew he was getting diabetes even though it was not yet on his chart. *You're also getting kidney failure, jaundice, Coxsackie, Cushing's disease, pretty much everything that's been named*, Carter's adult awareness thought. *But the day you force-fed yourself five boxes of Apple Jacks, it didn't kill you. I had to clean up the vomit, though.*

"Just give me," the soldier said.

Carter tried to ignore the demands. "You want to listen to the radio together for a while?" he asked, leaning down. "We could talk. Plus I need to have a look at your bleeding there."

"Don't touch me, you fuckass, I'll kill you with my bare hands," Philion snapped, voice tuned with honed menace. "I've killed VC, NVA, hooch bosses, Saigon hookers, I've killed mama-sans, I'm not going to stop at killing you." He flailed threateningly, and was a menace despite his reduced form. Supposedly Mad Dog obtained his byname on the night he earned his Silver Star. After his rifle jammed he charged an enemy position, shrieking a wolf's howl. He shredded up two men with a bayonet alone and then turned their guns back onto their own ranks. Stepping on the mine came later, when his unit wasn't even under fire.

"Come on, Mad Dog, you never killed any mama-sans," Carter said, trying to inspect the bleeding hands. "And I know what you did with the Saigon hookers."

"You don't know what I did over there!" Philion said, spitting it out with the intensity of madness, wanting others to fear him. There was a pause and he added in a lucid voice, "I like to say that tough-ass shit."

Carter took the opening. "Let me bandage your hand, we'll listen to the radio or talk about the eightfold path." He knelt and began to clean the self-inflicted cuts, trying to touch gently.

"Eightfold path," Mad Dog said, his fit now spent. "Prop me up so we can talk about that again. Tell me what I have to do to be released."

Carter lifted the fallen man, transferring him to the bunk. "We begin with the *prajña,* the steps of right wisdom," Carter said restfully. "We must acquire right views and right intentions. We seek to move beyond the chain of causation—"

He spoke on and Mad Dog calmed, eyes relaxing. Carter the orderly spent hours keeping the soldier from his fury in this way: reading from religious texts, from a library copy of *The Story of Philosophy* on which a child had drawn pictures and written "ex libris" in a child's hand, sometimes making up Buddhist-sounding terms and theories when memory faltered. As his younger self spoke lullingly to the suffering man, Carter the adult saw his memory of the manner in which Webster Philion was released. They found the body swinging from a steam pipe in the hospital basement. Mad Dog had dragged himself there in the abject hours before dawn, somehow moving quietly enough to rouse no one. The discovery came when a maintenance worker, bent over to walk among the pipes, struck his head against the base of Mad Dog's stumps. They had already gone cold, whatever made the man alive having dissipated into the inert subterranean air.

THAT NIGHT WHEN HIS DUTY ended Carter walked back to the dormitory, ate franks and beans from a can, and eagerly read the mail. Two love letters from Jayne Anne, who wrote florid, satirical missives about her activities in the ladies' home society as she awaited his return—letters of the type proper women sent to soldier boys a century before. It was her little joke, though Jayne Anne did seem to view Carter as away at war, since technically he had been inducted and unquestionably now served at the pleasure of the Selective Service Commission. In the mail was also a thick manila envelope of antiwar leaflets and broadsides, lots about Pentagon marches, invective against the soldiers with whom Carter spent his hours, puerile drawings of bomber pilots as Nazis and constant use of the term Amerika. Young Carter felt vaguely titillated to be reading such things on a military reservation, as if he were a fifth columnist. He read, began to feel sleepy, and laid down.

As Carter the hospital orderly drifted off, his adult awareness was in tumult. He expected to feel himself rise away and return to the present day, but the sensations of that peculiar journey did not begin. Was he to slumber with his younger self, and dream? Then awaken to the next dawn? That would be longer than he had ever "been" in his past, if that was the verb, and would mean, if he understood the rules of these happenings, that when he regained the present a substantial amount of his own time would have passed.

Then he realized something more immediate. He'd heard mentioned that it was Tuesday. That meant tomorrow would be Wednesday, dreaded day of his time at the VA hospital, for Wednesdays he spent behind door 386 with Mack. The thought made adult Carter want to leap up, flee the room, race away from his younger form, and be drawn back to the pleasingly impersonal present. But Carter couldn't make himself leap up, because he had not on that night, and no one can change the past. The young orderly fell into slumber, taking his older consciousness with him. They slept dreamlessly.

MORNING CAME UNBIDDEN. Young Carter woke mildly apprehensive, his adult consciousness snapped to in terror. There was a grimy breakfast, a shower, and then Carter arrived for duty, worked through some miscellaneous rounds, and as he did each Wednesday, reported to room 386.

"Hi. It's me."

"I know the fuck who it is."

Carter was never able to suppress his squeamishness about how Mack looked. Mack had been an Eagle scout, class president, straight-A student, effortless natural athlete, possessor of earnest charm, the town's best product in a generation—the gleaming rock star of Carter's youth. Now about two-thirds of him was left, balanced on a poorly fabricated support frame.

It happened when Mack's unit had been advancing during a small operation near Lang Vei, not at one of the great battles like Ia Drang or Hué, no magnificent attack jets streaking overhead or artillery crumping, just a routine squad movement. The cracking began all around where Mack was walking. He later told Carter that anyone who claims to have been in combat and to have had bullets whizzing past his ears is lying because bullets don't whiz, they make a pointed, hideous crack. The cracking grew worse when the report of rifles was joined by the jabbing horror of a heavy machine gun. Soldiers hate large-bore machine guns, they fire jacketed slugs that can kill straight through truck doors or earth berms, can ricochet and still kill on the bounce, that heat the ground where they hit, that do things to living tissue that should not be done.

Realizing he was in machine-gun sights, Mack lunged forward toward a low rise of cover. He hefted his body sideways, as a boy vaults a fence, to land prone and least exposed. As his left side came up above his right, Mack felt red pain. The gun kept firing a little longer, till a mortar team behind Mack's position walked rounds up to the source. One of the walking rounds fell a few meters from him and the overpressure broke both his eardrums. Soon the enemy had been silenced, the only sound Mack might have heard would have been the other soldiers shouting for him. Mack's left arm, left leg, and left hip had been dissevered from him by the machine gun, which was sweeping the field just as he vaulted and exposed himself sideways relative to the stream of bullets.

Within minutes a Cobra was orbiting the spot where Mack had fallen, laying down suppressing fire to cover the approach of the medical Huey. He could no longer hear the helicopters, but knew their presence from the unnatural downward vibration of the air. A corpsman from the Huey put a towel in Mack's mouth for him to bite. After a glance at Mack's wounds the corpsman tore open two morphine hypos using his teeth for speed and injected both, assuming all he could do was relieve the death throes of a man whose soul was about to depart his body. When they lifted Mack toward the helicopter, the medics had trouble finding places that weren't bleeding to grab. Somehow the field surgeons saved him, his left arm, leg, and hip gone, the remains of his left side extensively cauterized in extreme haste. A religious person might say it had not been Mack's time to die, but that would require an explanation of why it had been Mack's time to be cut in half, or why it was ever any young man's time to creep toward other young men in war.

"I brought you the paper with the baseball standings," Carter said.

"Cram the paper. I told you *Playboy*."

Mack always kept the room's lights low, to make his form harder to see. His face, once that of a men's magazine model, was now blanched and bony, eyes subject to precession as he tried to regard anyone. Mack was standing, held vertical by an Erector set of prostheses strapped around his midriff. A clanking stand, nothing sophisticated but formed at the AFB metal shop by two welders, allowed him to keep his balance and take a few steps if he could brace with his right hand. The structure was held to his body by a cut-leather harness strapped and tied with cloths that got bloody and pissy and had to be changed. It would be years until artificial limbs were available, and by then Mack's nerve endings would be too hardened for anything other than the inutile "social arm" he could sometimes wear. There was little hope of unaided walking, considering no limb or armpit to brace the crutch against on the injured side. Mack had been told it would always be the wheelchair or clanking a short distance on the metal stand with someone's assistance.

"Did you bring me dope?"

"I won't have grass again till next week. Somebody's coming through."

"Then get me extra morphine."

"Mack, that stuff is addictive—"

"I want some!" He slammed his one fist down on the table, losing his balance. Carter had to bound to his side to keep Mack from toppling. Mack sneered at being aided, kept from humiliating himself physically by a brother whom he once could hoist above his head.

"Don't you ever say the word 'no' to me. If our places were traded and you were hurting like this I would do anything for you, get anything you needed to make the pain go away—smack, whores, anything. I'd rob banks if I had to, to get what you needed." Mack looked at Carter with contempt. "Not that our fucking places could ever be traded, they'd close down the Marines before they took a freak like you."

Carter tried to absorb his brother's abuse with Buddhist equanimity. It didn't work particularly well, but then he was a novice on one of the early paths. The chief of the medical staff knew Carter and Mack were at each other's throats and wondered whether to ban contact. It was he who'd come up with the every Wednesday system, feeling that if fate placed brothers in the same facility, they should spend at least some time together.

"I've got the questions. Do you want to go over them for a while?"

"Sure, why not. You'll have a few laughs."

"Mack, there's nothing I want more than for you to go home. There's nothing Dad wants more. He's rebuilt the whole place—ramps, supports, he says you'll hardly recognize the house. Dad is going to look after you."

"And when you get out you'll go back to making a mockery of everything I almost died for."

Carter swallowed. "We can agree to disagree about the war," he said.

"We can agree that you have your freedom because I stood up to defend it! It's survival of the fittest out there and the reds are gaining ground every day. By protesting you give comfort to the nation's enemies."

"We're opposed to an unjust war, not in favor of communism." Carter tried to speak softly, avoiding provocation.

"Unjust! You're saying I gave up my leg and my arm for a cause that is not just!"

Carter backpedaled. "You didn't start the war. You did what you thought was right."

"What I thought was right but you know better!" Mack was

swaying, having trouble maintaining equilibrium on the makeshift strut. "Anyone who doesn't love this country is free to
leave! You, your faggot friends, anybody. Get out now!"

"Mack, let's review these questions."

"I mean it, get the fuck out right now." Mack was crimson.
"Don't come back until you have something I want. Don't fuck
with me."

Mack tumbled sideways into the chair that faced the window,
clanking the struts and swearing as one poked against flesh. He
turned away from Carter and would not look back for some time,
perhaps an hour; he often sat in silence and would not acknowledge Carter's presence. Carter would sit equally silent until Mack
chose to resume speaking. Each time Carter arrived to spend
Wednesday there was a bitter argument, followed by a period of
stillness that ended when Carter assisted him to the toilet; there
would be relative civility for the rest of the day. Mack always
wanted to see the latest picture of Jayne Anne—she sent curled-
up Brownie prints of herself at various rallies and appearances—
and it made Carter uncomfortable to show them, since Mack's
hometown steady had not written in months. At least they could
go through the baseball pages together without arguing.

While Mack sat mute and unmoving, Carter leafed the sheets
he had pinched from the psychiatry files. Reconstruction of the
Morris abode notwithstanding, the Marines wouldn't approve
Mack for discharge to go home because the psychiatrist from
Burlington had assessed him as disturbed. Mack initiated fights
in the rec room and mess area, swinging wildly with his one arm
and toppling over. He pounded on things and threatened the doctors, not just harangues but unsettling threats about revenge. Below some unreadable handwritten clinical notes in his file was a
blue-ink stamp impression that read UNSTABLE. The doc had a
stamp that said that—as if he came to this conclusion so often it
would tire him to write the word out by hand. UNSTABLE stamped

on the file of a man who couldn't keep his balance because he had given his country two limbs.

So Carter had lifted a military-issue list of psychiatric questions and was coaching Mack on how to respond stably when the next assessment came. He tried to compose responses that oozed normality, then put those answers into Mack's head. Knowing the questions in advance was the key, for the psych assessment scenarios were enigmatic, eerie:

Suppose you were married, came into the room unexpectedly, and found your wife on the phone. What would you think?

A stable response would seem to be, "What a fucking stupid question." Carter's suggested response: "I would think she was talking to a friend." One of the questions said,

You're walking down the street, minding your own business, holding your rifle. A dog comes out of nowhere and acts like it might bite you. What should you do?

Try to come up with a nondescript response to a hypothetical that begins, "You're walking down the street, minding your own business, holding your rifle."

After going over the psychiatric scenarios for a while, Carter turned to a letter he was working on. He had taken to writing their district's congressman, asking for assistance in getting Mack sent home. A year before Carter had been mailing the same congressman droning, tendentious antiwar epistles. He now forwarded polite, cautiously worded letters with formal salutations and closings.

One of the other orderlies, a Quaker boy who spoke very slowly, knocked on the door and told Carter to go to the hospital's main office, it was important. Carter asked Mack if he wanted to come—moving Mack through the halls was a production, but there was still some hope that with repetition he could become partly ambulatory. But Mack was in his post-argument trance and didn't answer.

Carter left for the office, adult consciousness already knowing what would be there—two discharges for Mack, one from the hospital and the other from the Marines, plus a letter of commendation, plus a memo from the Selective Service releasing Carter from the balance of his alternate service obligation. Allan Morris was well connected on the local draft board, composed as it was entirely of VFW members. Such boards were stocked with veterans on the theory that those who had already been compelled to serve would think the same must pertain to others, in the way that every physician despises the weary thralldom of residency, but once through it, insists the next generation suffer as well. Selective Service board members tended to believe a tour of duty in war was not just a necessary evil but good for a young man's character. Of course such veterans were by definition survivors of conflict. The dead weren't particularly well represented.

The memo to Carter said that considering his brother's extensive injuries from conspicuous valor "and your taxpayer-financed training in proper care of the crippled," under an extraordinary-circumstances clause he was being excused from the remainder of his commitment in order that he return home and attend to Mack during rehabilitation. The directive was signed by the board chairman, a lumber wholesaler with whom Carter's father did business. The memo noted that while the board had no power to compel Carter, once released, to be present to give Mack care, it assumed he would "do what any loyal son and brother would do."

The young orderly swelled with relief to read the letters. Mack would be going home, and he manumitted. Only later, aboard the

Greyhound bus as Plattsburgh receded, would Carter reflect that his release meant that much less consolation for the declining days of Mad Dog and others.

Seeing himself read the letters again, Carter's adult consciousness did not jump to the fantastic welcome party Jayne Anne would stage—a much better reception awaited him than awaited most genuine veterans. He thought instead of the period when he tried to care for Mack at home: the continuous denunciations, the impossible dynamic of father and brother triangulating their anguish against him, his mother's reclusion as she spent hour upon hour in her room with the door closed, Carter's own spite about being the disfavored son. Adult Carter remembered buying the used VW van with the small sum he'd saved, packing it while the others slept, and closing the back door forever on his sense of belonging; driving away, the car sputtering to gain speed.

Carter the orderly took the letters and sprinted down the hospital hallway, sure Mack would be delighted. His adult self realized his awareness was beginning to expand away, watching his young, skinny form trotting into a dissipating distance.

Decades after the war, disaffected Vietnam vets and leftover flower children would find commonality of cause as regards retro obsession and bitterness against government. The extent to which the two groups would converge was remarkable. Attend a present-day Grateful Dead concert and by the gates you will behold the faded hippies and the faded Vietnam vets clustered together, once opposing camps of a vicious culture war, now chattering amicably, each aware the other is the sole group that still cares about its destiny. Eventually, like old marrieds, they even grew to look the same.

Well has it been said that a sadness of aging is that with each passing year, fewer take note of your life's adventure. When young, most are surrounded by interest from parents, aunts and uncles, schoolteachers, countless little friends. By midlife, co-workers and immediate family members may still follow your saga, but the audience is ever smaller, while your story grows steadily less engaging, the sense that you might do anything grand evaporates and the surprise twists tend toward the negative. By the latter phases of life, there may not be anyone left who is keen to know what's happening to you. At least the leftover flower children cared about the disaffected vets and vice versa, if only to sustain their arguments as long as possible, and God willing each will care about the other's fortunes until the day all their eyes have closed.

As his adult awareness rose away from his orderly's body, Carter faced the ugly fact that in the present day not one person cared for Mack nor followed his all-negative story. Mack had his own home, a place of the type realtors call a bungalow. He survived on military disability and the small inheritance from their parents' deaths, passing his days watching video rentals and surfing the Internet and swearing aloud about all the things other people were doing that he was not. Carter sent him money but had not visited in a decade. Sometimes Mack ripped the checks up and returned the shreds.

Carter heard him again say, "If our places were traded and you were hurting like this I would do anything for you, get anything you needed to make the pain go away—smack, whores, anything. I'd rob banks if I had to, to get what you needed."

Then the hospital of miserable men became a vapor, and Carter Morris tumbled back to the present.

CHAPTER NINE

Lᴵᴳʜᴛs ᴡᴇʀᴇ ɢᴀɪʟʏ ᴀʙʟᴀᴢᴇ but no one in sight. Carter stood on an esplanade of the Mall to End All Malls, squinting into its infinity like an astronomer scanning for the edge of a nebula. Luminescence spilled along the shopping corridors, neon twinkled here and there, a few mirror balls spun. Yet the mall was mute silent, not another living thing present.

For a moment Carter entertained the notion he had returned to some parallel world depopulated except for him. Rapidly he advanced to the panicked thought that the review of life had concluded, he was now dead and his hell would be this place.

Hell Mall, where the condemned endlessly jostle to inspect the racks and become covetous, where those who thirst endlessly are served excessively sweet iced coffees that never satisfy and where the cineplex endlessly shows "The Best of Woody Harrelson" on every screen. Through all eternity, Hell Mall would just keep getting more crowded. A fraction of the damned would arrive smiling, thinking they had been sent to a consumer's paradise, but wait till they saw the prices! Lucifer strolls the piazzas, checking for receipts, prattling on about his philosophy of customer-oriented agony and passing out cards proclaiming that his mission statement includes Total Quality Torment. As their purgatory, some of the condemned would spend an initial eon circling in search of a parking space, endlessly seeing the car just ahead get one right by the door.

Then Carter looked at his watch and realized the mall was empty because it was three o'clock in the morning. He was in the part of the complex far from the hotels, miles from them perhaps given the mall's size, and apparently could be relieved that at least there was not yet twenty-four-hour mall shopping. Gates or shutters had been drawn across some of the stores, changing them from welcoming to foreboding. Each step echoed. Whether the thousands of interior lights were left shining as a precautionary measure, or to reflect the mall's operating premise that our duty regarding resources is to consume them, he could not know.

As Carter walked in the direction of his car, it occurred to him that he might run into a drowsy security guard. There would be an awkward situation with a policeman called, perhaps a public embarrassment—what possible explanation could a local attorney have for being in a closed mall at 3:00 A.M.? This realization made Carter quicken his pace, to pass through the zone of jeopardy more rapidly. He stayed dead-center on the promenades, not wanting to trip motion detectors that might be near shop entrances. Carter made it to the walkway to the parking structure without encountering any guard, and then pulled up and stood blankly before the metal handgrips of the outer door, wondering if alarms would go off when he pushed. Should he push and bolt? Activate a fire alarm as a diversion? Peering toward the parking lot, Carter noticed the reflection of rotating orange strobes. Squinting he realized the flashes emanated from the hazard bar of the tow truck that was, at that very moment, pulling off with his car. There was a news box by the door. Carter checked the dateline on the lead story of the displayed edition. It was six days after he met himself in the mall.

The tow truck bounced away with his car, orange oscillation faded into the distance. Drawing a deep breath, Carter pushed outward on a mall door. Alarms yelped electronically. Carter grabbed the news box and used it to prop the door open, so that security guards as they responded would assume thieves had just entered, and sprint inward to find them. He ran through the garage and down a series of curved automobile ramps to the nearest street—there were no stairs to the street, since no one ever arrives at a mall on foot. Finding a phone kiosk Carter attempted to call a cab, but the hack company wouldn't dispatch to a street-corner location in the dead of night. So he turned in the direction of the outer entry to the Hyatt, where there would be taxis. As Carter walked, two police cruisers screamed by and swung up the entrance ramp toward the mall. Soon he was riding home in a cab, discussing the weather.

Carter slept on the couch for an hour, then went to the office before dawn, to get a jump on figuring out what had happened in his absence. He learned that owing to his long truancy, there had been a coup d'état. The same stern message from Kendall Afreet was on his desk, in his e-mail, and on his fax: "This has ceased to be amusing." Ginny Intaglio, the memo went on, was now lead attorney for the Value Neutral settlement; Carter now reported to her. He cursed quietly as he read further. His original special compensation percentage was unchanged—Carter had gotten the share in writing in a countersigned MOU, so as the deal went up his take rose in parallel—but now Ginny and Kendall each were to receive special shares too.

Carter had not jumped at his chance to fuck Ginny but she had certainly jumped at her chance to fuck him. Must have sensed weakness. In retrospect, not fucking Ginny was poor professional judgment. As soon as she indicated interest he should have shoved her against his desk, bent her forward, yanked up her skirt, and given it to her, not so much for their mutual pleasure as for the sake of a favorable power dynamic. Taking what you wanted was, after all, the spirit of the age. If he had degraded her, she would have respected him. Treating her civilly exposed him as fainthearted.

Flipping memos, Carter found several from his new supervisor. They were cool and managerial, the come-hither tone having gone-yon. At least, despite reverses, his status in the deal remained secure. Value Neutral, the memos said, was upset but continued to insist that Carter's name be first on any accord. In professional terms he was doing steadily less work steadily less well, while his reputation kept rising. How very current.

Then there was the money. Ginny reported that in the wake of a new $4.9 billion tort judgment against General Motors, a heart-pounding sum no matter how much it came down on appeal, Value Neutral had again upped its settlement offer, this time quite substantially. Malison & Afreet was now being offered $180 million, several multiples of the opening figure. Even after the others claimed their cuts, Carter's payday would rise to a phenomenal $28 million.

If his objective had been money for the sake of what money can buy, Carter would have whooped to behold this figure. But as his objective was to dull his conscience by turning his life over to money, the figure mainly caused Carter to feel relief. Nobody could possibly fail to sell out for so much gold; only a saint or a bodhisattva would say no. Money like that would have a personality of its own, it would control Carter, pamper him but also make his life choices for him, let him spend his hours idly skimming brochures for Greek villa rentals or attending art shows. The money would take over and crowd out uncomfortable thoughts about how he should be using his life or what should be in his heart. And if Value Neutral's millions left him compromised, then he'd donate to Save the Children and leave big tips.

ABSENTMINDED, CARTER SKIMMED other materials on his desk. Several envelopes from Catholic Relief Services, a call from Mayhew Collins—please don't tell me you're in trouble again, Carter thought—an invitation to a moot court, and motions to be reviewed for a class-action suit involving people who'd been stuck in Otis elevators and wanted compensation for their lost time. One brief contained an incredibly elaborate calculation, performed on a consultant basis by an economist from Princeton retained by counsel, purporting to show that forty-five minutes stuck in an Otis elevator had cost one plaintiff exactly $1,383,904.65 in potential lifetime earnings, through something the economist labeled "opportunity deficit exponentiation." Fearless bullshit, Carter thought, the best kind.

Nothing could top another companion filing, however. A woman who had sex with two men she'd been stuck in an Otis elevator with had lodged a novel cutting-edge brief in conjunction with the class-action case. Plaintiff asked damages for loss of consolation on the part of potential lovers not yet met: she argued that no sex could ever be as hot for her as that day in the elevator, and thus Otis was to blame for making future intimate partners unsatisfactory by comparison. Loss-of-consolation litigation traditionally involved some event that caused a person to cease desiring copulation; this litigant's claim was that she had been caused to become insatiable. Maybe Otis could settle by providing her with an elevator she could get stuck in.

Miscellaneous work was stacked up in other cases. There was a letter from the ACLU, asking if Carter would assist its appeal of the murder conviction of a bank robber who killed a teller with a gunshot to the back of the head, first forcing her to kiss a photo of her children good-bye. Security cameras recorded the crime; the ACLU wanted the conviction thrown out on grounds that the cameras violated the killer's privacy. "It is a dark day in this country when Big Brother has the right to put up video cameras to monitor citizens' private decisions," the ACLU letter said.

A murder is a *decision*—mustn't be judgmental—a lifestyle choice. Such euphemism made Carter think of perpetual use by the media of the word "spree" to describe multiple killings, as in "shooting spree." *Spree* means "a carefree, lively outing." Television announcers shied from saying "rampage" or "massacre," mustn't be judgmental about people's lifestyle choices. Those to blame for rampages were invariably described by the media as "the shooter" or "the shooters," the word "shooter" sounding affirmative, almost like a skilled trade. Mustn't called them the "murderers," too judgmental.

Farther down in the stack was a letter of thanks from a woman in Norman, Oklahoma, for whom Carter had won a wrongful death suit when her husband was killed by a delivery truck. Now that the check had finally come, the woman said, she had employed the funds to enroll her daughter in college. Carter had to stop for a moment when he read that one. It was a constructive use of the law, and he'd come to the point that he had forgotten this could occur.

Next was a memo from Kendall announcing that the firm had landed a major new client, the Saudi Fuels Association. "We will be representing them in regulatory proceedings before the EPA and also with the Department of State, helping them negotiate the conditions under which U.S. infantry will be permitted to protect their assets," Afreet noted. "They need our help in getting the word out about the lack of scientific evidence of global warming and the dangers of too much stratospheric ozone."

Working quickly, Carter drafted a final settlement summary for the Value Neutral deal, along with a press release and FAQs packet for reporters. He wanted a pile of things to put on Kendall's desk before the office opened, so it would appear he had been working hard through the weekend. Carter banged the words out, well past the point of thinking about what he was writing:

Q. Isn't your law firm receiving a very large amount of money while the plaintiffs will only get rebate coupons?

A. Legal overhead expenses are higher than many people realize. Also, thanks to the tireless efforts of Malison & Afreet, the coupons have no expiration date.

Q. In other class-action suits such as *Grandits v. Forever-Freeze*, weren't individuals contacted and asked whether they wanted to participate in the settlement?

A. That's true, but they were also required to prove they had actually been struck by one of the exploding microwave corn dogs. Many found this process intrusive. In our user-friendly settlement, buyers will simply receive notices of their waiver of rights via mail, and opening the envelope to see what's inside will constitute acceptance of the waiver.

Q. Haven't your firm's statements about this case been evasive?

A. That depends on what you mean by evasive.

Carter finished the documents and deposited them on Afreet's desk, deliberately not channeling the paper flow through Ginny as the memos instructed. By now it was almost eight. Miss Lockport and some of the young associates were arriving for work; they greeted Carter warily. He went to the elevator to go down and get coffee, by mistake hitting P1 rather than L. When the door drew back on the parking garage, he saw Ginny and Kendall arriving together, she stepping out of the passenger seat of his Corvette. This rendered fairly obvious the circumstances under which the fine points of her takeover of Carter's case had been negotiated.

"Hey, buddy, nice to see you," Afreet said, with thin derision.

"About time you showed your face. Time to consummate the deal." Consummation was clearly in his thoughts. "Let's do it, okay? Let's lock and load." Like everyone picking up this pseudo-military phrase from Hollywood, Afreet got it backward, the way every swaggering action-movie star gets it backward. A gun is loaded first, then the action is locked; if you lock first, you can't load.

Ginny looked Carter over, as if she were an emergency-room admissions director wondering if this was one the docs could save. "You all right?" she asked. Told that everything was fine, she said in a managerial tone, "I need the final settlement summary and press release." Told they were already on Kendall's desk, she replied, "Reread the memo about changes in the chain of command during your unexcused absence," then swiveled and walked toward the elevator bank. The swivel was so technically impressive Carter was surprised it didn't set off every motion detector alarm in the garage.

Carter spent most of the day taking inconclusive stabs at the work that had fallen down the chain of command to him during his unexcused absence. He drank rummer after rummer of coffee from the specialty shop downstairs, each tasting worse than the one before. He called Dr. Andorra's receptionist to cancel the next appointment. A short time later Andorra herself called back to persuade him to reinstate. The conversation was aimless. It included such exchanges as:

"No, I can't remember where I am while these episodes happen. Can you remember exactly where you were at every moment in your life?"

"But tangible memory illusions combined with repression of location could be fascinating to my readers—I mean, fascinating to explore on a clinical level."

Late in the afternoon his intercom sounded. "A Reverend Collins to see you," Miss Lockport said. Reverend?

During his incarceration, Mayhew Collins had memorized extended sections of the Bible; too bad a person can't be paroled for that, as jails in some Islamic nations will release those who commit to memory the Koran. Mayhew's ability to recite lengthy scripture passages in his determined voice made the prison guards deferential and slightly taut, worried for the dispositions of their souls. But Collins never said anything about the ministry.

"Man of the cloth, probably can't pay legal bills," Miss Lockport whispered through the system. "Shall I bugger him off?"

Carter didn't want to see Mayhew Collins. The name alone made him think of arduous labor and extended loneliness. The case had taken over Carter's life for three years: endless inspections of paperwork, tracking down witnesses who had moved out of state, sweet-talking court personnel, arguing with policemen and their lieutenants and captains about access to file folders and Ziploc bags of hair and fibers. Finally Carter won the confidence of the retired detective who told him about the deal with the jailhouse snitch who claimed Collins confessed in his cell and about how the blood splotch that proved someone else did it had been "lost" by the evidence room. Even then, two full additional years of filings and motions were required to win Collins his freedom, including the harrowing night of the death-row countdown in which Carter had flown to the state capital in a rickety small plane hired by a legal-rights organization, waived the detective's affidavit before the governor's chief of staff, screamed at him about the governor's reelection strategy and that most droll of legal concepts, "*actual* innocence." When Carter thought of Mayhew Collins, he thought of incessant, forlorn work. Memory of the work and the loneliness stayed with him while the glow of the release day had dimmed. Carter's emotional filtering mechanisms were set all wrong.

WEARING A COLLAR, STOLE, AND SOUTANE of uncertain design, Mayhew Collins entered Carter's office. His face, severe and chiseled when he emerged from the penitentiary, had filled out from making up for the home-cooked meals he had missed. His hair had streaked to silver but was thick and healthy. The ameliorating effect of freedom had not changed his intensity. He stared tightly at Carter, a focused stare a jury once read as menace.

"Mr. Morris," Collins said. He scanned around. There was an unwieldy pause. Collins stopped for extended periods between thoughts, as if in agonized debate with himself regarding whether to speak further. "We always talked in the interview room, separated by Plexiglas. I have never seen your circumstances." Pause. "It is a nice office." Pause. "I believe your office is quite nice."

They exchanged small talk. Collins pulled down a law book to inspect, one of the many volumes of the CFR. "I thought about you a considerable amount." He paused. "You saved another man's life, my life. You were walking an admirable path. I envied that." Another pause, while Carter winced internally, fearing Collins somehow knew about the pending corporate payoff shenanigans. But he was thinking aloud on other matters. "I believe I could have become a professional, had my circumstances been different as regards formal education," the reverend said. Collins returned the reference book to its position.

"You got your job at the dispatch office back, didn't you?" Carter asked. "I remember negotiating that with some regional vice president. Job back plus seniority."

"Oh, yes," Collins said. "I was happy to be gainfully employed. The human being is an industrious animal, it is unhealthful to be idle. But I felt ill at ease." Long pause. Carter tried to steal a glance at his watch. "Then one day, while gardening, I heard the Lord call my name. Quite distinctly, in point of fact.

Heard my name aloud, not within my mind. Aloud through normal speech."

*You're not seeing people or hearing voices, are you? Ha ha.
Of course not.* Maybe he and Collins were a natural pair, both
slowly losing touch.

"What did you do?" Carter asked.

"I was terrified," Collins said. "My instinct was to run. But
the Bible tells us to stand tall before our Maker, so I asked what
business the divine would have with such as me. I was told I
must go back into the prison and preach the word." More quiet.
"It made me sick, physically ill, to think of returning to that man-
made inferno, even wearing the precious visitor's badge that
would let me back out. But I did as the higher power bid me do.
For the last six years I have gone there daily. So far I have saved
twenty-nine souls, including the soul of my brother in Christ,
Leydell Bell, who was executed last week. Which you might
have read."

A long pause followed. Carter hadn't read, he automatically
skipped death-penalty stories. Collins said, "Leydell was baptized
on the morning of his death. He renounced his sinful existence,
allowed the Lord to enter his heart, and threw himself on divine
mercy at the last. Today Leydell sits in everlasting glory by his
Father's throne. I could not have saved his life as you did for
me, for he was guilty of a horrible crime. But I was able to save
his soul, and I did."

Collins sat down. Removing his jacket, he revealed that his
shirt was soaked through with sweat, though the office AC was
running at its nuclear-winter setting. "Intense" was a weak ad-
jective for Mayhew Collins.

"How do you support yourself?" Carter asked.

"At the onset of my ministry, I resigned from UPS and let the
Lord provide," Collins said. "As my own needs are few, I could
exist on grace. Then I realized this was selfish, for my wife had

suffered privation during my incarceration and deserved not to experience the same again. So I explored options. Today my prison ministry operates under a modest grant from the Pew Charitable Trusts." Pause. "I wrote the application materials myself, unaided."

"Mr. Collins, I wonder if you would tell me how I could—"

"You are a rationalist," Collins said. "Talk of higher power makes you uncomfortable."

Carter tried to wave that off. "Every person is entitled to his or her—"

"It is conviction, not opinion," Collins said. "For example, I believe that every day for all eternity Leydell Bell will see the little girl he murdered, and they will embrace and love each other as brother and sister. This is made possible by transcendent power, of a higher nature that is comprehensible from the standpoint of our plane." A pause. "You do not believe in transcendent power. But consider that regardless of how our existence came about, there must be some force that surpasses understanding. *Something* made the universe out of nothing. Was it God? A life force? Some essentiality whose specifics we have not yet guessed? It had to be something, some great mystery. *Something* called forth a magnificent creation."

"My daily life is not exactly affected by how the universe was made," Carter said, trying to defuse Collins's mood.

But he did not waver. "I believe that something watches us and notes our choices," Collins said in a way that made Carter feel taut. "I further believe every person is contacted once during life by the great mystery at the center of existence," he said, his intensity making these words sound spooky. "Contact takes the form appropriate to the person. In my case, it was a charge to serve. In other cases it may be a consolation after tragic loss, or perhaps a demand that a man stop making excuses and become what he is capable of being." Collins paused. "Many do not understand, or refuse the message, or even fear the good that is within them."

Collins turned in his hand an expensive Corning glass paper-weight, in the shape of a puffin, that Carter had once ordered from an upscale catalog when he was desperate to think of things to spend money on. "Mr. Morris, when I am having trouble getting through to an inmate, I speak of the great mystery. Criminals feel contempt for fellow men and may be divorced from common human values, but they tremble at the prospect of the ultimate, as they sense the reality of a larger power. Our being is no biochemical fluke, Mr. Morris, no coincidence of amino acids and molecular heat exchange. The Ivy League may be unable to fathom this, but it is well grasped in prisons."

This wasn't the pallid, fretful Mayhew Collins whom Carter had known on death row. Was he now a man of God, or an emissary of the life force, or a long-winded crackpot? Carter sensed the answer would impose some obligation upon him. He cast another glance at his watch, this time making the motion deliberately apparent.

"If you would tell me how I could—"

The conversation shifted off the cosmic to Holden Roof, a death-row inmate Collins believed innocent. Switching from painfully slow speech to the kind of rapid whoosh of facts that lawyers and prosecutors use when filling each other in on cases, Collins told Carter a tale of a foolish man's choice of the wrong kind of friends, of misdemeanors for petty drug buys, of the chain of coincidences that led that man to be wandering late one night through an upper-class neighborhood where a woman had just been slain. Roof had been collared by one of the first officers on the scene and "walked out" to the media immediately as the killer, the state's attorney promising execution. The verdict came on circumstantial evidence: there were no witnesses and no physical links between Roof and the crime, other than his proximity and a neighbor who testified that she thought she might have seen someone like him near the house around the time of the murder. The deck was stacked against Roof: he even had a tattooed tongue which the judge had instructed him to stick out to show to the jury, though there was never any evidence introduced regarding tongues or tattoos. Roof had not been able to find a lawyer to handle his appeals—people have a constitutional right to an attorney at trial, but afterward it's whatever you can arrange—and now his date with the chemical drip was a month off. Collins wanted Carter to take the case.

"Every stiff on death row claims the cops got the wrong man," Carter said.

"I know prison talk," Collins replied, and Carter realized he had condescended to him. "Most to whom I minister I would not want to see released—I have to walk the streets, too. This man is doing the time but did not do the crime." Collins whooshed through information favorable to Roof, such as a perfect record of child-support payments, his broken-down car not far from the site of the arrest, absence of violence on his sheet, the minimal poor man's defense he had received. "There may be grounds for a stay based on malfeasant counsel while the rest of the case is reviewed," Collins said, clearly pleased that he knew such a term. And there was the matter of the skin cells from underneath the fingernails of the victim. "As you know DNA evidence is conclusive, but none was introduced at trial, though the state possessed samples of the killer's skin cells," Collins said. "I went to the court archives and looked up the Roof file." During the protracted pause that followed, it seemed Collins was reliving in his thoughts each stride of the trip to the courthouse as a free man rather than a captive. "There seems to have been a DNA assay whose results the state's attorney moved to have sealed," Collins said at last. "I suspect you know what that means."

Carter knew what it meant.

Collins placed on the desk a department-store shopping bag containing photocopies relevant to the case. "Anyone could tell from your demeanor that you are not pleased to be handed this. I was not pleased to be handed my cup by the Lord, either. But the great mystery need not explain its actions to us; it has already done us favor enough by placing us here." Collins rose to depart, and pronounced, "There is no doubt what you must do."

"Wait," Carter said. "How would I arrange to have the law firm send a donation to your ministry?"

Collins handed him a business card. "A tithe is all I ever ask," he said, slightly slippery. Then he left.

Carter's mind rolled from side to side, seasick. He did not wish any form of involvement in the matter of Holden Roof. What was this guy doing driving around in a wealthy neighborhood late at night anyway, didn't he have the half a brain required to know that was how losers like him got themselves sent up? And what kind of Einstein has his *tongue* tattooed? Carter paused, imagining how the prosecutor must have angled to get the judge to order that the tongue be extended for the jury to see. There's nothing like scaring the jury, and here the accused had been compelled to stick out his tongue in the literal sense at the twelve peers holding his fate. Any minimally competent defense lawyer would have blocked that ploy. Surely an appeals court would grant a stay based on inadequate counsel while an investigation could review the more serious—

Carter hoisted the shopping bag and hurled it into the trash, hard enough to knock the can sideways. He didn't need this good-for-nothing and the dumb-ass dilemma he had walked into. Where did Mayhew Collins get off bringing him this problem, talking in five-dollar terms like "malfeasant"? Carter had already done his good turn for Collins, owed the man nothing. He had asked about donations with an escape clause in mind. Carter would arrange for Collins's ministry to get a check—roll it into the Value Neutral settlement—and that would placate the reverend. Let some junior legal-aid lawyer deal with the Roof appeal. Junior lawyers need that kind of experience. Midcareer, what you need is seven figures. Carter had already done his share of saving the world.

That night, headed home, he stopped at a tavern and drank. Carter hadn't simply gone to a bar to drink in—how long? In his college days, tavern stops were a principal form of socializing, along with playing stump-the-bartender by ordering offbeat drinks like a sidecar or a Pimm's cup. Now Carter just sat sullenly imbibing, speaking to no one, entwined among other sullen, silent people like himself, the resigned cohort of middle-aged men and women who were at the acme of their life's bell curves but too fatigued to do anything with the moment except repeat daily steps.

The tavern was nice enough, in the sense of well kept. The worn-out middle-aged clientele looked middle to lower-middle, schoolteachers, salespeople, clerks, and assistant foremen maybe. An hour here was cheaper than an hour on an analyst's couch, and though neither would help you much, at least an hour with scotch was pleasant. Drink temporarily creates the illusion that things are just about to get better, whereas psychiatrists labor to convince you that things will never get better.

Looking around, Carter noted a few exceptions to the rule of most tavern patrons being middle-aged people sitting alone. In one booth were a pair of teen lovers, at the age when getting served a cocktail represents an illicit thrill. They snuggled and glanced about furtively, unsure whether their presence had been accepted. In another booth, two South American guys in the matching shirts of a lawn-chemical service were knocking back pitchers and clearly on a path to blowing their week's wages on the fines and license points for the DWI that awaited. A waitress shuttled among them. In the sunny, upscale restaurants Carter's social class favored, wine and cocktails were ferried by smiling college coeds working part-time as they moved ahead in life, whose perky outlooks made it all seem healthy and optimistic, part of prosperity. Here the waitress was a sixty-year-old woman with deep face lines who'd spent decades being called honey by strangers and who still roomed with somebody to share the rent, making it seem that the nineteenth-century English anti-cheap-gin reformers were right about affordable alcohol being a plan to lull life's have-nots.

Carter had made a dent in the best bottle of single malt scotch in the establishment—the brand had to be high-quality since he'd never heard of it—when he started feeling remorse about the shopping bag thrown into the trash. Maybe he should announce a Holden Roof appeal just before the Value Neutral settlement became public. Distract the press and keep his image liberal enough to make the corporate deal credible. Okay, he'd save Holden Roof but he'd do it for his own selfish reasons. That would count as ethics by the standard of the day.

Tipsy, Carter lurched toward the pay phone by the rest rooms, fumbling in his pocket for coins. Only then did he realize that a young man he had taken for a drywall worker or record-store clerk, who had been savoring the local craft-brewed ale and staring at him from across the bar, was one of his younger selves.

Younger Carter stood up: long-limbed, handsome, flat-bellied, composed. "Do you drink so much because you're unhappy?" he asked.

"Don't judge," said adult Carter. He was deeply annoyed that one of his earlier selves had been there to witness him sinking into scotch, since he hadn't been falling-down drunk in years.

The younger form indicated his ale. "I have to admit the beer has gotten a lot better, so maybe we live in an age of progress after all," he said. "Do you need help?"

"I need thirty-five cents."

The young man gave two quarters to his older self. With them Carter called the night desk at his firm's building. After some beseeching, the security guard beeped the overseer of the cleaning crew moving through the complex. Carter wanted to know if his wastebasket had been emptied yet.

"Sí, yes sir, all is cleaned," the crew chief said, upset by the call and thinking he was being quizzed on efficiency.

"The things from my wastebasket, can you get them back?"

"Oh no, señor, they already shredded. Everything is shredded immediately as Mr. Kendall instructed. The first we do is shred."

Carter hung up and habitually dug from the coin-return pocket the dime and nickel that clinked down. Then he stared at the currency.

"Your quarters worked in the phone," he said to his younger self.

"Why wouldn't they?"

"A psychiatric episode shouldn't be able to pay for a phone call."

Carter regarded his younger manifestation for a moment and said, "We need to find a minister named Collins. I think you better drive."

As Carter stepped toward the saloon door he stumbled and brushed against his younger self. The instant they touched, Carter knew the sensation of every part of his body flying outward from every other part—though this time, given inebriation, he also knew an additional sensation, motion sickness. Touching his younger self Carter experienced uncomplicated singleness of purpose, an impression of physical invulnerability, and a torrent of androgen hormones so powerful he felt his penis might burst straight through his pants. Then the tavern became a vapor and Carter tumbled backward, head reeling.

CHAPTER TEN

In the kitchen a mammoth brushed-metal cauldron, insti-tutional size, sat on the stove, stewing sauce for the spaghetti that was the nightly fare. The kitchen was expansive, designed for the days when a farm wife fed twenty hands, so the social life of the group house centered there. A floating cast of hippies and college students; money perpetually tight; unannounced arrivals sleeping on the porch or in the barn; always more at the table than planned; lean kids wandering in hungry and asking when was dinner and nobody even knew who the kids were or how they got there—every possible variation on spaghetti was Jayne Anne's solution to that web of circumstances. Some of the kids who lived at the farm or passed through talked of sabotaging an aircraft carrier or kidnapping Dean Rusk or seizing control of a microwave relay tower to broadcast their demands over national television. But though they discussed flamboyant plans that would entail daunting effort, advanced skills, and split-second timing, none seemed to be able to go into a kitchen and produce a meal. Everyone was waiting for Mom to do that, and Jayne Anne had become Mom.

Evensong was descending, almost time to light the candles whose wax overflowed from the tops of old wine bottles. Really there were quite an impressive array of empty wine bottles. Some had been converted to candles, others saved for their association with pleasing indulgences past. Kid wines—Boone's Farm, Lancers, Mateus, Paul Mason Crackling Rosé, that last the inspiration for the period song "Crackling Rosy." Glass milk bottles were stacked in a corner, quart containers of the refillable sort that a dairyman in a doorless lorry came to pick up twice weekly, dropping off a new supply. They'd talked about getting a cow to become more self-sufficient, maybe make some cheese to sell. They'd chosen a clever name, Emancipation Emmental. But nothing happened beyond talk. A cow seemed like quite a lot of responsibility, rising at dawn to milk her and all that.

Besides the deliveryman's name was Bob and he was always on time, he was neighborly and nonjudgmental, never cracked wise about can't-tell-the-boys-from-the-girls. Who could bear to take business away from a friendly Vermont dairy route driver named Bob? For some of the stoners at the farm, Bob's arrivals were the leading event of the week. They'd sit on the porch smoking grass and watching for his snout-nosed lorry, start to cheer and giggle when the truck began kicking up dust on the gravel drive, always exactly at the appointed hour. The notion of doing something on time was a real trip to the stoner faction. Once when Bob was delayed by a flat tire, the stoners became extremely anxious and wanted to alert the state highway patrol to search for him.

"Don't you like it when it's quiet like this?" Jayne Anne was asking. "I mean, in the twenty-eight seconds a day that it's quiet." She and Carter were looking out the kitchen window toward the meadow, where a heterogeneous collection of house residents and guests and passers-through and—say, who are those two guys in the army surplus?—labored fitfully to complete a maypole.

Carter walked up and ran his arm affectionately across her back. "Always checking to see if I have a bra on," she laughed. He stood behind and circled his arms contentedly around her waist. They watched the others continue their disorderly work in the declining light.

After his discharge from alternative service, Carter had decided he wanted the school without walls. Jayne Anne dropped out too, to be with him. One thing led to another and now they were paying the lease on a repossessed farm in the southwest corner of Vermont, just over the New York State border. Half a dozen joined them as "members" of the house, which meant they got a bed, though still had to be prodded to contribute their share of the costs: Jayne Anne called weekly meetings to explain over and over again that parents or government or anonymous benefactors were not providing the farm, they were responsible for it monetarily. Of the many friends, hippies, and floaters who arrived, a portion were charming free spirits, others obnoxious. The week before they had thrown someone out for the first time. He came uninvited, ate free for two weeks, did not a single chore, complained daily about the lack of television, and then started a drunken tirade against the "oppressive police-state atmosphere" when Jayne Anne told him that if he wanted to stay, he'd be responsible for cultivating the tomatoes.

Exactly how they were holding the farm together financially, Carter wasn't sure. He worked off and on as a carpenter's helper and sporadically pursued his goal of the time, starting a liberation news service; this in a period when alternative communication was done by mimeograph machine and second-class mail. Jayne Anne went into town three days a week to work as a paralegal. She found a job helping the local solicitor, who'd been doing the wills, deeds, contracts, and annulments of the county his entire working life; plowing through boilerplate increasingly tired the old custodian of everyone's secrets. Various hippies around the farm got odd jobs or finagled in-kind trades for supplies. Marshall Lelchuck was in residence and never performed a stick of work, endlessly holding his cell meetings for audiences of the gullible or weak-willed. But Marshall did place a phone call once a month to a trust-fund officer in Connecticut and a check would arrive endorsed over to the Azimuth Collective, name chosen by Jayne Anne. Since in this way Marshall was the sole farm member who reliably covered his share, the others made their peace with his presence.

The big shock in the first few months had been the hundreds of dollars in long-distance phone bills carelessly run up. There occurred a colossal display of collective immaturity when Jayne Anne called a meeting to try to figure out who made which call. According to those present for the meeting, no one had made any of the calls, not a one. All agreed that everyone was very, very upset that the existence of the bill was being mentioned. Jayne Anne got a lock for the dial of the rotary phone and kept it on a chain that dangled in her décolletage. Even Carter couldn't get ahold of it without logging in his call.

"Are you supposed to dance around the maypole at dusk or dawn?" Carter was asking as they watched the others.

"Little late if it's dawn," Jayne Anne replied. "I think anytime is okay. May Day goes at least as far back as the Romans, whose festivals lasted a week. Bacchanals, you know. A full week of drinking, dancing, and fairly advanced group screwing."

"You mean our generation didn't invent sex?" Carter aped amazement. "I would have sworn I read in *Time* magazine that ours is the first generation to notice sex. This has been confirmed by the media."

"My dear," Jayne Anne said, turning to embrace him, "here in our little commune we certainly have the Roman attitude about intoxicants, but we are two thousand years behind the times when it comes to creative screwing."

"Let's see what we can do about that," Carter said. They kissed and he felt the delectable sensation of her pressing her crotch against his, signaling willingness. The pleasure may be in the act but the excitement is in the partner's signal that the act is desired—making the moments before sex, in their way, the best.

A porch door swung, creaked, and clapped back shut, the rebound motion bringing in the encircling and confident air of spring. "The maypole is ready for the dance, assuming nobody pulls too hard," called Rigel. She glanced into the cooking pot. "Spaghetti, wow," Rigel said.

At that moment Carter's adult perception expanded into his earlier form, tight in amorous embrace with his young love. His consciousness struggled to focus on anything but that. The porch door began swinging and slapping anew, and most of the farm's cast of characters entered. To keep his mind off Jayne Anne, Carter reviewed them:

Marshall, his hair electric curls, trailed by a flashy-looks woman named Phyllis Caplan who rarely said anything beyond: "Whatever Marshall wants." *I'll be the one who picks you up from the hospital after he beats you senseless,* Carter thought. *On that day Jayne Anne threatened to get a gun and kill Marshall. Now that I've seen the mall I wish I hadn't stopped her.*

Rigel, her granny dress and crocheted headbands the archetype of flower-child correctness, embraced Phyllis like a long-lost friend though they'd been together only minutes before. Rigel smiled, hugged, and wowed her way through life, seemingly unhindered by any ballast of reality; she could wander across a six-lane highway plucking daisies and every car would miss her. They never learned her birth name or anything about her parents or family, Rigel maintaining the stars themselves had bestowed her cognomen upon her. *Children's books were the perfect place for you to land*, Carter thought. *I bought a couple of the "Fernando the Friendly Ferret" series for old times' sake.* Carter imagined Rigel now spent her days signing books for admiring schoolchildren, leading them in merry songs and blithe dances. *It's good to know life gives some people precisely what they want.*

Dave Drendel, his melancholy face rarely lit with expression, carried in leftover supplies from the maypole project. Dave was a math major whose dream for the farm was to establish a benign-control Walden Two exactly as Skinner described. But he sank too deep into the arcana of behaviorist theory, spending days on end trying to draw up elaborate rules in the name of freedom. His future was to become an urban cartographer for the U.S. Geological Survey, endlessly revising the plans that formed the official chronicle of suburban expansion. *I'm sorry, Dave, I don't know much about what happens to your head, and my guess is no one else does either.*

Audrey Graham, known as Lala-Lala, poured herself a cup of the sweetened wine she drank the day long, without any adverse effect to an estimable figure. They'd met Lala-Lala in a Cambridge movie house and on the spur of the moment she had asked to move to the farm, bringing one suitcase that, she said, held all her possessions. A high school dropout who worked as a secretary for a defense contractor on Route 128, her South Boston background and divorced mother on public assistance were things she dreaded to speak of but of which the others openly boasted. Revolutionary theory dictated alliances with the working class, making Lala-Lala a prized find. But her opinions were rarely listened to, the college types feeling they had best do her thinking for her. After one of her trips back to Boston, Jayne Anne got it out of Lala-Lala that she'd become a kept woman for a top executive of the defense contractor, each time taking an envelope of cash left on the night table. There was a tremendous dust-up, the women giving speeches about feminist consciousness-raising, the men scandalized that she would sleep with the enemy but not with them. Lala-Lala stormed out never to return, saying nothing about the company documents she had been laboriously copying the entire time, documents regarding denials of promotions to women. *Everybody in the law today knows the name Audrey Graham*, Carter thought. Graham v. Raytheon, *what a case, what a job you did on the stand. You pulled the whole company's pants down, Lala-Lala. And we treated you like a flighty tramp.*

Lucy Chadrow, a slight and quiet-voiced woman, entered with a basket of wildflowers. Lucy was the academic star of their group, blessed in IQ, but switched majors annually. She'd do a year of pre-med or architectural engineering, become good, lose interest, and move to something else. Lucy spoke more casually of destruction than anyone they had ever met—they were going to blow up this, sabotage that. Like others on the farm, the most radical act she ever performed was leafleting. Lucy went on to become the benefits manager of an HMO holding company, spending her days denying claims. *Guess you found your calling within the system*, Carter thought.

Don Kirman followed Lucy, who lived for his attention. Don was magazine handsome and possessed the languor of looks. He expected to be turned to as the group's leader in all things, interrupting others often and speaking as though he were making official announcements. Don seemed athletic but never joined games, always claiming minor injury and bidding for sympathy; he spoke of grand ambitions but couldn't be relied on to pick up the mail. He would become an anchorman for a cable-TV business show. *You found your calling, too*, Carter thought. *You look great, have no responsibilities, and spend the day asserting that you knew it all along.*

There were others in the floating mix. Randy, the philosophy major who would blubber "I'm going to die, I'm going to die" when his draft notice arrived and the next day disappeared, once sending a postcard from New Zealand without a return address, as he feared the commune mail was being monitored by the FBI. Jacko, a Vietnam vet with a flair for repairing things and a hazy focus on life, who hung around initially to score drugs but would become one of the collective's few dependable members. Libby, an Ivy League woman with a patrician background, who formalistically insisted that half the house's members be female and a tenth be black. The stoners, interchangeable harmless hippies whose appearance took on the blur in which they perceived the world. And at this particular moment the two guys in army surplus, whom nobody knew who they were.

"Everyone, it's time to dance," Rigel called out. "The moon is in the third house, and Jupiter aligns with Saturn. These are favorable signs." She began to twirl about, arms outstretched.

"Did anybody get more wine?" Jacko asked. His frayed green service wear was visibly authentic compared to the surplus-store vests sported by the two unknown arrivals, who were following the army-look fad that inexplicably coincided with opposition to the war.

"I think we need a written policy on wine," Dave offered. "Too many wine-acquisition decisions are being made without group planning."

"Everyone follow me and I'll assign places for the dance," Don announced.

"We should celebrate May Day by blowing up a power transmission tower," Lucy said, almost inaudibly. "Instead of engaging in indulgent debauchery."

"Indulgent debauchery, hear, hear," Jayne Anne cried joyfully. "Three cheers for indulgent debauchery!" She and Lala-Lala did a little whirl-dance together.

"You have no idea what it means to blow something up," Jacko said to Lucy. "Don't talk about that shit."

"Doesn't anyone here feel guilty that despite the assassination of Dr. Martin Luther King, Jr., we still do not have a Negro who is a full member of the house?" Libby asked. Even in a flannel work shirt, she managed to look like Miss Clavell. "I think we all need to exert more effort on feeling guilty. I personally feel very, very guilty."

Marshall shot back, "King was a tool of the desegregationist establishment and the tired old compromise groups like the NAACP. His talk was all milk and honey designed to stop the blacks from radicalizing. J. Edgar Hoover secretly pulled his strings."

"Dr. King was the most evolved human being since Gandhi," said Randy, the philosophy student. Randy took other people's comments in high seriousness. He turned to Phyllis and appealed to her, "You can't actually believe the FBI had anything to do with Dr. King."

"I agree with whatever Marshall thinks," Phyllis said. Marshall smiled; he liked to see his control demonstrated.

"If they were behind him why did they allow him to be shot?" Randy was agitated.

"Maybe he was about to talk, spill the truth," Marshall said. "So they had to kill him. Proves my point." Phyllis looked at Marshall admiringly.

"But, like, wasn't Dr. King stirring people up?" one of the stoners asked. "Like, how does that serve any conspiracy?"

"Create the illusion of dissent to suppress the real thing," Marshall replied. "Classic social control strategy. Come to my next cell meeting and I'll open your eyes to the truth about Rachel Carson, too."

"Kinfolk!" called Rigel. "It is time to dance to welcome spring."

THE GROUP STRAGGLED ONTO THE PORCH and across the meadow, faces lit by strakes of the declining sun. Carter and Jayne Anne held hands. *I don't remember this day exactly but please don't let it be anything romantic*, his adult awareness thought. *I don't want to feel again the things I once felt. Leave me alone, let me be embittered. Don't spoil my accomplishment.*

Seeking to avoid thinking about Jayne Anne, his adult consciousness rested for a moment on memory of the demise of this place. After the elites of the student movement abandoned the counterculture and decided to console themselves by making fortunes in medicine and law, Jacko was the last to carry the torch for the farm. He and sundry vets, bohemians, and teen runaways would keep the farmhouse open through the Reagan decade, using increasingly improbable financial schemes to stall the bills. The atmosphere changed from one of bright promise to a rearguard action against the inevitable, every day gotten through without something bad happening viewed as a day stolen from a voracious future. Always the farm observed the annual rite of the maypole dance and sing-along, though the songs went hopelessly south about the time of the Bee Gees. Jacko's gradual burnout diluted his competence to function as commune administrator; eventually he left for a VA hospital, babbling about government listening posts on the hill above the farmhouse. No one else had his ability to hold things together. Not long after Jacko's institutionalization, the property was sold at tax auction and the land converted to a refuse transfer station.

Arriving at the maypole they admired its makeshift garland of streamers and peace symbols. Rigel spread out her hands to begin a ceremony, then said with dismay, "My Druid book, I've lost my handbook of Druid incantations." She became completely flustered.

"That's okay. We'll sing 'Kumbaya,' " Lala-Lala suggested.

"And I was going to read the one that causes the moon to mate with the sun," Rigel said in great disappointment.

"Kumbaya, my Lord, kumbaya," Lala-Lala began to warble, off-key owing to her level of intake of Boone's Farm.

The stoners joined in first, the concord of the notes sounding just fine to them. Dave stood rigidly upright and began to sing as though doing so to pass a choral requirement. Phyllis hit a few notes but when she saw Marshall scowling, fell silent. Most of the others joined Jayne Anne with great amusement.

They worked their way through the numerous verses of "Kumbaya" then onto ones Lala-Lala added—someone's toking, puking, fucking, coming. Rigel danced and twisted streamers about the pole as they sang. A wine flagon and a joint were passed round.

When the many verses ended, Marshall snapped, "Okay, that's that," and turned to leave. But Jacko of all people piped up in a confident voice and began singing "Puff the Magic Dragon." (Later he would explain, "We did sing that in Nam, but mainly because we wanted the Magic Dragon gunships to show up and blow the other side to pieces.") Jacko, too, was joined; an old-fashioned sing-along had broken out. Soon they were all crooning along about little Jackie Pepper, Marshall mumbling, "This is so corny." There was more circling around the pole, more quaffing and inhaling. Lucy the aspiring international terrorist got teary on, " 'A dragon lives forever but not so little boys.' "

When that song concluded Phyllis, looking around nervously, began to sing, " 'Well my bags are packed, I'm ready to go.' " More verses, wine, timbrel, and dance.

When that rendition ended there was an interlude as everyone waited for the next song to be proposed. Don started in, confidently, " 'Come gather 'round people, wherever you roam, and admit that the waters around you have grown.' " He led them along the difficult lyrics, the women being impressed that Don knew all the verses and Don knowing they would be impressed by his knowing. The group felt they accomplished something by getting to the end of that one.

When the next pause came, Libby cleared her throat and began, " 'A winter's day in a deep and dark December.' " She looked around, unsure, then drew out the words just as the album did, " 'Eye-eye yam a-low-o-o-own.' " With many false notes she led everyone through the classic downer ballad of the era, one that you'd sing if you were depressed or aspired to be. The stoners happily bellowed, " 'I am an island!' " as if it were a sea shanty.

There was a bit of a sidetrack when Lala-Lala broke into, " 'Cherish is the word I use to describe.' " The group politely joined, Marshall making faces.

Next Jayne Anne offered, " 'If you miss the train I'm on, you will know that I am gone,' " which they belted out with boisterous dancing and wine-bibbing, though it is a descant of deep sadness. Next Randy offered a song that sounded upbeat owing to its jaunty air, but whose topic also was irreparable damage: " 'One day, you'll look, to see I've gone, for tomorrow may rain so I'll follow the sun.' " Carter's adult consciousness wondered why it was that so many songs of this era of seeming promise concerned wistful regret for loss. Maybe every generation's abiding emotion is wistful regret. Anyway, Carter had long since lost his ability to hear the whistle blow.

There was a break for wine as the sun reddened. " 'To everything, turn, turn, turn,' " Rigel offered, and they sang with authority. " 'A time to build up, a time to break down . . . a time to dance, a time to mourn . . . a time that you may embrace, a time to refrain from embracing . . .' "

When his turn came Dave straightened and began, " 'The eastern world it is explodin'.' " Soon they were all drunkenly, enthusiastically serenading the Vermont countryside, " 'We're on the eve of destruction!' " Nothing like a nice song about total global annihilation to make for a successful party.

Then Rigel trilled in soprano, " 'I am a child, I last awhile.' " She sang this song alone, the others listening respectfully, mute before truth.

The festival continued well after dark, until the point was reached when the group ran out of song ideas. Carter looked around and dove in, in a stout voice, " 'How many roads must a man walk down.' " The group became subdued and let him progress through the verses solo, then joined for each chorus, members of a gallant little band linking arms around each other and swaying as they intoned, " 'The answer is blowin' in the wind.' " There were smiles where there would not always be, and a floating sense of the possible.

As the young Carter sang, his adult awareness began to expand away and briefly viewed the group as if from above. He beheld himself in love with a radiant woman. He saw in their late hours of unlimited prospects those friends whose youth time had since claimed; each had been a child, and lasted awhile. *We were going to rebel against social conventions, ring in an age of happiness, play at the world and remain forever kids,* he thought. *We turned out closed, brittle, and covetous, like everybody does.*

Carter heard for the last time his youthful companions' yearning song about the winds in which answers would be found. But he did not return to the present day. Instead Carter discovered himself on the hill overlooking their homestead collective. Hours had been compressed into an instant; it seemed midnight of the same night, after the culmination of the May Day observance. Below could be glimpsed the lights of the farmhouse. Some of their friends were moving about on the porch or in the duskiness nearby, here and there the carmine glow of a joint or cigarette. Fragments of voices drifted upward.

It was a time to embrace. Jayne Anne and Carter were sitting together on the rise. She had peeled off her sweater and was leaning back against him, pressing the smoothness of her bare back into his chest. His hands were cupping her breasts, a circumstance more privileged than erotic, expressing partnership. Both had their heads tilted up. Jayne Anne loved to stargaze, and they spent many opportune evenings this way. The heavens held lights innumerable that night, a brilliant display since they were so far from the city. His young self felt contentment.

"I wonder which one is Rigel," Carter was saying.

"Which two. Rigel is a double star. But I don't want to tell her that, it would spoil Rigel's belief she was christened by a single astral being." Jayne Anne indicated a point of light in Orion, then nestled farther into Carter's embrace. "They are two stars, yet so tightly bound to each other they appear as one."

"Let's be like that."

"Oh, we could be a lot better than that," Jayne Anne said. "I look up at those stars, with their age and majesty, and think that what's here on this hillside right now is even greater."

"Greater than the stars? We can't even keep the mimeograph machine running. The VW van has been stuck in mud for three days now and everything we try just gets it stuck in deeper. I had to redo an entire recall petition because I spelled the congressman's name wrong." He paused, then added, "Though the stars should feel privileged that they are allowed to shine on you."

Jayne Anne purred. "Oh, we're incompetent all right." She gestured toward their friends below. "And they're a hoot. Yet together all the armies of the world combined could not defeat us."

"I thought we were antiwar."

"I mean the armies of the world as it is," Jayne Anne said. "There is no limit to the good that could be brought about by those who believe. Gandhi's followers were riffraff, and they defeated the entire British Empire. Christ's disciples were ordinary people, a little slow-witted and bumbling according to the Gospel accounts. But they believed, and that made them an unstoppable force. There are lots of examples in history of kings, dictators, and generals marching off as prisoners in front of the bayonets of a few completely disorganized dreamers."

That's where I got that line, Carter's adult awareness thought. She smiled and pressed closer. "We're bumblers, we're disorganized, we're dreamers—we meet all the qualifications. So we should try to accomplish something memorable."

"You're too optimistic."

"What matters is that we believe, in ourselves, our moment, our chance. That we never give up," Jayne Anne said. "The world could get better or worse, and it will be up to us to decide which it will be. But no matter what the future holds, there will always be causes to fight for. Do you promise, Carter Morris, that you will never give up?"

"Lady, I promise."

Oh, God. I did say that. I meant it when I said it. But I didn't know how badly I would stumble or how drear the world will become. When I gave up, I did it with dignity.

Jayne Anne pushed against him, enticing warmth. "And, my prince, do you promise you will always love me?"

"Lady, I will love you long after the stars have fallen dark."

That promise I kept, Jayne Anne. There has never been anyone else. Through eternal sleep I will dream of the days when it was like this between us.

"Let us then vow our love for the heavens to witness."

Carter laughed and said, "The heavens have larger concerns."

"Nothing exists in time or space that could possibly be more important than the choices we make," Jayne Anne said. Then, pressing tightly, said, "And I choose you." They held each other in a light wind. "The world offers so much if we have courage. Maybe the reason we're here is to make the stars proud."

Carter moved to kiss her, but his older consciousness was denied that transport. He felt himself expanding away, glimpsing the entwining forms of the lovers at a distance. From above Carter saw for the last time the young Jayne Anne, upon whom any star would be privileged to shine. Then the Vermont countryside became a vapor, and he tumbled back to the present.

CHAPTER ELEVEN

Kᴇɴᴅᴀʟʟ sᴘᴀᴛ ᴏᴜᴛ ʜɪs ᴡᴏʀᴅs as he completed paperwork at the county detention center. "You got a fear-of-success complex or something?" He was whipping through the paperwork, signing things he plainly hadn't read. "At your last annual performance review, you might have mentioned that your long-term career goal was complete destruction of yourself and your employer."

The processing area was eerie and dimly hostile—seemed designed to be that way. Sundry muggers, DUI regulars, support-payment jumpers, perverts, mules, fences, carjackers, winos, second-story men, insurance-scammers, ID-fakers, credit-fraud-specialists, and the like were being shuffled in and out for what cops call without irony "processing." Scent of fingerprint ink thickened the air. The place was full of people who started as bright children bubbling hopeful charm, fumbled away their one chance at life, and were now good mainly at passing their contagion on to others.

Carter, Afreet, and Tommy Pinguid, the criminal defense attorney Malison & Afreet had just retained, stood by in their pinstripes. Carter had been to booking areas before, but never as the subject of discussion. He wished he were holding a briefcase. Kendall did not feel completely comfortable, either. Given the way he worked over the company accounts, Kendall was not entirely sure there would never come a day when federal marshals arrived to take him off to be processed.

Proximity to the gates of prison ought to unsettle, of course. By the turn of the twenty-first century two million Americans were incarcerated, a higher proportion of the population than had been imprisoned in the former Soviet Union. U.S. penal demographics mixed the genuinely wicked with a larger cohort of check-kiters and shoplifters and first-time drug offenders, foolish kids or cash-strapped fathers or addicted single mothers, all locked away in caverns of monotony, beatings, and rape. Perhaps the genuinely wicked deserved to be tormented in such artificial underworlds. But American prisons held hundreds of thousands who'd never harmed anyone, merely made dumb mistakes. Their confinement improved various statistics, gave district attorneys and politicians something to boast about. Look around any kindergarten in the modern United States. Statistically, one beaming face per class is bound for an existence lived primarily in jail.

One shame of the contemporary nation, Carter knew, was that its tens of millions of well-off citizens didn't care about runaway prison growth because nearly everyone effected was poor or working-class. Not the affluent nor the suburban nor their children were being locked up to pad statistics—if caught at something they were usually allowed to slide or if accused, obtained the best counsel. The postwar age group had once made the mistake of glorifying lawbreaking; now it glorified prosecutorial excess. But then, putting so many of the have-nots into jail was a sweet deal for the haves. Streets were cleared not only of true criminals but also of the kind of people regarding whose existence and needs you'd rather not be reminded. The successful and suburban of contemporary America wanted to consider themselves admirably broad-minded. It's a lot easier to be broad-minded if the losers in life's contest have been removed from view and locked up.

At the booking desk, Tommy Pinguid was schmoozing one of the sergeants. Tommy was at ease in police stations, since he called on them often in his professional capacity. He carried himself as a regular guy, though he lived on a fenced estate with indoor and outdoor pools, tennis courts, and pastures upon which racehorses grazed; though on weekends he hired porn-star actresses to party on his twenty-six-meter yacht, *Mistrial*. Tommy's forte was winning acquittal for obviously guilty rich people. The celebrity or wealthy heir caught standing over a corpse holding a warm gun was his dream client: if Tommy could get somebody like that off, he could get anybody off. The more obvious his client's sin, the better Tommy liked it; those who know they are guilty do not quibble regarding legal fees. His cases often generated outraged television talk-show commentary about rich man's justice. Tommy liked that, too. Being publicly denounced served as free advertising, insuring other moneyed, obviously guilty people heard about his practice.

"Didya see that no-good mangy dobbin Bates Hotel placed in the fifth?" Tommy was asking the sergeant. "Two hunnert ta one. Made somebody's day, am I right? How's the wife and kids? Been doin' any fishin'?" The policeman laughed and kidded back. Few owners of yachts paused to banter with him. Seeking rapport with the common man, Tommy would slip into "dickhead" and "waddaya waddaya" in police stations, then have his secretary call to find out the correct way to pronounce the names of *Atlantic Monthly* authors so he wouldn't embarrass himself at dinners for the Council on Foreign Relations.

Carter had regained normal awareness in the tavern where, to his perception, he had just seconds before staggered up from his last scotch and used the pay phone to call the office-cleaning contractor. It was midmorn of the morrow. The tavern manager was at that moment unlocking the establishment to start preparing for the lunch crowd. Glimpsing someone inside, the manager secured the door with a dead-bolt lock and called 911. This time Carter was not as deft about stealing off. He was in the stockroom trying to figure out how to unbolt the rear exit when the local foot patrolman arrived.

En route to central booking the officer kept looking hard at Carter as if he recognized him but couldn't place it. Finally the policeman said, *Hey, you're that guy.* Patrol officers had been issued a likeness of Carter's face, recorded the previous week at 3:00 A.M. by security cameras inside the Mall to End All Malls. At the station, Carter was read his rights. He dialed Kendall, and Kendall immediately brought in Tommy Pinguid. That was good in the sense that Pinguid was sure to save Carter's bacon. Not so good in the sense it meant Kendall instantly assume guilt.

Once the forms were finalized, Carter would be released on recognizance. He slumped at the counter as Kendall slogged through page after page and Tommy did nothing but shake hands and receive well-wishing like a visiting dignitary. Pinguid's profession was to ruin good police work. But Tommy had been born in the projects and now lived large within the law: cops were not going to begrudge that.

Spying Carter, one of the uniforms stopped and addressed him. "You're the lawyer who freed Mayhew Collins, aren't you?" The officer carried so many weapons, radios, flashlights, cuffs, ammo clips, and various spares on his belt that he jingled with the slightest shift in his weight.

"That's right."

"You did a good job," the policeman said. Consequences of the Collins case had included public hearings, a corruption probe, and a reformed department that was a better place for the honest cop. The officer asked, "So what the hell happened to you?"

"Don't answer that!" Tommy Pinguid said in a winning voice, and the policemen laughed.

A shining black Town Car was waiting directly outside. The desk sergeant let Tommy's driver idle there among the ranks of police cruisers and ambulances, parking in the cop lanes normally a perk even city council members can't be sure of.

"Never bring a limo to a police station," Tommy volunteered as they got in the Town Car, seeming to feel he had to apologize for its mere two tons. "A limo says drug money," he explained. "Cops don't mind rich man's lawyers like me, we're just working the system. But drug lawyers, they wanna take 'em out and shoot 'em. The drug boss, he didn't inadvertently smother his exotic dancer girlfriend or unintentionally decapitate his ex-wife or some other crime-of-passion thing that's a regrettable misjudgment on an otherwise admirable record. The drug boss is killing kids he never even met. Cops, they boil when they see drug lawyers with their Patek Philippe watches bought with blood money from OD'd kids. Me, I never represented any drug lord, not once." Tommy added, "Knowingly, anyway."

As they rode through the downtown streets, Afreet and Pinguid discussed how to finesse the latest complication involving Carter Morris. On paper Carter was looking at several counts of breaking and entering. A plea could mean revocation of his license to practice law.

Twenty minutes later, arriving without an appointment, Pinguid received an immediate audience with an assistant DA. Tommy asked over and over, What was broken? Where are the signs of entry? How can you break and enter without breaking anything! Tommy got worked up and shouted, Your people can't even show where the alleged entry allegedly occurred! All you know is that a man was standing in a tavern. You have no evidence whatsoever that he entered!

By the end of the session with the assistant DA, Pinguid was arguing passionately that Carter was the central figure in a high-pressure class-action lawsuit that could represent a landmark victory for American consumers, and that the mayor would not want the newspapers saying his administration was harassing an attorney on trumped-up charges in order to prevent him from winning a landmark victory for consumers. Tommy had come into the whole thing cold on the facts of Carter's situation and within minutes jumped on such points; he had scant idea what was at stake in the Value Neutral case, but was a quick study and a master of bluster. Tommy thundered, Perhaps the mayor is accepting campaign donations from corporate interests that want to block this victory for consumers! Perhaps talk radio should be tipped to look into that! The assistant DA replied with irritation, What exactly was this legal eagle doing inside a locked mall in the dead of the night and inside a tavern that had been locked all night? Tommy bellowed back, Lost in thought! He gets lost in thought contemplating his landmark consumer lawsuit and doesn't notice that everybody's going home because all he can think about is the welfare of the consumer!

After the meeting Tommy expressed confidence the charges against Carter would disappear by close of business that day. He swung them by their office, and Kendall watched his Town Car hum away.

"Fifty grand he gets for that," Kendall said, with steeped admiration. "Three hours of his time this morning, plus later today he'll call the DA on a private number which he'll know even though only the DA's wife and the chief of police are supposed to have the private number, and he'll yell at the DA about are the charges dropped yet and probably he'll be getting a blow job from some hot-babe showgirl while he makes the call. The only writing he'll ever do is the invoice. Fifty grand for well-timed shouting."

Kendall looked at Carter with a drained expression and said, "Man, what I'd give to become him."

After a pause Afreet continued, "Of course those fifty Ks come out of your share of the settlement, not that you'll be able to tell considering how much money this whole thing is up to. Obviously if you weren't the key to this deal I wouldn't have been over there in a heartbeat with Tommy Pinguid, I would have faxed you the dismissal notice. Or maybe e-mailed it to your cell phone. Fax is getting kind of old-fashioned."

Then Afreet honed in. "Settlement is now three days away," he said. "Hold yourself together three more days and afterward you can go fruitcake, you can be abducted by aliens or climb into a tree and play the zither for all I care, just hold it together for three days. Three days of normalcy and you will be as rich as Tommy Pinguid. As rich as Tommy Pinguid, are you following me? You can hold it together for three days, can't you?"

Before Carter could reply, Kendall said, "Don't answer that."

UP IN THE OFFICE, silence ruled as Carter walked the halls. Even the interns, who normally lived for interoffice drama—and the more upsetting the better—looked jumpy. Everyone was acutely aware that Carter was veering toward blowing the best payday the firm might ever see.

In his office, Carter briefly reviewed a sedentary mass of documents regarding the Value Neutral closing. Probably they were in order, but he lacked the energy to determine conclusively. Ginny could deal with any problems—she'd run the palace revolt, she might as well pull the all-nighters on the documentation. Carter buzzed in a junior associate and assigned him to bring up everything on the pending execution of one Holden Roof.

The associate was puzzled. "Is this guy our client?" he asked.

"This guy is whatever I say he is," Carter snapped. "I'm going to do a good deed to help shore up my public image for the Value Neutral deal."

"Oh, like you're really concerned about your public image."

Normally law-firm associates are reverential toward senior lawyers. Even the most somnolent and senile partner, no longer good for much beyond posing for his oil, is treated deferentially. That an associate would diss him to his face told Carter his standing at the firm had all but collapsed. Probably he would be fired once the settlement was final. Though he'd be rich then, what would it matter?

The associate departed and Carter picked up the latest FedEx package of appeals being sponsored by Catholic Relief Services. It possessed no small considerable heft, and surely was filled with earnest pleas to come to the aid of penniless people whose circumstances were dissolving into wretchedness through no faults of their own. These, Carter thought resolutely, should be forwarded to somebody. There was a woman at Yale Law who specialized in indigent asylum cases—why weren't the do-gooders nagging her? Or maybe it was Duquesne. No, the University of Washington. Where *was* that woman? He tossed the parcel back onto the table, unopened.

SINCE THE MOMENT HE FOUND HIMSELF back in the tavern, regarding the late-morning light, Carter had known what must happen next.

Just the name Jayne Anne made him think of decades of bitterness, of the self-imposed melancholy that gave Carter his justification. He had said on that horrible night that he would never be happy again, and dedicated the years since to proving himself right. Decades of the comfort of blighted hopes, of blank days in which to dwell on what had been lost. Every year the mistake he and Jayne Anne made receded in importance and yet every year Carter renewed his vow to do nothing about it, as if once that moment were squandered, the possibilities for his life had expired.

But when he heard himself again making that forgotten promise to her, his footing changed slightly. Carter could not be the aggrieved party if he, too, had failed to keep his word. He resolved to apologize. The experience would be extremely unpleasant, and then he could founder in that.

Carter thought about one more call to Dr. Sonora Andorra, but it would have been a wasted dime. The tavern was intimate, the barkeep had a good view of the patrons; Carter simply could not have blacked out and spent the entire night there without being noticed. Nor could he have left, intoxicated, wandered the night without arousing suspicion from anyone and then gotten back into the tavern past dual dead-bolts without so much as creasing his suit. Some power or some office was leading him down corridors of time and forcing him to look through doors.

Toward what end? Perhaps all this was about the desire of the great mystery to compel a mortal to confront a forgotten vow. Yet why should a higher power care about reminding one pitiful man of his broken word? Such a memory might render an honorable person wretched, but Carter was already wretched, so it was hard to see what the great mystery stood to gain there. And it could not possibly be any sort of way of telling Carter to go back to being the idealist he once was. Idealism, like pro wrestling, had been exposed.

Rather than call Andorra, Carter dialed a number he did not have to look up though he had not used it in a very long time. He simply said, "It's me."

"Should I be glad?" Jayne Anne replied without a missed beat or indication of surprise. She sounded as if she had spent the morning calmly preparing for the call, though they had not spoken in roughly a quarter century, and waited for Carter to continue.

"I was thinking about that night of the May Day dance, when I made you two promises."

"Go on."

"I kept one promise. I've never loved anyone else and I never will love anyone but you. I broke the other. I gave up, on the world, on myself. Now I eat hand-rolled lobster ravioli and drink fifty-dollar bottles of wine while complaining about the capital gains tax. I hope for train wrecks because they create multiple parties to sue. Once in a while I hand a dollar bill to a bum. That's my contribution to the betterment of humanity. I wanted to tell you I am sorry."

Both ends of the line were silent for a moment. Then Jayne Anne said, "You saw Rigel last night, didn't you?"

Carter was thrown off. "I haven't seen her in years."

"I meant the star. Orion was out and Rigel was very bright near the celestial equator, five hours right ascension, ten degrees declination. I was lying on my back, looking up at Rigel, thinking of you."

"You can't possibly still think of me."

"Don't tell me what I can do."

"I called to apologize."

"I'm way ahead in apologies," Jayne Anne said, now cross. "I apologized in person, by letter, by phone, by gift, by prayer. That night I stood in front of you naked and handed you a doubled-over belt and begged you to beat me, if it would make things right and let us go back to being the way we were. Don't tell me about apology."

Carter hung up. No repetition of her repentance could matter, since he had long ago determined never to accept her apologies. There was a lot about life Carter was determined not to absolve.

The phone rang. "Caller ID," said Jayne Anne's voice. "You've had my number all these years. Since you sent me that envelope full of my letters of apology ripped into shreds, no return address, I haven't even known what city you were in."

"People make mistakes," Carter said.

"Tell me about it," Jayne Anne sighed.

There was a lengthy silence. In conversations between lovers, exact words chosen don't mean as much as tone and the timing of the breaths that precede onset of speech, the indications of whether the other party is favorably inclined. Something in the manner by which both of them fell silent and paced their breathing held possibilities.

"It's too late for us," Carter said. "Our moment passed. We were free spirits once, and young. Now that's gone."

"Speak for your own spirit," Jayne Anne said.

They talked awhile longer, she inviting him to visit. Nothing momentous was said. After the line went quiet, Carter stared at the phone handset a considerable time. He didn't have to ask if she ever married. Carter had always known she did not: he would have been aware somehow, the polarity of the Earth would have flittered in some manner he would have sensed. Should they have made up years ago? Carter was offended by the thought. It was as if he had to go to his grave brokenhearted in order to justify his decision to become brokenhearted in the first place. Perhaps the syndrome could be called Emotional Vietnamization—Dr. Andorra could use that on the talk-show circuit. In this phenomenon, the subject piles error after error atop the original mistake, in order to postpone the day when the original mistake must be admitted.

Jayne Anne had told him she wanted to sleep around before marriage, get that out of her system, and Carter had agreed. It seemed obligatory given the times. Jayne Anne was a bold and sensuous woman coming of age during a period that believed itself to be sexually groundbreaking; Carter almost would have worried if she had not wanted to try a little of this or that with boys or girls. And you could say a few words in favor of fooling around. The Boom generation might exhibit an insufferable prolonged adolescence, but was experiencing less of the midlife-crisis effect. Perhaps improving longevity simply will postpone the midlife crisis from age forty to sixty. But it seemed that relatively few men or women of Carter's demographic were in their middle years being seized by that dread-inducing I-missed-something feeling that caused many from his parents' generation to ruin families in pursuit of improbable fantasies. Because the contemporary standard is to fool around when young, today most enter the middle years with itches pre-scratched.

In the case of Carter and Jayne Anne, they'd agreed they would not tell each other about flings—neither need know if it was just a little experimentation, not love. Then from the day of marriage, they would be monogamous. A square deal considering the times. It might have worked, if only he hadn't seen.

The guy on the expensive motorcycle, Michael, the actor with the cigarette-advertising looks, came up from New York in the last days they were all together at the farm. She'd met him at an off-Broadway cast party—Jayne Anne got invited to New York events in the period after the Whole Life Square demonstration, for a while she chaussed on the boundary of minor celebrity. Michael drops by the farmhouse on his cycle, just touring Vermont to see the leaves, says he. Hihowareya. He was the best-looking man Carter had ever met, the male equivalent of the swimsuit-issue models in whose presence it is said men cannot keep their heads. Jayne Anne seemed to be cueing Michael that it was important he be friendly to Carter. That pretty much announced that they must have slept together in New York, and now Michael had come here to make sure everyone knew that he knew that Jayne Anne belonged to someone else. Yes, that had to be it, and the decent thing to do, considering. The guy would leave and it would all be back to normal.

Jayne Anne asked Carter to go to town to buy groceries so they could make their guest a nice dinner. This would be an hour round-trip, but ten minutes down the road Carter realized he left without his wallet. He drove back, walked into the house, kids downstairs sitting around arguing about the Cambodia bombing and the new Crosby-Stills album, everything ordinary and propitious. He walked upstairs and opened the door to their room.

There she was on all fours, the male model kneeling behind, her face exulting in pleasure. They must have scampered up the stairs the moment his VW pulled out of the drive.

Maybe if he'd only glimpsed their outlines and not so clearly seen her expression, for the imprint of his lover's features alight in an ecstasy caused by someone else simply refused to leave his thoughts. Jayne Anne had a moment of weakness when offered significant temptation—if a swimsuit model had ever come on to Carter, surely he couldn't have resisted either. Why not just forgive? The pleasure part of sex can flow with a beloved or a stranger, that it felt so very good for Jayne Anne when she was with someone else did not mean she preferred to be with someone else. Yet Carter thought they were born to be each other's rhyme, and now confronted the fact that anyone can finish a sentence.

So much from that era was fragile, balanced on unlikely assumptions. As the ideals of the period would end wrapped up in recriminations regarding the mundane, so did the ideal of their love. That evening at the farm when Jayne Anne ceased to be a perfect goddess and diminished to the status of merely a grand human being, something within Carter toppled, hit the floor, and shattered.

FLYING TOWARD BUFFALO THAT AFTERNOON, aircraft straining upstream against the currents, Carter tried to order his thoughts. He'd surrendered his young illusions of changing the world. He'd given up a life and home with Jayne Anne, children for consolation. He'd dropped his calling as a crusading attorney. Now he was in a cramped metallic tube moving through the wind between himself and his forsaken love, when at that very moment wealth, the final thing he sought, must be won or lost. Would he bungle away riches, too? That would set Carter up for embittered aging to be followed by a lonely death and obituaries noting squandered potential. *When they write my obituary,* Carter told himself, *I just hope they spell "debonair" correctly.*

He was bound for Buffalo because since not long after their falling-out, Jayne Anne had lived in Jamestown, New York, a rural community on Chautauqua Lake, the place for which the nineteenth-century lyceum movement was named. Her great-grandmother had lectured on the classics in Chautauqua tents and stumped for the Woman's Christian Temperance Union. Then she founded a boardinghouse in Jamestown for unmarried pregnant girls from the industrial belt between Buffalo and Erie, Pennsylvania. By the turn of the century, the factory of the Welch Grape Juice company alone provided enough teenagers in trouble to fill out the boardinghouse census.

Ownership of the home descended through the female line of Jayne Anne's family, who converted the facility into a girls' orphanage and later into a group residential facility for teenagers whose parents were jailed. That had been in the year Jayne Anne returned to Jamestown. Everything had flown apart, her love and her counterculture; she planned to help her mother temporarily while thinking through new goals for her life. Jayne Anne knew six surprisingly happy months working with and learning from the woman with whom she had quarreled so bitterly in adolescence. Then one morning her mother did not come down for tea. Jayne Anne found on the bed a motionless form, mouth frozen open in a gasp. That afternoon her mother's assistant told Jayne Anne the true financial condition of the group home and immediately resigned, leaving the facility to fold unless Jayne Anne took over. She took over and it proved a market-savvy move, as any facility that could win contracts from jails would become a boom business.

At the Buffalo airport, Carter rented a car and drove south along Lake Erie, whose flat panorama occupied the distance. On

Main Street in Jamestown he found an old clapboard inn with a screened verandah—he would have guessed there were no more such places except in Maine tourist towns—and took a room, leaving his bag. Other than accepting Amex and receiving e-mailed reservations from other continents, the old clapboard inn differed little in structure or social function from the previous century. The desk clerk gave Carter directions to Jayne Anne's boarding home—knew her, had known her mother. His mother knew her mother's mother. Carter turned up the drive toward an old, vaguely institutional structure on the lakefront. Jayne Anne was standing on a second-story porch watching for his arrival, like a sea captain's wife scanning the harbor.

He had not told her he was coming.

Walking the approach, Carter reminded himself that he must not betray any shock to see her no longer young. The surprise instead was how little she seemed altered by the years—her face smooth and figure still glamorous, though he couldn't know about the lumpectomies that had taken their toll on those storied, so-often-displayed breasts. By close inspection the thinnest creases could be seen at the fulcrum points where her eyelids met, and a streak of light gray accented the median of the hair that, artistically braided around a thin golden cord, extended to her waist. Otherwise Jayne Anne appeared little different from the nubile dynamo who once challenged him to a basketball game. She wore a necklace from which dangled a small locket Carter bought her, and had placed a daffodil in her lapel.

The two sat in wooden rocking chairs by the lake and watched twilight approach. A girl of seventeen or eighteen, turned out in all-black fashion, approached and spoke inaudibly to Jayne Anne about the administration of the house. To Carter she only offered a glancing "hey," but toward Jayne Anne was respectful. The girl had five or six piercings running in an arc along the auricle of her left ear, and the glinting flash as she spoke gave away a studded tongue. Was this a symbol of rebellion? Something to excite lovers? Did it double as a radio antenna?

The teenager departed. Jayne Anne told him of the kids she worked with, some sweet, some intolerable, all from poor backgrounds—deprived not only of the material but of constant parental attention and coaching from the earliest age, without benefit of which even the privileged may struggle. Jayne Anne worked, worked, worked them on behavior, academics, and the concept of delayed gratification, which she had come to see as, at some level, the essential secret of the successful classes. "I'm the disciplinarian now," Jayne Anne said.

She took the kids rowboating, to Chautauqua concerts, shopping in Erie as a reward for good grades. About a third rejected Jayne Anne's help and spiraled inexorably toward drugs and jail, repeating the failings of the parents from which they had been removed. About a third were transformed by tough love, faced the world, pulled up their grades and got into college, wept and embraced Jayne Anne and called her mom on their last day. This third Jayne Anne adored, and she pined for their return. Of the final third, Jayne Anne said, she had no idea what effect she was having. The girl who'd just left was in that group.

"Their lives are so ripped up," Jayne Anne said of her charges. "I know some people are evil, but most of these kids' parents never harmed anyone." Most of their parents had been jailed not for violence but stupid mistakes like buying drugs to get some release from the pressures of existing with little when others have much. Or for selling drugs to obtain cash, which everyone must have and which they saw coming to others with apparent ease based on good fortune or the God-given IQ they were denied. Jayne Anne said, "America swells with blessings, yet we forget there are millions who live from paycheck to paycheck and whose whole world can come crashing down because of one medical invoice or car repair bill, and people like that make stupid legal mistakes about checks and debt and drugs. What they need is help, education, and treatment, not vindictive punishment." She seemed pretty steamed. It was good to see Jayne Anne steamed.

The sun expanded and reddened. She was talking about political concerns because otherwise they would talk about—what, exactly?

They had reached the point in life at which, as a man and a woman alone by a scenic lake, they spoke not of romance or longing but money. Carter told her about his downward slide from public-interest law to the current borderline swindle. She said what he knew she would say, that he had to walk away from the deal: he could have the millions or his soul, not both. Carter tried to convince her there was nothing tainted about reaching into the till of a Fortune 500 company; he would be a Robin Hood. Imagine how well that argument went.

They tried to go forward with mannerly small talk, steering clear of many hurts. Jayne Anne told him of her plan for the boarding home. Following the family matriarchate tradition, she, too, wished to revise its purpose. Her ambition was to build a new wing that would serve as the headquarters of an organization to lobby on behalf of have-nots. The lobbyist staff would be the third of her kids who straightened out. After college they'd return and work for her, while providing positive role models for the latest batch of troubled teens who arrived to the residential building.

"The system doesn't respond to street tactics anymore, it responds to lobbying, so I'd like to learn how to lobby," Jayne Anne said. She would assemble a squad of courteous, clean-cut kids who had lifted themselves out of the worst possible situations and could talk firsthand to legislators and the media about the fifth of society that was being left behind. "I'm not sure what issues we would focus on—maybe the minimum wage. I'd let the kids decide. Once we asked the older generation to trust our judgment about what was right and wrong; we should do the same for today's generation in turn. Anyway, there will always be causes for them to fight for."

Carter said, "This is a good idea." So idealistic and hopelessly naive, it might even work.

Jayne Anne drummed her fingers. "Nobody will fund me. The foundations think it's blue-sky, they see people as an old issue. One foundation said they were looking to fund a program to oppose genetic modification of canola oil. Another asked if I could come up with a proposal on albino polecat habitat preservation." After making the rounds of the philanthropy world, Jayne Anne had tried cold-calling on a few wealthy businessmen, who told her they would be more comfortable funding something like art outreach.

"If it's too blue-sky, that's the reason you should do it," Carter said. He was taken aback to hear himself speak as he once would have.

After dusk diffused around them there were voiceless interludes reflecting the fact that neither knew where the conversation should be leading. It grew dark enough for starlight, and they looked up at the constellations. Jayne Anne pointed out Aldebaran, Betelgeuse, Castor and Pollux. Her grandfather, a Methodist minister, had been an amateur astronomer who spent hours gazing at the same stars from the same shore, tinkering with telescopes. His life's goal had been to make the first scientifically confirmed celestial sighting of a supernatural effect. Jayne Anne inherited his gene for optimism.

At one point Carter asked her what was in the locket. A strand of your hair, she replied.

Around midnight Jayne Anne said, "We should try again."

"I wish we could start the whole thing again—us, the times. Maybe we could get it right if we had eight or ten more tries."

"Can't change the past," Jayne Anne said plainly.

"We might have done something useful for the world, and had a great love."

"We *did* have a great love."

"We screwed up everything," Carter said. No part of him wanted to be cheered.

"We were beautiful, bewildered children and we took the first step."

"Toward what?"

"Let's find out."

"It's too late," Carter said. "The moment passed."

"Darling," said Jayne Anne, using the word exactly as she had long before, and as if there had been no intervening haze of lonesome remorse, "perhaps the entire future of society was never on our shoulders. Perhaps what it was always about was whether you and I, in our one chance to live, could make a happy and constructive life."

"Either way, we failed." The noctilucent constellations had slipped behind high clouds, handing the night to a cloak of darkness.

"When we met if I'd told you the two of us could spend thirty years together, what would that have sounded like?"

"Unimaginably long and luxurious."

"We could still spend thirty years together, maybe forty if the actuaries know their business. We still have time to impress the stars."

"Maybe you still have time. There's nothing left impressive about me."

Carter had not really heard what Jayne Anne had said, nor wanted to hear. His disappointment was now his glue to life, and its hold could not be severed.

Shortly after this exchange they parted, brief and awkwardly touching lips. During the bungled kiss it was clear to Jayne Anne that Carter didn't really mean it. Carter could not be sure at that point if he could mean anything. Seeing Jayne Anne again had not ignited emotions within him, as he had slightly hoped. He had left his emotional self on a Vermont hillside above what was now a refuse transfer station.

Jayne Anne, by contrast, understood that their youth had been lived out in a period when great changes occurred but also when foolishness became respectable. Now people remembered the razzle of the times and enjoyed mocking its folly retroactively, but had lost touch of the romantic dream of closer personal relations and a better world. Jayne Anne had not lost touch with these things. She knew, of course, that some people adopt a dim view of human promise because it relieves them of the obligation to try. She would have never guessed Carter would join this group. But then a lot happens you would never guess.

AFTER SLEEPING AT THE INN Carter drove back to Buffalo, went to the gate to await his plane and to listen to incomprehensible public address announcements. The airlines can make machines that fly around the world but are incapable of producing loudspeakers whose enunciation can be understood. The typical airport announcement could say, *"Attention please, a large comet has been sighted headed straight this way, you have an estimated thirty seconds to pray"* and not a single person would flinch.

Somewhere within the electronic garble of an announcement he heard his own name spoken, along with instructions to "meet your party" at an airline service desk. Approaching the desk, Carter spotted a bearded young man staring incredulously at the front page of *USA Today*. By now he had no trouble picking out his earlier self.

"Don't be amazed, all the newspapers have switched to color," Carter said as he approached the figure.

"I wasn't looking at the newsprint. I just cannot believe Bill

Clinton became president of the United States!" Carter's prior manifestation was transported with delight. "I know him, he's a radical, we worked together on the McGovern campaign. Clinton became president, this is so far out. The country must be totally transformed. And at last integrity in the White House!"

"I'd better fill you in," Carter said.

Regarding his parallel form more closely, Carter realized the fashion markers were out of phase. This manifestation was attired in a puffy frilled-collar shirt accented by broad white vinyl belt, ambled on the cumbersome waffle-soled Nike sneakers that started the athletic-shoe craze. Mention of the McGovern campaign, which occurred in 1972, meant this fellow issued from the mid-seventies.

"We can't be going back to disco era," Carter sputtered. "That was the low point of human history."

The younger man smiled and touched his older form on the shoulder. Immediately Carter felt the weariness of all-night studying, the enervation of far too much caffeine, the dulled anxiety of wanting but not getting sex. His mind filled with the back beats of some of the worst music ever preserved by recording devices. Then the airport terminal became a vapor, and he tumbled into the past.

CHAPTER TWELVE

THRUMMING SOUNDS FROM THE CLOTHES DRYERS filled the apartment around the clock, punctuated even in the numb hours before dawn by the strident buzzing of machines announcing a completed cycle. As his sleep was interrupted yet again, Carter would mumble, "Who does laundry at 4:00 A.M.?" The flat was always warm owing to heat that rose from the bank of coin-op dryers in the brownstone basement just below this "garden" apartment, whose subterranean windows opened to no garden. Though allowing only slants of light, the stunted slit windows did provide a scenic view of people's feet. Shoes, boots, sandals tromping by; from his reading chair Carter could have extended a hand and tripped anyone in the pedestrian traffic. He'd reached a low station in life, all right. But the place was cheap and at any rate, Carter spent most of his time in the law library.

Wooden planks stretching between cinder blocks formed a bookcase. A platform bed, fashioned with his dwindling carpentry skills, occupied half the room. Carter built it king-sized with the muzzy intent of being prepared for the ménage à trois that was the erotic epitome of the moment. He'd meet two delectable women at a party and they'd all go at it together. That was the plan, anyway. To be ready for this improbable event, Carter sacrificed much of the usable floor space of the apartment to the huge three-bodies-sized bed in which he slept alone.

A tennis racket was propped by the door, emblematic of the

decade's sports fad. A one-butt kitchenette stood to the side, the only countertop a square Formica board that could be placed over the sink during food preparation. Copies of the moment's magazines, *Ramparts* and *Psychology Today* and *[More]*, were crumpled under newspapers. Textbooks were scattered around, a phonograph turntable perched on two cinder blocks, stacks of albums in every free space. Paul Butterfield, Country Joe, Ritchie Havens, Chuck Mangione, Tom Rush, Al Stewart, Ten Years After. Carter hadn't even finished school and already his tastes were nostalgic.

A percolator worked at its task near the sink, *blub-plop, blub-plop*, this being the period before coffee went high-tech. The law student bent over an assignment, a too-bright reading lamp focused on the text. Words and phrases were marching past his eyes: replevin, dispositive, res judicata, collateral estoppel. *McDonnell-Douglas v. Green, Bivens v. Six Unknown Named Agents, Thermtron v. Hermansdorfer.* No sign of *Plessy v. Ferguson* or *Marbury v. Madison.* The clock radio read 2:18 A.M. A buzzer on a clothes dryer sounded.

Carter's adult consciousness scanned the mélange. The newspaper headlines seemed to have come from another century. MOROCCO INVADES SPANISH SAHARA, MADRID VOWS RESISTANCE. Morocco invaded someone? Carter couldn't even remember that war, let alone that a place called the "Spanish Sahara" still existed in the 1970s. WHITE HOUSE DEFIES SUBCOMMITTEE ON MAYAGUEZ TESTIMONY. What the hey was that? KEY WATERGATE FIGURE MARDIAN SENTENCED. Huh? Carter had followed the Watergate prosecutions with obsessive glee, they were more fun than the baseball scores, but now had no inkling who "Mardian" was.

Law school was a scorched period in Carter's life. The counterculture was over, though some clung to its remnants. People said that if you went to San Francisco and remained exclusively within the blocks that bounded the Haight-Ashbury alternate universe, it was as if nothing had changed. But cloistering was no answer, and anyway Haight-Ashbury was the redoubt of the period's fecklessness, not of its larger dreams. The antiwar and civil-rights crusades had concluded and that was to the good, since many underlying problems had been addressed. But when these movements ended, the sociological galvanometer showed a big drop in electricity. Free love became *Hustler*, starting sex on its way to getting a bad name. Counterculture leaders decamped to med school or to seek MBAs, signed up with Mudge, Rose, or Arthur D. Little, protected places with high pay where their brains would be admired and all emotional expectations waived. A few movement figures staged ridiculous public conversions, desperate to maintain the limelight. A few true believers went to Nepal or India to catch the Maharishi fad, but that turned out to be mainly a marketing pyramid. Infuriatingly, drugs seemed the only counterculture idea with staying power, spreading during the 1970s and 1980s to the inner city, the suburbs, to privileged prep schools, across age groups and races and classes. When Janis Joplin and Jimi Hendrix OD'd within days of each other, both at age twenty-seven, that should have been all the warning anybody required about anything stronger than grass. The warning was not heeded: drugs would become a plague to society and a bane to individuals.

Thus the worst thing about the sixties was the main thing kept. This seemed, to Carter, a good reason to give up. The love of his life had broken into pieces; the movement he thought would make a better world had instead unleashed and glamorized something harmful; careerism was taking over, so he'd need a career. These influences left Carter pessimistic, money-hungry, and estranged from the warmer values of his fellow citizens: so it was only natural that he would turn to the law. Carter the law student not only was in the process of discarding his ideals, he had, consciously or sub-, chosen a profession that rewards the discarding of ideals. This seemed to him somehow fitting, though he planned to keep his sideburns.

Expanded into his younger body, adult Carter felt dead-weight fatigue. It wasn't only the hours of studying. Nobody ever knocked on the door of his flat. The free-flowing enchantment of the farm and of protest life, kids in constant interaction, peaks of anger and joy, five or six emotional crescendos a day, that sense they were all in something together—gone, replaced by kids competing to screw each other on grad-school class standing and at job interviews, by every day being like the day before, by culture being John Denver and politics being Gerald Ford.

Carter fell asleep at his desk, adult consciousness experiencing his younger self's insecurity and ambiguity. Awakening he found that the percolator, left on, had burned through its element, hanging a ferrous fetor in the air. Carter showered and dressed for class. He remarked to himself that it had been one year to the day since he had spoken to Jayne Anne. For a while to come he would carry in his mind the precise figure on how long they had been apart, marveling as the number expanded from weeks to months to years. Eventually the specifics would become hazy.

It was cold and he shivered on the sidewalk. A garbage truck mawed in its load of green bags stacked up higher than parked cars. Every city block in Manhattan seemed to have a garbage truck working it all day long, they seemed to shuffle endlessly up the block and back again, never able to keep ahead of the garbage piles. Carter glanced at the newspaper rack for the latest edition; another city hall scandal revealed. From a skim of the article he learned there were accusations, suspicious circumstances, angry denials, and complex statutory details, but he couldn't be sure what, exactly, it was that the officials in question were supposed to have done. Sure sounded bad, though. At least a person could count on New York to produce one entertaining venality after another. Just when you thought every possible form of misdealing had already been indulged by someone in government or finance, you picked up the morning paper and found new proof that imagination knows no bounds.

Freezing wind off the river hit his face, refreshing him. As he walked, Carter passed a museum he hadn't had time to visit. He entered one of the halls of the law school, a splendid shrine of learning but covert within the city streets, seeming not to want to draw attention to itself. As if the delivery-route drivers and waitresses and garbage-truck workers didn't know that the kids trudging in and out of the law school's doors, hunch-shouldered in their beat-up field jackets, proud of the deteriorating conditions of their boots, were going on to five-bedroom homes and Italian vacations and boardroom sinecure from which to step on the fates of those they now walked among. Most of the law students prided themselves on the fact that they stopped at local diners for cheeseburgers and at local bars for beers and talked shop with the regulars, but always letting a law text show from the book bag just so there'd be no misunderstandings.

Inside one of the hallways, Carter's glasses fogged up. He rubbed them in the fabric of his ski cap. A professor, hurrying to finish grading papers so that he could work on a corporate consulting report, offered a fleeting hello.

Stopping at the student bulletin board Carter read, disconsolate. Nothing outrageous to protest, no marches to join. ROOMMATES WANTED. COUCH FOR SALE. USED CELICA LOW MILES. Poster for a Joe Papp play, advertisements for a bar-exam cramming service. A petition to ban smoking in the student union. Sign-ups for office hours. RIDE NEEDED TO PHILADELPHIA FOR SPRING BREAK, DRIVER MUST BE NONSEXIST. Sorry, a notice said, all appointments for recruiting interviews by the representative from Cadwalader, Wickersham have been booked.

Ninety minutes of a class in securities law. Carter kept his attention alive by telling himself that someday he'd participate in a landmark case. A few of the other students were likewise motivated by interest in legal theory, hoping to clerk for one of the smart judges. Predominantly, though, Carter's fellow students were one-dimensionally focused on lucre. Many had a beadiness about them, perceiving a predatory world in which the law was a spear they would use to catch game.

After studying through the afternoon Carter went to a diner for a cheeseburger, then returned to the library. He exchanged pleasantries and gossip with a few students, none of whom he knew well. A popular professor was retiring, there ought to be a party thrown, but everyone was too busy to organize one. Carter realized he should write his mother, but was too busy for that as well. Why didn't she send brownies more often? At this point, regular brownies were the kind Carter hungered after.

Staying at the library till it closed, Carter skulked home through the winter darkness, ski cap pulled low. He walking purposefully, trying to not attract the attention of lowlifes. Pounding homogeneous disco radiated from apartments, cars, and clubs. Carter passed a woman with a baby daughter at most two years old huddled inside her frayed coat, and the woman asked him not for a quarter or a dollar but for ten dollars. A cold street, late, a run-down part of town—hardly a promising place to panhandle. The woman didn't looked drugged out, rather in plain despair. Carter pretended not to hear her. His gait quickened, to put distance between his book-based problems and her surely less interesting difficulties.

Carter unlocked the door to his apartment, where no one was waiting or would be. He took off his coat and cap and went to start the coffee, then remembered the percolator was kaput. He sat down, put his head into his hands, and wept.

His adult awareness began to expand away. From above Carter saw his younger form stooped and wailing, alone, and could provide no consolation. During this excursion he had reviewed nothing of moment, lived again nothing memorable, encountered again no person who influenced his development. *All this just to see myself cry?* Carter wondered. Then he tumbled back to the present.

CHAPTER THIRTEEN

BRUSQUE PAIN SHOT THROUGH CARTER'S BACK as the luggage pushcart struck him. "Look out!" someone cried as a general proposition. Whoever was pushing the dray was unable to see ahead because the stack of suitcases blocked any view of where the wheeled mass was going. Carter stumbled sideways into a shoal of passersby, each staggering with a burden of luggage. None could swerve, owing to momentum from the weight of their outsized possessions being lugged or tugged. "Well!" a middle-aged woman exclaimed as Carter brushed against her.

The long glass walls of the concourse sagged inward as a jetliner spun up its engines to push back from a gate. Carter looked around at the commotion. His awareness had been regained directly in front of a moving luggage cart on a bustling concourse in the Buffalo airport. At least this time he was reinstated to the present during normal business hours.

Carter worked to recover his balance among a profusion of suitcases, satchels, valises, cartons, garment bags, shopping bags, and shoulder bags that occupied more space than the flow of passengers. Our forebears arrived at Ellis Island with a single trunk per family, if that. Now people wouldn't dream of going away for the weekend without taking along their own body weight in luggage. Hotel bellhops stack entire carts with the baggage of a single guest, and not an arriving aristocrat. The buses of rental-car agencies have been redesigned to leave as much room for belongings as for passengers. Schoolchildren march off to class with backpacks larger than the astronauts took to the moon. New-home designs incorporate storage areas the size of bedrooms, offer walk-in closets that could enclose a snack bar, yet still buyers complain there isn't room for their stuff. In many suburban homes, people are starting to stack stuff in hallways because they have run out of space in the basement and attic, though the typical American basement roughly matches in square footage the floor area of the typical European home. At the current logarithmic rate of growth in personal possession, not Homo sapiens or intelligent machines or radiation-enhanced termites but consumer goods will be the ultimate winner in the conquest for control of the Earth.

Mumbling excuse-mes, Carter maneuvered himself out of the luggage tributary. Nearby was a waiting lounge with TV monitors. Several were tuned to those midmorning shows where the host asks smirking questions while the audience but not the person being questioned sees an imposed legend such as, HER BOY-FRIEND DOESN'T KNOW HER JOB IS GELDING HORSES. Pop psychology dominates such shows:

> HOST: So, Judy, the reason you started dating the lesbian former nun who posed for *Playboy* was to get back at your mother for not mistreating you as a child, because not mistreating you left you no childhood trauma to blame your adult failings on?
> JUDY FROM SAN DIEGO: That's right! It was cruel of my mother not to mistreat me!

But then one era's pop psychology is the next's profound insight. Freud adjusted his theories in accordance with what he thought might catch on; his ideas seemed to deepen as people grew removed from his attempts to promote them. If Freud were alive today, he would be hosting a midmorning show and writing books with titles like *Dream Power in Thirty Days.*

In the airport lounge another TV monitor was tuned to a financial news cable station, stock-market vacillations now covered as the first year-round sport. On such channels, commentators endlessly depict all trends as obvious to them in retrospect, while confidently projecting that interest-rate changes will drive markets either higher or lower.

On the business channel that was showing in the airport lounge, commentators' forms floated above a border where ricocheting prices, symbols, and arrows seemed to oscillate by the second. This data trot also displayed the date and the time to the tenth of a second. Was there some stock-trading advantage in knowing what tenth of a second it was? From the trot, Carter ascertained that his latest absence had consumed two days. That put the closing of the Value Neutral deal at tomorrow.

The call to his office didn't exactly go well, but the closing was still on. Carter gave his arrival time. "Someone will be there to meet you at the airport," Kendall said. "Don't worry about finding them, they'll find you." They? The way he said it sounded capitalized: They. Afreet reported that the Value Neutral corporate brain trust was very favorably impressed by Carter's decision to take on a high-profile death-penalty case just before the settlement. "They say it gives you perfect vibes with perfect timing," Kendall said. "They think you're a virtuoso tactician. Only in America could someone who has produced a lengthy sequence of fuckups and deceptions be viewed as a master."

"It's worked for several presidents," Carter noted.

"That's why I love this country," Afreet said.

Waiting for his plane, Carter swallowed hard and placed another phone call to Jayne Anne. It wasn't a rapturous reacquaintance and wasn't horrible either, just felt vaguely natural to be communicating with her. Jayne Anne was perplexed about why he was only now arriving at the airport, since he'd left her lakeside citadel two days before. She expressed the firm view that he must not under any circumstances go through with the settlement. It was one thing to fail to change the world, no one should be judged by that standard; another to abandon principles, this invites judgment. If you sell out, she told Carter, you will be exchanging your honor for a few million dollars—

"Not a few. Twenty-eight million dollars," he said.

"Don't get technical with me," Jayne Anne snapped. "Whether you compromise for one dollar or one billion dollars is irrelevant. Honor can be sold for very little but not bought back at any price."

"What if I used the money to do good works?"

"That's what they all say. Good works always turn out to be vacation homes, art collections, and a twenty-two-year-old trophy wife."

"Suppose I gave away half on the day the check was received."

"Madam, we've established what you are, now we are bickering over the price," Jayne Anne answered. Her suggestion was that Carter quash the Value Neutral settlement—bare it publicly, make a stink. She counseled that this would allow him to recover his sense of worth and purpose in life.

"Don't tell me you're trying to save my soul, too," Carter said.

" 'Too'?"

"Never mind."

OTHER THAN BEING EXCRUCIATINGLY UNCOMFORTABLE, the plane ride was uneventful. As he stepped out onto the jetway at the other end, Carter saw two tall, dark-suited, stout figures with broad shoulders and impassive faces, the sort who play Secret Service men in movies.

"Mr. Morris," one said. "I'm Hadron. This is Lepton. We'll

be your companions. Do you have any bags we can carry for you, sir?"

These must be They, the greeting party to which Afreet had referred. Carter asked Them who They were.

"Sir, we're from Wackenhutt, sir," Lepton said. "We are to companionize you at all times in the next twenty-four hours to insure your safe arrival at the event tomorrow. We will be staying this evening at the Four Seasons. We're already checked in. Hadron and I will drive you directly there. Tomorrow morning we will fly with you to the meeting."

Rental cops. Afreet was putting him on ice until the papers were signed. It was a smarter move than Kendall himself realized—presumably, no younger manifestations would be able to get past these bruisers.

"I need to stop at my place and get some things."

"I'm afraid that won't be possible, sir," Hadron replied. Law-enforcement types always say "sir" when they don't mean it.

"Sir, any legitimate business items that you require, one of us will be happy to obtain for you from your office," Lepton added.

"I'll need a suit and fresh clothes for tomorrow."

"Already in the hotel, sir. Brand-new and quite expensive. Mr. Afreet said they would bring you luck."

"How did you know my size?"

"A Miss Intaglio at your office said she was adept at guessing men's sizes."

There was no point in resisting these two, although technically of course Carter was free to tell them to buzz off. He walked between the Wackenhutt men, allowing one to carry his overnight bag. If they had first names they weren't letting on.

The three went to the Four Seasons and entered a suite that must let for a pretty penny; it was big enough to start a magnet school. Carter's things were placed in the master bedroom, while the galuts had their choice of sitting rooms. Hadron commented in an offhanded, businesslike way that they had chosen the Four Seasons because the windowpanes in its suites were bulletproof. Were they concerned about assassins? Did the hotel have a regular clientele that was?

The suit hanging in the closet was magnificent to behold, Savile Row stuff; its price tag had been left on so Carter would know how much the garment cost. Afreet was a believer in spending lavishly in the hours before a settlement. His theory was that this conveyed an air of confidence to the opposing side, while propitiating the gods of fortune. Often he'd rent out a conference room in the most costly hotel in town, even if perfectly adequate space was available at the office. Buried in the presettlement big spending were sure to be expense-account violations, watches or suits for Afreet or jewelry for whomever he was seeing. Kendall figured such little acts of kleptocracy would get lost as long as he made the overall figure very large, which is called a sliver strategy. If you managed to waste huge amounts of money, nobody would notice the sliver you diverted to yourself; whereas if you were frugal, expropriations would stand out. Entire governments operate on such assumptions.

Carter sent Lepton back to the firm for several lawyer's accordion files, including one containing papers Value Neutral had not seen yet. Hadron sat ramrod straight while his counterpart was gone, eyeing the captive. Carter wasn't offended. Those in the law-enforcement professions deal only with other human beings at their worst, and so assume the worst about humanity.

After Lepton's return, Carter ordered an extravagant room-service dinner, red wine from an admirable vintage, numerous courses he grazed upon and didn't finish. The rental detectives took turns going down to the lobby café for steak. During his dinner Carter laboriously wrote out three letters by hand on hotel stationery, placing them into FedEx envelopes to be certain they would be delivered. When Lepton went for his supper, Carter gave him the FedEx envelopes to post.

Standing by the welded window, Carter watched the glittery shopping-district street below. Insouciant lovers strolled hand in hand, on upward arcs, eager for what lay ahead. Carter was not eager for anything that lay ahead, whether the next day or in years to come. He pondered Jayne Anne's idea to train a new generation of cockeyed idealists. Even if she got the money, the project was odds-on to fail. But with society growing more satisfied, cockeyed idealism might be in critical demand someday, and there was comfort in knowing civilization still contained people willing to lower their lances and gallop directly toward a rotating windmill. Helping the downtrodden was an admirable path to walk; Jayne Anne belonged on it.

For a moment Carter wished he could join her cause—every public-interest group needs a lawyer, after all. He'd been a genuinely happy man when he was a dreamer, and reasonably content as a professional when his work was in service to others. Carter could not join her cause unless he first recovered his idealism, and joy of life. That hope didn't seem terribly promising.

Thinking of what was in the FedEx envelopes, he wished Jayne Anne's project well. It caused him no pain to know he would never be a part of it. Carter worked on the remaining legal papers for a few hours, neither sad nor pleased about the final choice he had privately made. When the hour grew late he hit the sack and slept deeply, nothing troubling his thoughts, for he had resolved himself to what would happen.

BEFORE DAWN THEY left for the airport for the hour-long flight to the city that held the insurance-company skyscraper above the square that had once seemed to carry the import of Carter's life. The rental detectives informed Carter that Afreet and Ginny had gone the night before "as a security precaution." Surely a polite ruse to allow them to spend an evening together at company expense in the presidential suit of the most expensive hotel that could be found. Aboard the plane, Carter sat in first class with his sentries. Along with breakfast, Hadron swallowed a dozen capsules of vitamins, bee pollen, DHEA, gingko biloba, lysine, omega acids, and pulverized tiger shark penis extract, plus numerous glasses of orange juice, complaining that the juice was not fresh-squeezed. Several of the firm's associates, the support team, sat back in coach. They stared forward at the scene of their lead attorney minded by two heavies, unsure as to what this boded.

Black cars were waiting to take them to the conference. This time they bypassed the walk across Whole Life Square, driving directly to the skyscraper and entering through an unmarked ingress to the garage. "It's the secured VIP access and it's already been swept," Lepton explained. Swept for—land mines? Carter did not turn to look toward the square. He fingered an envelope in his suit pocket. It held a copy of something that a paralegal Carter had hired to work for him, rather than the firm, should be faxing to the Value Neutral lawyers just about now. The paralegal had been in Carter's employ for two weeks and done excellent work, though expressing puzzlement about gaps in his ability to contact his client.

Reporters were waiting in the lobby of the Whole Life Tower, not just the business press but CNN and two network affiliates. Carter kidded with them confidently and posed for pictures like a politician, but said they'd have to wait till afterward for comments. The man from the *Financial Times* groaned and asked, "Couldn't you just say something generic so we could leave?"

"Something generic? Okay, I am withdrawing from the campaign not because of the special prosecutor but to spend more time with my family." The reporters laughed. They'd be on his side in the postmortem press conference, Carter felt sure.

Upstairs the physical scene was roughly as it had been the first time around, but the languor had been replaced by amperage because so much more money was to change hands. Excitement was higher than if a bacchanal had been about to begin, or a global peace treaty signed. In the modern ethos nothing tops money for excitement, perhaps because it's the only thing money can't buy.

Afreet and Ginny were waiting, she wearing a glistening string of rose pearls that Carter assumed would crashland on the expense account. Jennings Guerdon was there at the center, his tan looking especially mechanized. Since they'd seen him last, Guerdon had been indicted for price-fixing, played golf with Michael Jordan, dined in private with the secretary of State, married for the fourth time, and been named *Newsweek*'s "Ego of the Year."

Guerdon smiled broadly at Carter, offered no greeting, and instead asked, "Tell me one thing before we hand you far too much of our hard-earned capital. You scripted this, didn't you?"

He was in earnest, and his side fell silent to listen. "First you made us think your firm would do anything for money," Guerdon said. "Then you made us panic that you were unstable and we were stuck in a bad deal. Then you let us twist in the wind while the tort market zoomed and the medical studies came out. You must have known that was in the pipeline, that's why you walked out on the first settlement conference. You needed the delay to look like a personal behavior screwup because if your firm had made a standard request to postpone we would have sensed a business reason. Then you started this good-guy-public-relations offensive with the death-penalty thing. Now you end up taking us for ten times what we initially bargained for. It all seemed so random, unprofessional, and poorly managed that it must have been a plan." He paused. "Am I right?"

People in thousand-dollar suits and four-hundred-dollar pairs of pumps waited for Carter's answer. "Of course," he said. "The whole thing went exactly like I laid it out."

"I knew it!" Guerdon jumped up and slapped the walnut table with delight, as if he'd heard just what he hoped to. "I told you this man is a Zen master. Nobody's ever played me like this, nobody." He chortled. "Ladies and gentlemen, a round of applause for the Zen master. Both hands clapping please."

Value Neutral's team proceeded to clap for Carter at their boss's directive. "Deal with us, deal with the best," Afreet mumbled, bouncing on his heels, already calculating what line of revisionism would allow him to claim that what happened had been his strategy all along.

Guerdon did not seem troubled to have been played. He knew, and Carter knew as well, that Value Neutral stock had been rising all morning, as traders judged the company to be unloading exposure and a potential PR ordeal in return for a payment that was tax deductible anyway. Carter also knew from SEC filings that Guerdon had an options-vesting cash-out point at the end of the week; pumping the company's stock right now was thus good for his purse. Even if Value Neutral wasted a huge sum on the settlement, its CEO would, in effect, receive a commission on the waste—a classic sliver strategy.

As the acclamation subsided, an aide whispered in Guerdon's ear. He shot Carter a hard sidelong stare, displeased. Guerdon was being informed about the text of the fax.

"Since we're showing our cards, there's something I would like to say," Carter declared loudly. The room stilled. Kendall went from jovial to nervous in a single beat, and glanced to make sure the Wackenhutt men were blocking the exit.

"When I was young I dreamed of making the world a better place," Carter said. "I certainly never dreamed that years of effort, hope, and study would culminate in an ethically repellent deal whose primary effect is to shore up the stock price of a Fortune 500 company that deludes consumers and exploits labor."

Ginny put her hand to her mouth. Afreet fell into a syncopal deficiency, frozen, a swoon of suspended breathing. Guerdon's aides looked around at each other as if someone had just pulled the pin out of a hand grenade and was holding it aloft. Guerdon alone remained the picture of equanimity, because only he had seen the back-channel traffic that Carter had been sending in the last hour.

"I take that as a compliment," Guerdon said. "There are countless firms trying to delude consumers and exploit labor, and most of them fall by the wayside. We, on the other hand, are spectacularly good at those practices."

Carter checked the faces around the room and said, "If I accept this money, I betray what little is left of my ideals."

He and Guerdon were staring each other down. "Don't overreach," the executive said. "Here's this fax with your bank routing number and demand that you have confirmation of the transfer of your personal share to your account before we close. Also a series of demands for special waivers for you, prospective injunctive relief, hold-harmless clauses on every major point, and even a confession of judgment signed by us that you can hold in reserve. This isn't standard."

"Honor can be sold for very little but not bought back at any price," Carter said. "I will not go ahead unless I am damn sure I get my cash."

"These faxes include a stipulation of immunity for you personally. We'd never be able to sue you. How can I have a business relationship with someone I can't sue?"

"Reporters are waiting downstairs," Carter said.

Guerdon hesitated, slapped the table a few times as if playing the drums in a bad rock band, then said, "Okay, deal. You'll have your confirmation in twenty minutes." He initialed the fax and handed it back to the aide, who bolted the room.

The executive laughed lustily, as if he'd just watched the Broadway hit comedy of the year. Guerdon indicated Carter and declared, "A shaman, a rabbi, a mage! For the crowning touch, he even starts into a charade speech about his imaginary fucking principles, to make us sweat and create timidity about his last-minute demands. And with this final ruse he accomplishes what? Cuts off his own people's balls, that's what! Now he's got his personal payday secured and can't be touched legally, while the bloodsuckers in his firm start their internal fights over division of the spoils, and everybody but him has to deal with the ten years of secondary litigation." Guerdon practically giggled. "Zen fucking master! Give this man a standing O!"

As instructed, the Value Neutral team rose to its feet and applauded. Guerdon began rapidly flipping papers and initialing them, chuckling. Afreet stood with a pleasingly duped expression on his face, the look of a cartoon character who has just seen the suspension bridge vanish out from under him but has not yet begun his fall onto the jagged rocks. Ginny instinctively unfastened a button on her blouse, leaned Carter's way, and tried to draw his attention.

Details were finalized quickly. Carter's cell phone vibrated; he looked on the display and saw a prearranged code sequence that meant the $28 million had arrived at his bank by wire. Through the paralegal, Carter had already retained Williams & Connelly to protect the account against legal raids. The firm was expensive, but it would be like having rabid rottweilers chained to the ledger. Carter had also already retained a tax attorney, who was already at the task of structuring the transaction so as to defeat the top rate. After taxes and fees and the rest, close to $20 million would be his.

Carter and Guerdon went down to the lobby to bob and weave

with the press. Carter was the picture of poise, missing no chance to mention his new death-penalty case, though it was hardly germane to the matter at hand. The hostile questions went to Guerdon, who rambled about his golf handicap and how Jennifer Lopez looks even better in person. He had to be prompted twice by the company's director of communications before mouthing the obligatory patter about his commitment to protecting the well-being of consumers.

On the elevator back up Guerdon said, "Most people sell out for whatever they can get. You negotiated an impressive price."

"I'll take that as a compliment," Carter said.

As darkness approached, Jennings Guerdon blew out of Whole Life Tower at the center of a cyclone of aides. Lesser Malison & Afreet lawyers stole away, wondering how much they dared put on the expense account that night. Carter handed Kendall his letter of resignation, along with carefully typed instructions regarding the disposition of his 401(k).

Afreet looked him up and down and pronounced, "Truly you are a modern-day mercenary." He and Ginny left to a future of wealth together, or perhaps one should say quasi-wealth, given the years Value Neutral would stall the payments, discounting to present value the fines that courts would eventually impose for dilatory tactics. And perhaps one should say quasi-future, since it would only be a matter of time until Ginny milked Afreet of whatever he had to offer and then left him once again standing in midair looking down.

Carter Morris walked out into Whole Life Square. He went directly to its hub, where the odious modern-art statue now stood but the speaker's platform had once been. No one was there. The sculpture, which taxpayers had paid to have pre-rusted, was performing its intended function of driving the public away.

Leaning back against one of the I-beams of *Prometheus on Toast*, Carter watched the last sunset drain from the square, sup-

planted by the orange glower of sodium lights. He felt emotionally spent, which perhaps is better than feeling nothing—
implying at least that emotion exists to deplete—along with a
building nervous energy, because he was certain what was coming.

A figure emerged from the sodium chiaroscuro. Again it was
Carter when he was the Daffodil Man, at the height of his infat-
uation with life. "Sellout! Collaborator!" he heard his younger
voice declare.

"You cannot betray causes that have died," Carter said calmly.

"I didn't mean that! You sold out yourself."

"Reach and grab is the contest of our times, and I will not
apologize for playing the game well," the grown man said. "I
now possess what is valued by the world."

The young form regarded his older self with detached mourn-
ing, the expression of soldiers encountering a bombed cathedral.
"If I had known it would come to this—that *I* would come to
this—"

"And are you so worthy? You walked right past that woman
with the baby on the street on that freezing night and wouldn't
even give her a single dollar, as if you needed what was in your
pocket more than her."

The younger man shook his head and asked, "What are you
talking about?" The evening in question had not happened to him
yet.

"Come on, let's go," Carter said. He was anxious, edgy. "I'm
ready. I want to go right now."

Unconvinced but apparently obliged, the bohemian figure held
out a hand. Coming into contact with his younger self, Carter's
awareness nearly detonated. Carefully cultivated enervation was
replaced by jubilance, by a weeping, laughing, shouting, embracing exultation at the very fact of existence. Then he tumbled
backward to Whole Life Square.

CHAPTER FOURTEEN

THE STEEL WORKERS HAVE TURNED OUR FLANK!" Marshall Lelchuck was bellowing above the din. "The state troopers have cut off our rear and the National Guard is forming up for frontal assault. We'll have to mount a breakout."

"Use nonviolent terminology!" a nearby demonstrator interjected.

"And talk slower," a hippie remarked. "Some of us, like, have a hard time with linear thinking."

On the back of one of the demonstration posters—a bright pop-art silkscreen daffodil—Marshall had sketched a diagram of the current deployment of forces and factions. He was attempting to plot maneuvers, and lacked only for binoculars, terrain maps with pins, and a corncob pipe. The issue of immediate concern was that the protest organizers had set up their post at the far corner of the square, a significant hike from the speaker's hustings, and the downtown had filled with demonstrators and counterdemonstrators and bobbies and gawkers so much faster than expected that moving into position to start the speeches was looking like a real problem. To make matters worse, the television vans were by the speech platform and unable to reposition. If the speakers couldn't reach the cameras, airtime would go to desultory interviews with the crowd, not to the meticulously planned program.

"Man, there's never a dustoff when you need one," said Jacko, blearily studying the diagram. Marshall had asked Jacko to use his soldier's eye to survey the tactical situation. But after sleeping on the chartered Greyhound until its wee-hours arrival, Jacko had been knocking back Mogen David 20-20 since breakfast, asserting early drunkenness to be a Druid good-luck custom for public ceremonies. He was already in the gray area of coherence and not likely to be much help on anything that required mental acuity.

"Let go of your socially determined metaphors and feel the positive energy of the universe coursing through you," Rigel was telling Marshall. Somehow her lilted, happy inflections were audible above the tumult of thousands of shouting, chanting protesters, mixed in with thousands of hard hats and whole companies of police with their whistles and bullhorns, overlaid with rock music playing through power-tower amplifiers at considerably above the decibel level of distortion. "Trust the spheres," Rigel continued. "Exist in the flow of your dharma and all will unfold as is intended." Slowly Rigel rotated the daffodil in her hand. Waist-length tresses and flowered dress puffing out in the light breeze, she looked for all the world as if standing serenely in a William Merit Chase meadow, not at the apex of a confrontation that had taken over an entire city center.

"Off the pigs! Off the pigs!" Some militants were trying to get the crowd to take up that chant.

"Jesus is just all right with me!" a group of peaceniks intoned in response.

"Jesus, sure, that's it," Marshall said. "We'll start talking to the cops about Jesus. It will change the whole situational dynamic." Marshall scanned around the demonstration command post at the jumbled aggregate of flower children, tie-dyed freaks, New Left automatons, thrill-seekers, delinquents, bikers, potheads, dropouts, college naifs, and kids in Nixon masks. "Does anyone here know a Bible verse?" he hollered.

Nearby a red-faced revanchist-crypto-Trotskyite was shouting, "You're not seriously going to hand out Amerikan flags!" He was able to pronounce the country's name in a way that aurally converted the second-to-last consonant into a K. The revanchist-crypto-Trotskyite gaped at crates of small stars-and-stripes, the kind intended for waving at parades, that were being opened. Jayne Anne had ordered them from the One Nation Indivisible Bunting Co. of Sheboygan, Wisconsin.

The revanchist-crypto-Trotskyite seemed jumpy, which meant the social engineering experiment had worked on him, since jumpy is how the red student factions trained each other to be. He cried, "The American flag is a symbol of oppression!"

"Hey, asshole, I fought for that flag," Jacko said, with drunken bravado.

"You were compelled to fight by a neo-fascist social order controlled by secret councils of international bankers!"

"Nah, my grades weren't good enough for college," Jacko replied. "Besides if the bankers are secretly controlling everything, how come the world's finances are falling apart? How come, huh, trust-fund boy?"

Jacko smiled; he found it a parlor trick to intimidate the grad-school types who cowered before anyone who'd done anything real. Then Jacko announced, "Peaceniks fall in, we need to start distributing these flags." He began passing handfuls to various hippies, who fanned out to spread the flags into the crowd.

"Watch that guy, he could be the FBI plant," one of the peaceniks noted of the revanchist-crypto-Trotskyite.

"Negative, he's just an asshole. The FBI plant is over there, the one in the hot pink dashiki," Jacko said. He gestured to a pseudo-hippie so obviously wearing a wig and costume-shop clothes he might as well have had a nametag reading, HELLO, I'M A SPECIAL AGENT. "His name is Steve and he's from the Bureau office in Atlanta. This is his first field assignment. He's

GREGG EASTERBROOK

alright. I rolled him some regular tobacco in joint paper so he can blend in better."

At that moment Carter's adult consciousness expanded into his youthful self and beheld Whole Life Square on a fine spring day. Senses jumped from limp to maximum amperage in a single beat.

In every direction were college kids, wide-eyed teenagers, freaks, dropouts, bikers, earnest crew cuts, street performers, butch dykes, radical priests in collars. State troopers in their comic-opera broad-brimmed hats. Metro cops, some ominously fingering nightsticks, some having a grand time. Enough National Guardsmen to seize a Caribbean nation. Helicopters coursing overhead, one bearing the governor—rather "the commander in chief of the state," as Guards officers had been instructed to address him by a memo received that morning. Journalists from the news mags and the papers and the underground press, plus camera crews from all three networks. Ambulances parked in neat ranks. Paddy wagons lined up across the square in radials, to deploy if the powers that be decided to make mass arrests. Fire trucks with water cannon. Enterprising hawkers offering jays or Uncle Ho buttons or tuna subs. Bedlam in every direction and midmorning sun warming the scene, smiling down.

Life! No portable belt-clip fax machines, no PDAs with GPS, no synthesized voice mail, no twenty-four hour celebrity-confessions channel. *Life* with all its possibilities for glory or fiasco. Delighting in life, Carter's youthful awareness almost short-circuited his wearied adult mind.

Adult awareness stretched out into a body that felt elastic, finished growing but still bursting power. Carter realized his hair was unfashionably short for the moment and his face felt scratchy. The night before Jayne Anne, plying him with bourbon, had made him tonsure his beard, so that he would be clean-cut when he stood on the speaker's platform. After the shave she had

224

given him a haircut and saved a lock for her memory box.

The adult consciousness found his earlier spirit lighthearted and his reason at high alert, despite the quantity of bourbon before, during, and after the barbering ceremony. Young Carter was still at the point when the hangover was a subject he knew only from complaints by middle-aged writers in *Esquire,* which is today a fashion magazine, but was then the publication that middle-aged writers with hangovers imagined to represent the cutting edge of the revolution.

Viewing his youthful memories of the previous night, Carter remembered Jayne Anne had conducted the barbering ceremony unclothed, the better to win his cooperation. The year they lived in the city apartment she walked around starkers quite a bit, he'd forgotten that; just came home, yanked the sweater over her head with hands crossed to each side like a porn starlet, wiggled out of her jeans, went about her business naked because it was something nice she could do for him. Whenever they were the only ones at the farm during summer, her clothes were the first things to go. Carter wondered how he could forget something so captivating. Like many men and women of genus Homo, Carter vividly remembered all disappointments but was foggy on the details of past delights.

As young Carter shifted his sandals and wiggled his toes, his adult consciousness realized, *I can feel my toes.* Breeze across them was a sensual indulgence. Once again at the point when he was lighthearted and clearheaded and could feel his toes. Everything wasn't diminished to weary irony. Embracing spring air floated over Carter's skin.

And the young Jayne Anne was once again by his side, luminous. "Look how many!" she was shouting to him. "My prince, who could have believed this!" It was the period when her diminutive for him was my prince.

For a year they had worked together organizing what was

planned as the first pro-American anti-America demonstration. People were to wave flags and praise the country while demanding change on a range of issues. The farmhouse had been a fascinating place during the planning months, a running drop-in destination for protest leaders, clergy, writers, poets, all hoping to create a dignified demonstration to atone for those many events where Yippies ran amok with middle fingers raised. The plan was to keep everyone in line and make rational appeals based on the Constitution and the intent of the Founding Fathers.

Jayne Anne ran the organizing committee, labored to keep off the speakers' list the Hanoi apologists and trendy self-loathers and well-born Ivy League professors obsessed with their personal journeys of discovery. She'd found an earnest, clean-cut Medal of Honor winner, missing most of a leg from action in Vietnam, who would speak respectfully of God and country but declare his opposition to the war. *Senator Kerrey,* adult Carter thought, glimpsing the man at the organizers' tent, *you look younger and less troubled.* Putting the demonstration together, they had even had the unions in their corner. Had the unions until the last minute anyway—when the SDS announced it was coming despite being disinvited, and labor switched sides. Now nobody was exactly thrilled by the thought that busloads of Teamsters were inbound.

Jayne Anne turned her notice and wiles toward a metro cop standing nearby. "Will you accept my flower?" she said, proffering a daffodil from her basket. "Will you accept the love?"

The policeman flipped up his plastic riot shield. "What's a looker doing with this crowd?" he asked.

"We're trying to change the world, why don't you join us?" she replied. "We need brave men like you." Jayne Anne could suck up with the best of them.

"Quit dreaming and get a job," the cop said.

"Dreaming is a job," Jayne Anne answered.

Carter asked with excessive politeness, "Officer, do you know if it's true that Walter Cronkite is here?"

"That's what the radio chatter says." Cronkite was the second-most famous person in America after the president; his movements and safety would be a matter of keen concern to law enforcement. But the cop was not pleased by the arrival of an eminence. "CBS wants to make you kids look good and us cops look bad," the officer exclaimed. "We could be cracking heads right now and we're not. Will Cronkite point that out on the air? When the riot starts we'll get the blame. Uncle Walter should of stayed in New York where he belongs."

"There won't be any riot. All participants are sworn to non-violence," Carter said. The officer replied with an expression that said, *Who's this guy, Howdy Doody?* Jayne Anne repeated, "Will you accept my flower?"

The policeman let her attach the daffodil to his windbreaker and delivered a smile when she smooched his cheek. Carter's adult consciousness, conditioned to the packaged sleekness that reigned as the female ideal of his day, marveled at how womanly Jayne Anne looked in old jeans, work shirt, and braless glory.

"Listen, you two seem okay," the cop said, and with the inflection of his voice took them into his orb of confidence. "The governor is looking for a pretext to order the Guard to charge. Cops, we just want to maintain the peace, fulfill the parade permit, and disburse the crowd. But the governor controls the Guard. You see any sign of this turning ugly, you get yourselves and your friends out fast. Tear gas will only be the beginning."

"Our cause is just and our people will be orderly," Jayne Anne said.

"It may not be up to you." The policeman used a foreboding tone. He walked off, keeping the daffodil in his windbreaker.

Carter's youthful awareness was animated with adoration for Jayne Anne, including at this moment a prideful sense that his beloved had expertly handled a thorny confrontation with an authority figure—though she had only briefly chatted up a cop. On this day Jayne Anne could be but a genius, a beauty, an orator, a princess of the coming utopia, a gift from God to the temporal world.

"Maybe he's trying to tell us something," Jayne Anne said. There was a worry line on her countenance. She took a maternal attitude toward the demonstrators, even the Teamsters and the yahoos, dreading the thought of anyone being harmed. Jayne Anne's nightmare was that the demonstration would turn into a melee, as if Chicago and Paris had not already proven the bankruptcy of that approach. Some of the reds and cryptos argued that rioting that leads to police brutality was desirable because bloodshed will radicalize the uncommitted. But this was just lingo they had picked up from lectures by tenured professors who drove Alfa Romeos and crossed the street to avoid bums who would ask them for quarters. No one who spouted the anarchy-is-good line volunteered to be beaten up personally by police, the way the sainted freedom marchers offered their bodies to swinging nightsticks during the King years. Jayne Anne had noted that among intellectuals, the more privileged the background, the more likely to believe it was noble for other people to suffer. And don't get her started on the Norman Mailer types who arranged to be arrested as a career move, then spent years lauding themselves for My Twenty Minutes in Jail.

"There mustn't be a riot," Carter said. "Today is our chance to make a better world. We must not fail."

"Nobody will judge us if we fail," Jayne Anne said, locking eyes with him. "What the stars require is that each person *try* to make a better world. The rest is out of our hands. Unrealistic expectations only lay the ground for disenchantment."

They pressed their way through the rumpus to the organizers' area. Carter's adult awareness focused in on faces in the crowd, and somehow he was given to know which of these rebels would end up as investment bankers funneling illegal campaign contributions to politicians: *that one there, the one with the chin-length sideburns and Chairman Mao hat.* He knew which would be destroyed, either medically or legally, by the drugs they extolled: *there, the woman with the flower garland, giggling nonstop.* He knew which would end up at the bottom of the knowledge economy, forgotten by the student leaders who would abandon the average person's concerns to chase after wealth: *that one there, the guy in the Fly United T-shirt.* He knew which would simply be left behind by the passage of time: *there, there, there, there, there, there, and there.*

"Hey, the Daffodil Man," a kid said to Carter as he passed. "Right on. Didn't you last appear at Bowling Green? Or was it Brandeis?"

"That was an impostor at Brandeis," Carter replied. "I am the original Daffodil Man. Accept no substitutes."

Kids clapped and Carter handed out flowers. He put his arms around several hippies and they took snapshots with a flashcube Brownie, the smell of burnt chemicals miring the air each time the cube fired, melting one of the miniature bulbs. A chant of "Daffodil Man, Daffodil Man" went up from the nearby crowd, followed by cries of "Speech, Doctor!" Carter stood atop the hood of a BMW 2002 and spoke for a few minutes about the Bill of Rights, the Founders' belief in national self-determination, Locke and Jefferson, the Constitutional clause against involuntary servitude—the highly respectable points he hoped to hit later.

"Wow, that was deep," said one of the kids of a talk that lasted maybe four minutes.

"Hey, Daffodil Man, let's get drunk and screw," a hippie chick called out to him. "He's taken!" Jayne Anne called back. "We'll share!" the chick answered. "Death to Thomas Paine, death to

Descartes, death to all apologists for the technocrat-industrialist regime," screamed a militant from the back of the crowd.

He and Jayne Anne walked farther. "That talk was good, maybe you should run for Congress someday," she said. "Do you know what you want to do when you grow up?"

"Anything but law school."

At the staging area they found discombobulation had reached an advanced state. Somebody had moved a black-and-white television down to the street, trailing multiple extension cords from an apartment, to try to get some idea of what the networks were saying, or just news from other corners of the demonstration. Today, at a public march, everyone would have cell phones and miniature radios and laptops with wireless Internet access and know every detail from every point in the event, to say nothing of receiving real-time feedback from commentators in other hemispheres. But from an information standpoint, demonstrations of the sixties were like battles of the Civil War. Much time was spent trying to figure out what was going on.

Carter's fellow organizers gathered around the little set, watching its grainy images in mounting indignation. Walter Cronkite was interviewing the governor, the speaker's platform framing the backdrop.

"—subversive anti-American elements, Mr. Cronkite. We have sensitive intelligence information confirming that the leadership of this demonstration is composed entirely of Stalinist cadres under the direct, active control of Moscow." The governor was sitting on his suit tail, as his wife had instructed him, to prevent the shoulders of his coat from bunching up. His eyes seemed unnaturally small for a Homo sapiens, more like those of our arboreal primate ancestors, whose fossils have been found in Africa.

"Are you saying there has been spying on this protest group? Isn't domestic spying illegal?" Cronkite asked. Even then, not yet fifty years of age, he had attained the status of "avuncular." Cronkite's baritone was so impressively graveled as to sound as though it were emanating from a mechanism of gears and pulleys in his throat.

"As commander in chief of the state, I have authorized any and all means to safeguard our citizens from subversive anti-American elements. I am more interested in protecting democracy than in legal niceties."

"I doubt the Founding Fathers would have called the Bill of Rights a legal nicety," Cronkite said. A big whoop went up from the crowd on that line.

"No one is proposing suspending the Bill of Rights at this time," the governor replied. "I am sworn to uphold the Constitution, and I will do so whenever appropriate."

"Now about the charge that the demonstration is led by subversives," Cronkite said. "We are told that a Congressional Medal of Honor winner will speak today. Surely you are not saying this young man is a communist."

"I know for a fact there is no Medal of Honor winner in this city. No matter what you have been told it is false. The demonstration is being staged entirely by Marxists under the direct, active control of Peking. That is why, as commander in chief of the state, I am declaring that this demonstration is canceled, and giving the crowd thirty minutes to vacate the city limits. After that, the National Guard will restore order on my command."

Hoots and cries rose up around Whole Life Square. Car horns and air horns sounded. Policemen flipped down their visors and clenched riot shields. Carter and Jayne Anne looked at each other unhappily.

"Governor, these demonstrators have a valid parade permit."

"By the powers vested in me, I am revoking the parade permit."

"It is a county permit signed by a county judge. Are you declaring martial law?"

"Not at this moment. First my pollsters, I meant to say my intelligence sources, must ascertain the full threat to my reelection, I meant to say our precious freedoms."

"The demonstrators will make speeches. Why are speeches threatening?"

"Mr. Cronkite, I have in my hand a list of the planned speeches." The governor waved a sheaf of paper. "Just listen, good citizens, to these topics. 'God Is Dead and a Homosexual, Too.' 'Burn Your Bra and Kick Your Husbands in the Balls.' 'Nicholas Lenin, Our Lord and Master.' And this one, Mr. Cronkite, as a veteran I find this one so offensive it is difficult to read it on the air. But I will: 'Blow Your Nose with the American Flag.' Now you see, Mr. Cronkite, why I have no choice but to prevent such revolting anti-American propaganda from being given a platform."

"Jesus H. Christ, did you feed him that wacked-out stuff?" Jacko asked Steve, the FBI plant, who was standing with them.

"No, I'm federal, we don't coordinate with state law-enforcement agencies," Steve replied. Then catching himself, "I mean, like, what do you mean, man, I'm just here grooving on life, man."

"May I see that paper?" Cronkite asked, trying to snatch it away.

"Unfortunately I am not at liberty to share this document," the governor said, stuffing it into his suitcoat. Cronkite thought he caught a glance at the top, which looked like statehouse stationery, and decided to call the bluff.

"Governor, those speech topics may not be accurate. If there was proof a Congressional Medal of Honor winner was present, would you put the National Guard on hold?"

Handlers had not prepped him for this wrinkle. "Well, I—well, in the interest of fair play, I will order any spontaneous violence temporarily suspended."

"Alright," Cronkite intoned, the pitch of his voice on this simple word carrying the authority of a cathedral bell striking. "CBS News will find out what is really happening here. In the meantime we return you to our studios in New York to rejoin *The Knucklehead Game,* already in progress."

"He's signaling us," Carter said as the outline of Cronkite faded from the little set, replaced by images of a gigantic gong and shrieking couples dressed as Easter bunnies. "We've got to act fast. We've got to get Kerrey where Cronkite can see him."

They turned to look at the medal-holder, who leaned against a crutch. "I'm not exactly fast on my feet and what with the crowd—" There was no reason to complete the sentence. Moving him rapidly to the center of the square was out of the question.

Since the governor gave his dictum Whole Life Square, scene of hours of cacophony, had fallen nearly quiet, the demented din subsiding. Thousands of people could be heard shuffling feet, bumping and exhaling, while the residue of voices seemed to be of uncountable whispers rather than uncountable shouts and chants. Such absence of sound was ominous. Around the edges of the square they could see National Guard units forming up ranks and the guardsmen didn't just have riot batons, they were holding carbines. Half a mile away, police captains were arguing with Guard officers to keep back their inexperienced, apprehensive troops and let street-hardened cops handle the situation. But the governor was calling in orders about wedge tactics and assault formations and other subjects on which he knew absolutely nothing. A psychology of self-fulfilling prophecy was taking root among the guardsmen.

"Something bad is about to happen," Marshall said, and the man of huffing was visibly fearful.

"Like, why don't you take off your shirt again," Jacko suggested to Jayne Anne, sloshing words. "It's worked before."

"Dear, this is no time for a party," she replied in a school-mistress tone.

Jacko felt hurt. "I just really like it when you take your shirt off," he sniffed.

Wheels turned in Carter's brain. His adult self remembered this moment, the exhilaration he was about to feel when he put it all together.

Carter said to Kerrey, "You've got the Medal of Honor with you, right?"

"It's not as fancy as you expect."

"Will you trust it to me? I'm taking it to Cronkite."

They wanted to know how he could get through the multitude. "I won't go through. I'll go over," Carter said. He gestured to the radial lines of paddy wagons the police had set in place before the throng arrived. One line of wagons pointed end to end right to the speaker's hustings. Carter had realized that if someone ran on top of the wagons and jumped expertly from one to the next, there was an express lane to the centerpoint of the square.

Within moments they had buckled the medal and a mimeograph copy of the true program of speeches into a leather pouch slung across Carter's chest. They'd given him all the daffodils he could carry. Jayne Anne put a headband around his temple and slipped one of the tiny American flags onto each side, behind each ear, suggesting the winglets of Mercury.

Carter, Jayne Anne, Jacko, and Steve the inept FBI plant wriggled their way through the crowd to the spoke end of one of the paddy wagon radials. Several policemen stood by. How would he vault past them to begin?

Jayne Anne assessed the situation, shrugged, and mumbled, "Here we go again." She tore off her work shirt, creating an instant sensation.

Jacko stumbled to the cops by the endmost wagon. "There's

some free-love chick over there with her boobs out," he told the officers. "Shouldn't that be illegal?" Consumed with concern for their duty, the police immediately departed toward Jayne Anne. Jacko knelt to offer a knee-boost for Carter, and he was atop the van.

From that vantage point the demonstration at Whole Life Square was a sea of bobbing, rolling combers and whitecaps, this sea composed of heads. The metal tops of paddy wagons formed a highway to the square's innermost point, and Carter took off running.

Impacts of his feet made clunking echoes. Everything became vertiginous as he adjusted his gait to maintain balance atop the crowns of the vans. The van roofs, hardly intended for running, shimmied and rebounded under his weight, making stability difficult. He jumped awkwardly from the first truck to the second, almost losing his balance. Carter kicked off the sandals to improve his footing, picked up speed, and jumped more easily from the second to the third to the fourth. He felt athletic and chosen; there was no one ahead of him.

Spectators realized what the moving figure was up to and began to cheer Carter on. Carter began to toss daffodils to either side as he ran. He ran faster, leaped, ran, slowed to toss flowers, ran, leaped, closed toward the center of the square. Straight toward the paranoid governor and his inexperienced armed guards Carter ran. At that moment Steve the inept FBI plant pulled from under his dashiki a foot-long heavy walkie-talkie of the old military kind and began shouting on every law-enforcement channel that the running man was under the protection of the Federal Bureau of Investigation and all weapons were to be holstered— an act of competent quick-wittedness that saved Carter's life.

Running atop steel Carter heard the cheers, as once before he had heard others cheer for him running. Tossing flowers he ran in promise and hope, ran as every child dreams of running to the town's approval, as every child deserves to run. He could not hear Jayne Anne's calls of encouragement, but knew them to follow.

Carter arrived at the center of the square and was escorted to Cronkite, who botched the in-the-know salutation of the moment by greeting him, "Right arm." After Carter unwrapped the medal and showed the actual program, Cronkite persuaded a police detachment to part the crowd and bring the speakers forward. The anchorman went on the air to accuse the governor of fabricating charges and of planning to use the National Guard to cause a riot; in that simpler and less knowing time, people listening to the broadcast were shocked and indignant that a public official would lie about an important matter. Humiliated, the governor withdrew his troops and fluttered off in his helicopter. That night he was mollified by a congratulatory phone call from Vice President Spiro Agnew. "You talked tough," Agnew told him. "What America needs is tougher talk. Louder talk, too."

The speeches then occurred more or less as planned except for electrical outages, and if few in the crowd actually heard the words, the gist was what always mattered anyway. Carter had his national television one-on-one with Cronkite and spoke about the common ground, respect for differing views, freedom of conscience. He even remembered to praise the cops for restraint, winning a roar of approval from the officers clustered around the central platform. For a few days, at least, Carter Morris and Whole Life Square entered the American national consciousness as exemplars of the kind of principled protest the Founders had in mind.

And if the circumstances of the demonstration went downhill somewhat as twilight fell, the success of the occasion was undiminished. When the night-shift police commander decided the time had come to move 'em out, Carter was one of many snapped up in an arrest sweep, his brief detention only adding to the mythical quality of the day.

"Lady, you would flatter that flower if you wore it," Carter cried to Jayne Anne, leaning from the police van, as he handed her the last daffodil. "Until your return, my prince!" she called back as the sliding door whammed.

Carter's adult awareness saw the door close from inside of the van, felt the lurch as the driver headed off toward the lockup. His younger self collapsed to the cold steel floor, exhausted, exhilarated, full of surety he had just done something remarkable, knowing there would never be a greater moment in his life. Carter watched his tired and happy form as if from above and felt his consciousness begin to expand away from a place and time to which his entire generation could never return. Then the past became a vapor, and he tumbled back to the present.

CHAPTER FIFTEEN

Wᴴᴼᴸᴱ Lɪꜰᴇ Sǫᴜᴀʀᴇ stood before him in its paved expanse, once again a coolly bustling city center where tiny telephones were pressed against the ears of all who scurried, where FedEx and UPS and catering trucks were more numerous than lampposts, where crushed Super Ultra Lights from smoke breaks were strewn about the entrances of buildings, where Avalon was an automobile model. Carter felt certain his contact with the great mystery had concluded. It was the present day, where he would live the remainder of his life.

Carter walked to the point in the square at which police vans and television cameras and a raucous chanting crowd had congregated, to his perception seconds before. He could still see the setting as a ghost image, but the eidetic scene was dissipating and would never grow vivid again. People with CD headphones over their ears and eating PowerBars were walking straight through the ghosts, just as in years to come others would walk through wearing telepathy projectors and munching gene-replenishment wafers.

Though our memories are a cast and our futures pliant, what can no longer be changed too often dominates what can. Some allow the fixed character of the past to weigh them with mortmain disappointment, endlessly revisiting and regretting what can never alter. A better approach might be to accept the fixed past as incentive to face the present, even if, as is the norm, the present turns out considerably different from what had been expected. The early moments of life need not mean more than the later—the assumption memory too often makes. Later moments might exceed earlier in import, coming as they do with perspective added, and if they are allowed to happen.

Looking around the square, Carter at last felt released from the confinement of memory, and from his belief that once there was specialness, but could not be again. Of all the foolish ideas his generation had entertained, that was the corker. The moment he had been born into, the labels his contemporaries had worn, were nice mementos but in themselves possessed no larger meaning. Only the experience of life possessed such meaning, and this was the same for all places and times.

Looking around the square, Carter at last saw not what once was but what is. In that place and time was hope, despair, promise, hardship, love, heartsickness, friendship, loneliness, a life's work for a company of saints. People milled about with unmet needs. There is always someone wandering in a cold night of need and until there is not, there will never be an end of causes to fight for. And the city square was a point of relative privilege; for the 37 million Americans who live below the poverty line, or the billion men and women of the earth who live on a dollar a day, life was an unending struggle of need. It is not necessary, Carter at last realized, to belong to any particular group or to live in historic times in order to be called to service by the world. The world never stops calling. It's only a question of whether we listen.

Everything depended on whether Carter had returned in time, since the last act he intended for Whole Life Square had already been set in motion before the final settlement conference began. He tapped the breast pocket of his suit; the envelope of unseen legal documents remained there. Perhaps it was too late for Carter to rekindle his engagement with the ontology, and too late for him to love. But so long as he had returned in time, he might still be able to do an act of good—and to make small amends to the three people who should always have been the focus of his life.

Had he returned in time? Judging from the sun and the tally of passersby, the juncture seemed late afternoon. But of what day?

Carter took the cellular phone from his pocket and switched it to the Web data position. Within seconds, information from around the globe began flowing into the device. Price ticks of thousands of stocks; barometric readings for the planet's major cities; flight schedules in Japan and train departure times in Denmark; tide charts for the ports of the Adriatic. Casualty figures on the chemical spill in Bangalore; commentary on the trade between the Packers and Raiders; technical details of the hertz frequency of a new chip. Headlines BRITS BLAST FRENCH IN LATEST TIFF; CONGRESS, WHITE HOUSE CLASH ON BILL; NICOLE KIDMAN TO STAR IN MUSICAL VERSION OF *HEDDA GABLER*. In seconds the phone was primed with more information than anyone could process, even if doing nothing else.

Carter only wanted the date and hour. It was 4:00 P.M. on the third day after the closing of the Value Neutral deal—exactly the moment he had specified in the letters. Would they be here?

He regarded the square, its bustle of public liveliness and private loneliness, and across in the distance recognized an approaching form. Ward looked even heavier than he had a few weeks before. His drooped eyes and the rim of remaining hair that skimmed the medial of his head were incongruous beside the lithe images of boyhood verve that filled Carter's mental file under the name Louvain. Once, in a place like this, Ward would have been the one being ushered to the private entrance of a glistening skyscraper for an important meeting. Now he appeared uneasy, glancing around, very much the rural salesman called to the big city on an errand he would rather forgo.

"Well, I came," Ward said. "Thanks for sending that check. I couldn'ta otherwise. Did you—are you really rich now?"

The two men stood unspeaking in the winded square, Carter with his hand in the pockets of an expensive English raincoat, his childhood companion wearing a seed-company jacket block-lettered with the logo PIONEER HI-BRED.

Carter was silent because he was looking over Ward's shoulder toward the silhouette of a man struggling forward with protracted, robotic steps. Mack looked awful, like he never knew the sun, though he owned a tanning bed among the many other insurance-paid therapeutic contraptions in his home-prison.

"I sent extra money so you could travel with a nurse's aide," Carter said.

"I can fucking walk," was Mack's greeting. He indicated his new limbs. "Full-leg prosthesis with a mechanized hip and choice of social or functional arm. The latest." Mack had chosen the functional arm, with a grasping appendage he was learning to control. The effort his sibling had exerted to follow Carter's injunction and travel to this spot must have been fantastic, to say nothing of surprising considering their estranged state.

"This better be worth it," Mack pronounced.

"Hi, Mack," Ward said, slipping into the deferential tone that a little brother's pal uses when hoping the older brother will acknowledge him.

"Hello, Ward. Glad you beat that special prosecutor thing."

"There was never any formal finding. I resigned before—"

"I see her," Carter said. His heart almost quavered, a feeling he had forgotten. Jayne Anne, the third person to whom he had sent extraordinary letters the night before the Value Neutral deal, was crossing the square. She walked unnoted, not parting admirers as she had walked in youth.

"Did you take the money?" she asked.

"Without hesitation," Carter said. "The entire pile. Laughed all the way to the Swiss bank."

Jayne Anne's eyes smoldered. She was speechless, and seemed poised to leave without any further conversation.

"I took the money but I don't deserve it," Carter told her. "Which leaves me no alternative but to give it to you."

He pulled the envelope from his suit and removed folded pages of red-pinstriped legal typescript. "Here is a summary of the irrevocable instrument that transfers the entire after-tax sum, approximately $20 million, to a foundation to be headquartered in Jamestown, New York, and controlled by Jayne Anne La-Monica. The gift funds construction of a new building, then places the balance into a trust that will produce at least a million per year in perpetuity for staff and expenses; the figure may rise if the stock market rises. The trust instructs Jayne Anne La-Monica to use its proceeds as she sees fit in service of the public interest. The sole stipulation is that the foundation must employ on generous terms Wardman Louvain and Mack Morris, for so long as they should desire employment."

He paused for effect. Ward was whistling, and seemed to give off a soft light on the word "employment." Mack was squinting as he tried to be sure what was happening. The woman was poker-faced.

"These are not Rockefeller numbers, but great deeds have been accomplished with less," Carter said. Indicating Ward, he addressed Jayne Anne. "Ward Louvain is extremely skilled in politics and could serve as excellent instructor on lobbying and legislative matters. I commend him without reservation. We've been friends forever." Then he indicated Mack. "As my brother has overcome many hurdles in life, he is well suited to teach and mentor others trying to rise above hard fortune."

"You are out of your mind, right?" Mack was amazed. "I live behind closed drapes so nobody will see me. I can't call out for pizza without losing my temper."

"That will change," Carter said, pacing words. "Once everything in your life was right, and changed. Now everything's wrong, but can change again. Our pasts are cast, but our futures remain ours to choose. Mack, I want to call you back to the world."

His brother showed the slight smile Carter could not remember seeing since their youth. Jayne Anne took the papers, still betraying no sign of reaction. "I have complete control over this trust?"

"Complete. Use the money as you see fit to serve the public interest. No idea too blue-sky. My advice: advocate vast, sweeping reform and then settle for whatever you can get." Carter regarded her and for a moment spoke in a voice he had once used often. "Jayne Anne, make this a better world. I know you can do it."

"And you, sir, what exactly is your role in this enterprise to be?" she asked.

"None," Carter said. "It's too late for me. I'm faded. I plan to go off somewhere and pick up the pieces. Maybe I'll work as a carpenter and store up karma for my next life." He paused and looked hard at Jayne Anne, who remained impassive. He added, "The trust is irrevocable, so don't bother trying to give anything back."

Carter Morris shook hands with his childhood best friend, awkwardly hugged his only brother, and offered a gesture of jaunty salute to Jayne Anne. He pursed his lips slightly and said to her, "Make the stars proud."

Then he turned and began to walk toward the far end of the square where he could catch a cab and go figure out what a broke, tainted cynic might do in the years remaining to him. Carter was faded, that statement was true, but also set free from the harm he had done to his hopes of self. Twenty million dollars to be released from illusions? A bargain.

Walking away from his brother, his best friend, and the love of his life, Carter found he felt no remorse. He and Ward should always have been close, but weren't. Part of growing up is accepting that you won't have true friends. He and Mack should have fought side by side in some good fight, but instead just

243

fought. Part of growing up is accepting family unhappiness. He and Jayne Anne should have had wonderful decades together, but didn't. Part of growing up is accepting that most love fails. Perhaps it was just as well for things to end in this way, with their dream for an instant revived and no chance to descend to another disappointment, because they would not try again.

By the time Carter was nearly to the far side of the square, he was glad to have managed the entire distance without succumbing to the urge to look behind him.

He heard a woman's voice cry above the wind, "I can really do anything I want with this money?" Without turning, he gave a thumbs-up gesture.

"Then get back over here, that's an order from your new boss," Jayne Anne cried. "And this time, kiss me like you mean it."

Carter was poised on the cusp between what might have been and what is. The gravitational field of bitterness almost pulled him the wrong way. Bitterness likes nothing better than to attract more of itself, and life can be a struggle to break free of its grip. Yet sometimes, just sometimes, the gravitational field of love can be ever so slightly stronger.

He walked back toward Ward and Mack, who were both smiling joyfully. He took Jayne Anne in his arms, and they held each other in the wind. Her touch was every bit as good as it had been the very first time. The two men looked away and prepared to talk sports.

They kissed. Jayne Anne LaMonica said to Carter Morris, "I waited, and my prince returned."

People moved about the square, stepping through the ghosts and revenant hopes there. Four shadows of children, beautiful in a way the constellations themselves must envy, stood in the wind in which answers might be found. It was the only moment that ever really matters, the here and now.